# Summer Dreams

Helen Dale

ISBN 978-1-9996329-4-6

*Summer Dreams* is set in the UK in 2003-8 during the introduction of the Gender Recognition Act 2004. The background is historically accurate and includes actual individuals and organisations involved at that time. Most of the incidents described are based on real examples and experiences. Summer Dreams is, nevertheless, a work of fiction and any similarity to actual people or organisations, other than as part of the background, is purely coincidental.

## Acknowledgements

I am indebted to Brilliant Beginnings for their information on surrogacy. Brilliant Beginnings is a UK based non-profit surrogacy agency. Founded in 2013 they have helped a number of people complete their families through surrogacy. They were consulted in relation to the surrogacy aspects of this story, to advise on but not write these segments. Surrogacy is a real option for LGBTQI people and for more information please visit www.brilliantbeginnings.co.uk

I am also grateful to members of Manchester Women's Writers' group for their critiques of many of the chapters and to Joanne Whalley who read the whole manuscript for me.

## Inspiration for Summer Dreams

In 1966, while living in a tiny bed-sit in SW London, I caught a train to Bournemouth. It was an old styled corridor train and I changed in the toilets; putting on an orange bikini under my skirt and top. I took the Sandbanks ferry across to the beaches and dunes at Studland where I swam then sunbathed. As I lay there, I noticed a guy watching me so I quickly dressed and left.

But what if I hadn't noticed him?

What if he'd approached me?

What if he hadn't minded that I was trans?

Maybe, then, Summer Dreams wouldn't have been a work of fiction.

Also by Helen Dale

**A Tale of Two Lives:**
A Funny Thing Happened on the Way to the Palace
Autobiography

**Transgender Tales**
Adventures & Misadventures on the Journey from Transvestite to
Transsexual

**Understanding Gender Variance -**
A Practical Guide: including Intersex, Trans, Non-Binary & Gender
Fluid Individuals

# Chapter 1.   On the beach
## Saturday 10th May 2003

"You need to be careful you don't burn."

I must have dozed off for a few moments, lulled asleep by the scorching May sun on the white sand, the gentle breeze wafting through the dune grass and the swish of waves breaking on the shoreline. I'd been fantasising about meeting someone, falling in love, getting married and making love. The last two not necessarily in that order.

I opened my eyes. I'd thought the little secluded depression I'd found would hide me from prying eyes, but I'd been mistaken. A guy was squatting a couple of feet from where I lay. He looked to be mid or late-twenties, certainly a little older than my own twenty years. His well-defined body was tanned and his hair was sun-bleached. I assumed he was a local and worked outdoors most of the time. Perhaps on a building site or on a farm? It wasn't easy to tell with him squatting on his heels but he seemed about five foot ten tall. He had an air of confidence about him and, if I'd still been fantasising, he would have scored an eight or even a nine.

What was I thinking? This wasn't a fantasy and I could be in trouble.

"The sun can be very deceptive here — it reflects off the sand as well as directly from the sky. Even half an hour can be enough to burn you if you don't take precautions," he continued.

I rose up on my elbows, forgetting I'd undone my bikini top's strap. His gaze dropped to the bikini top now dangling away from my flat chest — the fillers I used resting in the cups. A knowing smile appeared on his lips. Hoping he hadn't noticed too much, I dropped back down and reached behind me to refasten the strap. My shape, and a modicum of modesty restored, I, again, lifted myself onto my elbows.

"It's a nice secluded spot you've got here. I often use it myself. My name is Roger, I hope I'm not bothering you."

"Well, I had hoped for some privacy. I'm Vicky."

"OK Vicky, I'll leave you alone if you like — but it would be remiss of me to let you burn your back. As there is no one else around, I'd better offer to do it for you. Have you got sun cream?"

I hadn't brought any with me. There had been too many other things on my mind that morning.

"No matter, I've got some here."

Roger pre-empted any chance of me declining his offer. He poured lotion on my back and I felt his hand gently spreading it. His hands had none of the roughness I'd expect from someone involved in manual work and the words he used implied education beyond the bare minimum. I reconsidered what he did. He unfastened the back of my bikini top again and slid the straps down my arm while he massaged the cream into my shoulders. His touch sent a shiver down my spine. I wondered if he'd try to take advantage. How would I react if he did? But he then refastened the strap and sat back on his haunches.

"Here," he said, passing me the sun cream, "I'm sure you'd prefer to do your front yourself."

"I'll do it later," I said.

"Well, that's a problem. You haven't any sun cream, I'll need mine and you want me to leave you to some privacy."

I was trapped. I'd stayed lying on my front to hide the bulge in my bikini bottoms. If I sat up, he would see it. But I couldn't stay as I was.

"Your secret is safe with me, you know. I saw you earlier as you took the path into the dunes and I noticed the outline of your bikini top through your t-shirt when you took your jacket off. You look fabulous by the way."

As I often did during outings as Vicky, I'd planned to use the toilets on the train from Waterloo to Bournemouth to change out of my jeans and t-shirt into a skirt and more feminine top and put on my wig and some make-up. But the train had been busy with people standing in the corridors and near the loos. I'd used the gents' at Bournemouth station to put my bikini on underneath my trousers and t-shirt. I'd zipped up my jacket to hide the outline — but it seems I'd taken it off too soon.

I looked at Roger. He'd realised I was a transvestite but didn't seem to be threatening. Far from it. I'd been much more vulnerable while he applied the sun cream. He could, equally, have assaulted me while I dozed.

I should have just told him I was going and put on my t-shirt. But I didn't.

I sat up and reached for the bottle and thanked him. He watched me with an amused smile as I applied the lotion, then handed the bottle back to him.

"Do you smoke?" he asked, offering me his packet. I took one gratefully to calm my nerves.

"So, Vicky, do you still want me to leave you on your own — or would you like some company? You know, it might be useful if I stayed. Anyone else coming along is more likely to sneak up on a single girl than on a couple."

That made sense, so I agreed he could stay. He spread his towel out next to me, stripped to his swimming trunks and lay down. My earlier assessment of a well-defined body was confirmed; not overly muscular but lean. I tried not to glance at the bulge in his trunks but couldn't help myself.

"Are you here on holiday?" Roger asked, the smoke from his cigarette drifting lazily upwards.

"Just visiting for the day. I can't afford to stop. I'd love to if I could. Do you live locally?"

"Yes, I've lived in Bournemouth most of my life."

We continued to chat – Roger was very easy to talk to and related amusing stories about goings on in the dunes. I didn't take long to relax in his company. I was glad he'd stayed. '*Definitely a nine*,' I pondered.

"I'm hot," he blurted, breaking my train of thought.

"Fancy a swim?" he asked. He stood up and held out his hand for me to take to help me up. He continued to hold my hand as we ran into the sea. I don't think I'd have been able to break his grip if I'd wanted to. But I didn't want to.

The water was fabulously refreshing as we swan towards a small raft moored off the beach. I held onto the side of the raft catching my breath as Roger came behind me, I turned to face him. He put one hand on each of my hips and lifted me up onto the platform where he soon joined me.

We lay down side by side and Roger took my hand again. When I didn't pull away, he leant over me, his face a few inches from mine. He looked into my eyes and paused, his own blue eyes sparkling. Was he giving me the chance to turn my head away if I wanted? Perhaps, but I didn't. Not seeing any signs of resistance he kissed my lips. I responded and slipped my arms around his neck. His hands slid under my bikini top and his fingers tweaked my nipples. I'd never experienced such ecstasy and didn't want it to stop.

The thought shocked me. I'd never considered myself as gay. I hadn't particularly fancied any girls I'd known — but nor had I fancied any of the guys either when going out as male. But being Vicky made a huge difference. She had taken me over. I wasn't playing a part, I *was* Vicky.

"There are some other people coming," Roger told me. "Come on, I'll race you back to the beach." He did a graceful dive into the water.

I didn't stand a chance. My legs were weak from the kissing and cuddling. As I got out of the water, Roger slipped his arm around my waist.

"What time is your last train tonight?"

"I'm not sure, I'd planned to catch one about seven – but there are later ones. Why"

"Because I enjoy your company and I'd love to take you out for dinner. I know a fabulous Italian restaurant"

"But I have nothing with me suitable for a restaurant."

"That's not a problem – we can go shopping now. It's only 3 o'clock. I'll treat you."

Well, how could I refuse?

It didn't take long to slip on my skirt and top and apply some powder and lipstick. I'd let my hair grow and it was just about passable when pulled back into a short ponytail. As Roger's elderly, but beautifully maintained, green MGB convertible was parked on the edge of the dunes, next to the path I'd taken, we were soon over the ferry and parked in the town centre.

Our first stop was Debenhams where I had a good look through their rails of dresses. I was like a kid in a sweet shop. I tried on four outfits. The first, an oriental style dress with a blue and white pattern. Then a short sleeved, mid-thigh length, dress with boat neckline with horizontal sections – white at the top down to the top of my bust, light brown from there to just under the bust line and dark brown for the rest. The third was a red skirt and white blouse. Finally a purple mid-thigh, sleeveless skater swing dress with a round neck. Roger said he thought the purple dress was perfect and I agreed, so that was the one I chose. When I came out of the cubicle after changing back out of the dress, I noticed Roger had made a separate purchase which he didn't show me.

We then went to the lingerie department and found a bra and pantie combination in almost the same colour as the dress. They joined the dress in the shopping basket together with a pair of 'barely black' tights. Back on the street, we found a Saxones. I tried on half of their stock before settling on a pair of black court shoes with two inch heels and a matching hand bag. Roger didn't seem to mind the time I was taking. Our final port of call was Boots where I picked up eye shadow and liner, mascara and blusher to supplement the foundation and lipstick I already had with me.

Back at Roger's house, I took advantage of his shower then dressed myself and completed my make-up before going back downstairs.

"Wow, you look fabulous," he said – taking my arms in his hands and kissing me.

"Mind my make-up, darling. I don't want to have to re-do it." 'Darling' had slipped out – but it felt so appropriate.

Locking his front door behind us, Roger opened the car door for me to slip into the passenger seat and then put my sports bag in the tiny boot. When he came to start the car, it wouldn't go, so we had to call for a cab instead.

Our dinner reservation was for seven and we were a few minutes late arriving. The maître d' showed us to our table and asked if we wanted something to drink. I was a complete novice in such surroundings but Roger suggested a 'Harvey Wallbanger' cocktail. I went along with his recommendation, it was delicious. The menu had a bewildering array of dishes – most of which I'd never heard of but, once more, Roger came to my rescue. He suggested garlic bread to start followed by pasta with a chicken Carbonara sauce. I simply handed the waiter the menu and said that sounded fine. I had no idea what it was but really didn't care.

The Bella Rosa restaurant had a small dance floor. Roger stood up held out his hand and led me to it. I put my left hand on his shoulder as he held my right, his other hand slipping around my waist. It felt marvellous as the hem of my skirt swished against my legs. When the music stopped, Roger pulled me to him and we kissed.

As our starters had arrived, we returned, hand in hand, to our table.

The cocktails were followed by white wine with the food. Not being used to so much alcohol and dizzy with what was going on, I was very light-headed.

With the first course finished, Roger led me back to the dance floor in time for a slow number I recognised from my parent's collection as 'Bridge over Troubled Water' by Simon and Garfunkel. Roger held me tight and I felt something pressing against my thigh. I completely lost track of the time as we danced and didn't want the evening to end.

We saw the waiter bringing our main courses so I reluctantly unwrapped myself from Roger's embrace. I then realised I'd left my sports bag in Roger's car. Most of the items didn't matter – but my flat keys and my train ticket were in it.

"What's the time Roger?" I asked urgently as we got to our table.

"Nine fifteen. Time enough to finish our meal, the station is across the road."

"The station may be but I've realised my keys and my railway ticket are in my bag in the back of your car."

"That's awkward. We don't have time to get there and back in time for your train. There is only one thing for it you'll have to stop at mine tonight. I DO have a spare bed." There was a smile on his face and a twinkle in his blue eyes as he emphasised the last comment.

I didn't *have* to return to London so I relaxed.

The meal had been everything Roger had promised. As we smoked and drank coffees, he said as I no longer had a train to catch, we could have another drink at the restaurant, go back to his place or go on to a small club he knew.

"I think you'll find the company at the Blue Peach interesting," he remarked, with a smile I was beginning to recognise hinted at some deeper meaning. The club sounded intriguing and I said I'd love to go to it; so he asked for the bill and for a taxi.

The Blue Peach was on a corner with the entrance at an angle between the two roads. The bouncer standing by the door stepped to one side and smiled as we approached. He resembled Frank Bruno and I wouldn't have wanted to get on his wrong side.

"Good evening sir, good evening madam," he said as we reached him.

"Good evening Graham," answered Roger, "this is Vicky a good friend of mine."

"Welcome to the Blue Peach, Vicky I hope you enjoy your evening."

"Thank you Graham," I replied.

I was surprised to see we didn't have to pay to go into the club – but Roger told me trans people were admitted free. I wasn't sure how that worked for him.

Inside, the décor was predominantly dark red with blue peach motifs. There was a bar over to the left, sofas with coffee tables between them around the other three walls. Higher tables and stools surrounded two pillars in the centre of the room. The ground floor gave an impression of an old gentleman's club with subdued lighting.

Stairs led up to another floor from which the sounds of music emanated. Another staircase led down to the basement containing, according to signs, toilets and a cocktail bar.

As I looked around, I realised the clientele was mainly same sex couples. It was a gay venue – I'd known such places existed but I'd never been to one before.

Roger suggested we go upstairs to the dance floor. There was another bar there and a tiny dance floor full of TVs looking at their reflections in the mirrors that surrounded it.

"What would you like to drink," asked Roger.

"I'll stick with the white wine please," I told him.

We sat on some high stools along the edge of the upstairs lounge and I watched the other girls on the dance floor.

Some of them came over to chat to us; Roger was clearly no stranger to the venue. It was the first time I'd actually met other transvestites — I'd been too scared to risk exposure and losing my job. Roger introduced me to some of the others. I immediately made several friends and found I fitted in here much more than I ever had in South London.

Roger led me to the dance floor. He held me tight regardless of whether the music called for a slow dance or something more energetic. I wasn't complaining though, I was in heaven.

The club closed at one in the morning. As we were leaving, I promised everyone I'd return as soon as I could.

Back at Roger's he led me upstairs and offered me the spare bedroom.

I could have used it, but I didn't.

Roger took me into his arms and I felt him unzipping my dress. I dropped my arms so it fell to the floor. I then wrapped them round his neck again our lips crushing each other's and our tongues intertwining. Roger slipped his thumbs into the top of my knickers and pushed them down my legs. I kicked them off when they fell to my ankles.

As we lay together on the bed, Roger's mouth switched from my lips to my nipples to my neck. When he wasn't nibbling my nipples his fingers were tweaking them. My whole body was screaming for his touch. He took my hand and placed it on his cock. I fondled it, feeling it harden.

I asked him to be gentle as I'd never done this before.

"Never?"

11

"Never."

"You don't have to do anything now if you don't want to."

"I want to, I'm just scared of it hurting."

"I won't hurt you. We'll take it one step at a time. Tell me if you want to stop."

He climbed on top of me and pressed his prick between my legs and started to slide backwards and forwards. I squeezed my thighs together as his rhythm increased. Then I felt his cum squirt over my thighs and I wrapped my legs around him and pulled him tightly against me.

After cleaning ourselves up we lay there smoking. I was wearing a red nightdress Roger had bought for me in Debenhams.

"You really like being treated as a woman and being seen as one, don't you?"

"Yes. It's not just wearing clothes – it simply feels totally right when I do."

"And I like treating you as one. I've enjoyed your company today. Do you have to go back to London? Can't you stay longer?"

"I'd love to, but I've got work on Monday so I have to go back later today."

"So when will I see you again? Can you come back down next weekend?"

"I'd love to," I told him. "I work late on Friday but can catch an early train Saturday morning."

I snuggled into Roger's arms again and eventually fell asleep when my excited thoughts finally allowed me to do so.

I woke again about five and needed the loo. I slid out of the bed and, as quietly as possible, did what I needed to do before slipping back in, trying not to wake Roger as I did so.

As I lay on my side I felt his arm slide under me and his hand fondled my nipples through the nightdress. His mouth nuzzled my neck. I pressed my bum into his crotch. Then I felt his other hand pull the hem of the nightie up around my waist before finding my anus and a finger penetrating. I felt something cold as he lubricated my entrance. I imagined I had a vagina and it was that which he was penetrating. Our movements synchronised, he increased the speed bringing us both to a climax. My whole body went into a spasm. I let out a long moan and felt totally spent.

The next day, Roger, having sorted out the car — I don't believe there had ever been anything wrong with it — dropped me at the station.

"Promise you'll come back next weekend," he pleaded.

"I promise, Guides honour!" Ok, so I hadn't been in the Guides, but in the Scouts. I wasn't entirely sure what we had in mind for the next weekend quite fitted with 'honour' either.

One final kiss and I boarded the train.

Later, as the train pulled out of Woking, I reluctantly took my bag into the toilets. I, regretfully, changed back into David. I had never previously spent more than a whole day and night as Vicky. My earlier outings had been a few hours here and there.

Back at Waterloo I took the Northern Line tube to the Oval. It was then a ten minute walk down Clapham Road to my flat on the corner with Dorset Road.

Flat? Well, bedsit. I had one grotty room on the upper floor of a two-storey, flat roofed extension at the back of the original house. There was one window which was overlooked by the pub across the road and a tower block beyond. The two flats beneath were accessed by an entrance on Dorset Road immediately below my window. My motor scooter was parked in the street

The room had a bed, a cupboard, a sink and a Baby Belling cooker and a second hand television I'd bought. The corners of the room below the ceiling were damp, the wall paper was peeling off and the ill-fitting windows let in draughts. The shared bathrooms and toilets were down the corridor. I had no idea, nor cared, who lived in the other flats. For this I spent more than a third of my meagre pay.

Electricity was through a coin meter controlled by the landlord. As the property was damp and cold, it was expensive to heat. Compared to this, Roger's semi-detached house on the northern edge of Bournemouth was a palace.

The following weekend couldn't come quickly enough and Roger was waiting for me at the barrier at Bournemouth. He took my case from me and hugged and kissed me.

"I wasn't sure if you'd come back."

"Well, here I am," I smiled, delighted at his welcome.

"Indeed you are. What do you want to do this evening?"

"I'll give you two guesses."

"One of those is easy, I think. What's the second?"

"If the Blue Peach is open, I'd like to go back there."

"It will be open later and we can do that. Do you want something to eat first? Perhaps an Indian or we can pick up a take-away."

"Let's go back to your place first then we can decide afterwards."

"Afterwards?"

"After item one on the list!"

"Oh. I see. Do I get the feeling you only want me for my body?"

"Don't blame me – you rubbed the magic lantern and unleashed the genie!"

"Vicky! I'm going to have to watch you."

My hand went to my mouth; I hadn't meant the double entendre. I buried my head in his shoulder to hide my embarrassment.

Back at the house, Roger poured us both a glass of sparkling wine and we sat together on the sofa in the lounge. After we'd taken a couple of sips each, I stood up, held out my hand and said "Come on." He picked up the bottle. Holding it in the same hand as his glass, he followed me, fondling my bum, as we climbed the stairs.

We put the glasses and bottle down then came together in each other's arms. I soon discarded my skirt and blouse with his shirt and trousers. Our underwear followed suit and we climbed beneath the sheets. As he lay on his back, I straddled him. As we climaxed, I felt my own body spasm – the shiver running down from my head to my toes. I collapsed on top of him, pressed my lips to his and kissed him as hard as possible. He hugged me so tightly I thought my ribs might crack.

"You are so fucking marvellous Vicky," Roger gasped when we finally came up for air.

We showered together then dressed. He wasn't impressed with some of the things I'd brought with me.

"Mmm," he remarked dismissively. "I think you need a new wardrobe."

I didn't earn much and having to maintain two wardrobes wasn't easy. Inevitably a lot of my female items were from charity shops and, I suppose, it showed.

"I can't afford it," I protested, "and I can't let you buy stuff for me."

"Why not? I can afford it and I like spending money on you."

I knew when to give in gracefully and accepted we'd go shopping again the next day. Now it was time to head for a restaurant then the Blue Peach.

Several of the members I'd met the previous week were at the club. They seemed genuinely delighted to see me.

All too soon the weekend was over and I was back on the train to London. But not before I promised to be back again next weekend.

When I visited for the third time, Roger said he wished I would stay longer. I had leave due, so we agreed I'd come down the following month for two weeks. Each weekend seemed to fly past. By the time I got to Roger's and we'd slaked one appetite, it would be time to go out for dinner then on to the Blue Peach. The following morning we'd be in bed until lunch time and it wasn't long before I'd have to leave. Two weeks together would be marvellous.

## Chapter 2.    The Adventure Begins
### Friday 6<sup>th</sup> June 03

Friday 6<sup>th</sup> June arrived. It was the anniversary of D-Day — and my own 'invasion' date. My intentions were rather more peaceful.

Travelling in a busy period meant I might have problems using the loos on the train. I decided, therefore, to change at my flat and take a chance on leaving it as Vicky. I had a quick bath in the communal bathroom next to my bedsit, then dived back into my room. I dressed and put on my make-up and finished packing my case. Closing the door behind me, I made my way down the passage to the front door. As I reached it, one of the other residents opened it from the outside.

I stood aside as the other person came in.

"Afternoon," he grunted, glancing at me. Chances are he wouldn't give me a second thought. Like me, he probably didn't know, nor care, who the other residents were.

Back at Waterloo, I checked for the next train to Bournemouth. I saw I had time to pick up something to eat and a magazine to read on the journey. Having bought what I needed, I headed over to the platform, and joined the train. I put my suitcase on the overhead rack then settled back into my seat. I smoothed out my skirt and lit a cigarette. I called Roger to tell him what time I expected to arrive.

As usual he was waiting for me at the barrier. He took my case, held me in his arms and gave me a lingering kiss.

"I'm so looking forward to the next two weeks," he told me.

"Me too," I gave him a squeeze.

He put my case in the boot of the MGB and we headed home. Now there's a Freudian slip — regarding Roger's place as 'home'.

Following an interlude in the bedroom, I changed into my favourite purple dress. We then phoned for a cab to the Blue Peach.

It all felt so 'right'. For years I'd thought about spending time as Vicky. At first I'd work out how to find an hour to spend dressed and how I'd use it. Then for an afternoon or an evening. Then, eventually, to spend a whole 24 hours. Planning how I'd wake in a nightie, dress immediately as Vicky and stay that way all day.

But this had exceeded all those dreams. We did all the usual touristy things: drives in the MGB with the top down, walks in the New Forest and feeding the ponies, visiting the motor museum at Beaulieu, wandering around Lymington, swimming in Lulworth Cove and a trip over to the Isle of Wight. On one day, we went sailing in Poole Harbour. Roger had asked if I liked sailing and I told him I did, but it had been a while since I'd done any. It was the truth, but not quite the whole truth. I'd pretended not to know what I was doing. He'd then have to hold me while I followed his instructions. We visited our favourite spot in the dunes at Studland a few times and had a look round the Tank Museum at Bovingdon.

We chatted a lot, but mainly at a superficial level. I was still unwilling to expose details that might make me vulnerable. I'd found this typical of the friends I'd made at the Blue Peach. In most cases we didn't know each other's surnames or where the others lived. We all had our secrets but some were more concerned about them becoming public than others. So you didn't share too much. I obviously knew more about Roger but I didn't pry into where he worked or what he did for a living.

I loved his wicked sense of humour and appreciated he was a kind and generous man. I'd realised he was considerate that first weekend I met him when he had allowed me the opportunity to easily avoid his advances, pausing before kissing me, offering me the chance to use his spare bedroom rather than sharing his bed. Asking me to tell him to stop that first time we made love if it hurt. Even then only using my thighs instead of anal.

I hadn't needed to plan to do anything special while dressed in my dreams. Just routine things such as shopping or having a coffee were fine. The activities weren't the point — it was being able to be Vicky. The more domestic the activities the better. I hadn't included a boyfriend in my fantasies — that had seemed too much to hope for.

In any case, surely a guy who would want me because I was a transvestite would be gay. I wasn't sure where that would leave me. Somehow Roger was different. He treated me completely as female and didn't seem at all interested in my penis. Yet he'd known I was TV when he followed me. So what was he? Was he bi-sexual? It had been a whole new world for me. How long before he tired of me? Was it only a holiday romance for him — perhaps one of a string of such affairs? Would our relationship, such as it was, survive when I had to go back to work? It was one thing to come down for a few weekends but it would cost a lot to do it as often as I'd like. Certainly more than I could afford.

I put having to return to London out of my mind. I didn't want to think about it. I couldn't think about it.

# Chapter 3. Goodbye
## Friday 20th June 2003

On the second Friday, Roger had a phone call. I heard him swear before he told me he had to go into the office for the day. He needed to deal with a problem that had cropped up. I said not to worry. I'd relax around the house and might even sun bathe in the garden — something I couldn't do at my flat. It was so liberating to be able to wander from room to room; plumping up the cushions or tidying away a newspaper. Or go into the garden and smell the flowers or the new cut grass next door. Perhaps picking a few blooms for a vase in the lounge. All I had in London was one room and diesel fumes.

When he'd left, I sorted out the laundry, made the bed and tidied the house —as I had so many times in my dreams. Laundry at the flat was a trip to the laundrette.

I decided to make a baked tuna salad for dinner with a strawberry Pavlova for desert. I would use recipes from a book I'd found in the kitchen. There wasn't much in the fridge so I walked down to the small supermarket on the corner. I picked up a few supplies, then to a local fishmonger for some fresh tuna.

Walking back up the garden path, I stopped and looked around the neighbouring houses. It was an idyllic setting, at least compared with London. I would miss it.

The hot sun had dried the washing so I brought it in, ironed it and put it away. I prepared the salad, marinated the tuna steaks and put them in the fridge ready to cook later. I then prepared the Pavlova. I had cheated with the meringue base, buying one at the supermarket.

As I sat drinking a cup of tea and smoking a cigarette, I reflected that the last two weeks had answered whether I would tire of being Vicky. Far from getting bored — even doing mundane chores like today — it felt so natural.

When Roger returned about six o'clock, I told him dinner would be ready in ten minutes.

"Let me wash my hands first and change out of these clothes," he said as he ran up the stairs.

---###---

"That was delicious," he remarked as he cleaned his plate.

"It was the least I could do to repay your hospitality the last couple of weeks."

"I don't think that's all you've done though, is it? I noticed you've been busy cleaning the house."

"Well . . .," I dismissed his remarks with a wave of the hand.

He stood up and came round the table and put his arms around me. He kissed me and said "You'll make someone a marvellous wife one day."

"I wish!" I responded wistfully.

"You really would like that, wouldn't you?"

"Yes I would. I don't mean doing housework but getting a job and simply being me. The last few days living as a girl have been fabulous and I really don't want to revert to living as a guy." I struggled to hold down the lump in my throat at the thought of it.

I tried to put the thoughts to the back of my mind but they wouldn't stay there.

The comparison between what I'd had in Bournemouth and what faced me in London was stark. Oh, my job was OK. I got on well enough with my colleagues and my boss but I didn't have what I'd call friends. It's difficult making close friendships when you can't share your real self with others. Especially when you are always looking for opportunities to get changed. Even if I'd lived in a nice place, I wouldn't have wanted to invite friends back. I'd often thought about getting a better flat. But I'd have then made it as feminine as possible so I still wouldn't have been able to entertain. Assuming I could afford something better, which I couldn't.

We spent Saturday at the beach. Then had a meal at the restaurant Roger had taken me to that first time then on to the Blue Peach. I felt totally dejected knowing this was my last full day as Vicky. At one point, Roger got fed up of my long face. He left me alone while he danced with one of the other girls. It was my fault but I felt I'd blown it with him.

Roger had to go back into the office on the Sunday morning to deal with something. He promised to be back by lunch time for a last afternoon together before I had to go back to London. I'd had a sleepless night feeling despondent about having to revert to living as male. I knew that wasn't possible now. Over the last few weeks at my flat I'd been waking up in the morning, swinging my legs out of the bed and sitting there with my head in my hands thinking "I can't do this anymore."

But what else could I do? The chances of getting a job as Vicky were nil. Only one of the girls at the Blue Peach was working as female and that was behind the bar. Every single one of those that had come out as transsexual had lost their jobs. The advice was 'keep it secret if at all possible'. That was fine if you were transvestite. I'd been doing it for years; but if you could no longer switch between roles then what did you do?

As well as problems finding work, I'd have to come out to the family. I didn't think Dad would accept Vicky. The only comments I'd ever heard him make about homosexuals had been negative. Supported by quotes from the bible.

It seemed certain he'd have the same views regarding transgender. In any case, he'd probably see my relationship with Roger as gay. Mum might support me privately but wouldn't go against Dad in public.

My twin brother Peter took after Dad and was quite macho. The most likely to support me was my sister Sandra. But even she wasn't likely to want me around her own two children. Her husband Ian would do anything for a quiet life. The prospect of telling them was frightening but unavoidable if I was to transition.

Perhaps they were right. Perhaps the bible quotes were right. Perhaps I'd been tempted to live an 'abomination' wearing clothes of the opposite sex. Having to give up and revert to male role was my punishment. But that wasn't fair. I'd been born like this so why should I have to fight against it? Why should I feel guilty or ashamed? Life isn't fair though.

Everything was stacked against becoming Vicky full time. There was no possibility of continuing to switch roles. I could no longer live as David. There was only one way out.

Once Roger had left for the office, I wrote him a note and left the house. I called at several shops for what I needed. Then I caught a bus to Sandbanks and the ferry back to the beach and the dunes where we'd first met. I expected him to get back to the house after work and knew he'd be distressed to find the note I'd left him. It just said 'Sorry.'

I poured the painkillers I'd bought into the quarter-full bottle of vodka I'd taken from Roger's drinks cabinet. Then, with tears flowing, I drank it down. Some half dissolved tablets caught in my throat and I drank water to help me swallow them. The last two weeks had shown how I should be — but how could I? The freedom I'd enjoyed had been a double edged sword.

---###---

A fog surrounded me, an over-riding feeling of confusion penetrated by an emptiness in my stomach. I had a sore throat and an aching head.

Where was I?

As I lay there, I became aware of something stuck in my arm. I opened my eyes, squinting against the light. I saw it was connected to a bag hanging over my bed.

Shit. I was still alive. Then I remembered hearing Roger's voice as I'd passed out after taking the tablets. As the fog cleared, I recalled him shaking me, trying to get me to my feet. I remembered him calling for an ambulance. I had vague memories of something being put over my mouth and of being carried. And of blue lights and a siren as I had drifted in and out of consciousness.

Fuck.

Why hadn't he let me die?

I was sure he'd only been playing with me during our holiday. Why would he want a silly twenty-year old?

At best it was just a holiday romance, one of a dozen he'd probably have every year.

I licked my lips to get moisture into them — they felt so dry.

My eyes focused and I realised Roger was sitting next to me. He took my hand in his then lifted it to his lips.

"Hi. How do you feel?"

"Crap," I said.

"You gave us a hell of a scare last night."

I looked at him. He looked worried and his eyes were red. Had he been crying? Did that mean he did care about me and we hadn't been just another holiday fling? I wanted to think it might be true but it was too much to hope for. And I certainly didn't deserve him. It was all very confusing.

"You should have left me alone," I told him.

"How can you say that?" he demanded. "Do you think I want to lose the girl I love? I'd been worried about you since Saturday night so I returned home and found your note. When I saw what you'd written, I guessed what you planned to do and where."

"Shit," I replied. "I'm so, so sorry."

"Hush. Everything will be OK."

How was that possible? Why hadn't they let me die? What was the point of still living? It would have been so easy — everyone would have got over me eventually. Nothing had changed. I couldn't live any longer as David and it wasn't possible to live full time as Vicky. So where did that leave me?

At that moment a nurse came in and asked Roger to leave for a few minutes. "Why don't you get a coffee, you've been up all night. She'll be fine now."

Roger kissed my lips, squeezed my hand, then left.

I had no idea what the time was — I seemed to be in a side ward without windows and no clocks visible. My watch and everything else had been removed. I was dressed in a gown and there was a drip into my arm. From what the nurse had said, I assumed it was now Monday. Hell, I should be back at work this morning. She noted various readings on my chart. Blood pressure, heart rate, temperature and the rest.

"You're bound to feel rough at the moment, we had to pump out your stomach. Your fiancé is a lovely guy. He was so worried about you. OK that's you done. We'll serve breakfast soon but I can get you a cup of tea now if you'd like."

Did she call Roger my fiancé? Where did that come from? I guessed he must have told them a white lie to be allowed to stay with me. It didn't mean a thing. Except . . , except didn't he just tell me he loved me? And he didn't want to lose me? Or was I still hallucinating? I wished my head would clear. Perhaps a drink would help.

"Yes, please, a cup of tea would be lovely. What will happen to me?"

"We'll be keeping you in for a day or two for observations. But you're young and fit so there shouldn't be any lasting side effects."

She came back a few minutes later with the tea.

"We had a surprise when we undressed you."

I blushed.

"No need to get embarrassed," she continued, "I used to work at Charing Cross Hospital. I'm well used to seeing transsexual patients. My name is Carol."

Carol looked mid to late thirties, shortish with flaming red hair. I suspected anyone who got on the wrong side of her would regret doing so.

"Can I ask, was what you tried to do yesterday because you are trans?" she added.

I nodded. "I can't go on living as a guy and can't see how I can live as a woman so what's the point?"

"I thought so. You know eight out of ten trans people consider suicide and nearly half make an attempt. They think there's no hope for them for the future — but there is. I've seen literally hundreds go through Charing Cross gender clinic. Almost all of them are happy with the outcome. I'm not saying there aren't difficulties. Society can be dreadfully cruel to anyone who is different. You're luckier than most though, having a fiancé who accepts you as you are. Look, I'll come back later and give you more information if you'd like, but Roger's back."

I wasn't sure anything she might say would help but it wouldn't hurt to listen. I had nothing better to do.

Roger leant over the bed and kissed me again. I smelled and tasted the coffee on his lips. "Feeling any better?" he asked.

"Yes, thanks, and sorry again."

"Stop saying 'sorry', just promise me you won't try anything like that again."

"I promise. But did you tell the nurse you're my fiancé?"

"Yes — I had to say I was or they wouldn't let me stay."

"Did you also say just now you love me? Or was that another white lie?"

Roger took me by the shoulders and looked straight into my eyes and said very firmly, "Vicky, I *do* love you. You're the best thing that's happened to me and I want to spend the rest of my life with you."

I burst into tears. Desperately unhappy because I'd caused him so much pain over the last few hours, joyful because of what he'd told me. The emotions made my head spin.

I think I blurted out I loved him too.

Carol came back after the shift change, despite the fact she was now on her own time. She explained the processes involved in transition. The options of NHS and private routes and a lot of other useful information. She mentioned a support group that met each month near the Blue Peach.

"What do you think?" I asked Roger after she'd left. "How would you feel about me transitioning, even having surgery?"

"Darling, it has to be your decision but you're obviously not really a guy. As far as I can see, you're a woman inside. But whether you've got male or female bits makes no difference. It's you I love, not what's between your legs and it's obvious you'd be much happier if you did transition. You need to do something. It's a lot better option than suicide isn't it? As for how, it seems to take ages with the NHS but that private psychiatrist can cut years off the process. Perhaps you should see him."

"But what would I do? How would I live?"

"Come and live with me."

"There's nothing I'd like more but it's not that easy."

"Why not?"

"Well, for a start I still need to earn a living, I can't sponge off you. My official documents are all in my male name. That's even if I can find a job where they'd employ a transsexual."

"Look, you told me you work in admin, right?"

"Yes, Why?"

"Well, the reason I had to go into the office on Friday was because our admin lady has quit. She got married on Saturday and is moving to New Zealand with her husband. So there's a solution to your job problem."

"Wouldn't you need clear it with your boss? Wouldn't I have to have an interview? What would he think about me being transsexual?"

"Can you use Microsoft Word and Excel?"

"Yes."

"You've got payroll experience? And book-keeping and petty cash?"

"Yes. But.. "

"Are you good on the phone?"

"I think so."

"Dealing with the public?"

"Yes, I sometimes cover on reception."

"How about organising a boss's diary?"

"Yes. But.."

"Would you want the job?"

"Yes — but —"

"But what? You've just passed the interview. I *am* the boss. I own the company. I didn't mention it before because I've had a few gold-diggers chase me. You're the first not to care about my background. Hell, you even argued about me buying you a few clothes. You've said you can't sponge off me so I'm damned sure you're not after my money."

"Are you serious?"

"Yes, darling."

I was amazed by this revelation. Working for Roger's company would certainly solve most of my immediate concerns.

"Next problem?" Roger asked after a pause. I couldn't think of any that mattered.

"I'll have to go back and work out my notice — it's only two weeks, thankfully. What does your company do?"

"It's a chandlers and we charter yachts. We hire dinghies and sailboards from the slipway in Poole where we took the dinghy out from. That's why you might have to cover the odd weekend. You already know a bit about sailing, you can train as an instructor if you wanted. The company will pay for it and you'd get more money afterwards."

"I'm already an RYA Dinghy Instructor and Coastal Skipper on cruisers," I laughed, "I've sailed since I was about five. I pretended not to know much so you had to help me more."

He shook his head in mock despair.

"Holding out on me were you?" he said with a smile.

"No more than you held out on me about owning the company. I have one more question though. If I'm your fiancé, when do I get my engagement ring?"

Life had gone from despair to elation in less than twenty four hours. From seeing no hope for any future, it now seemed exhilarating. 'Mrs Vicky Dalton' had a lovely ring to it as I whispered the words to myself. When breakfast came, I found I had quite an appetite.

# Chapter 4.   Appointment in Earls Court
## 26th June 03

When I got through to the private psychiatrist's receptionist, she told me the usual waiting time for an appointment with Dr Wright was about two months but if I could be at his consulting rooms at one pm on Thursday, she'd just taken a cancellation and he would see me then. The fee would be £130. I immediately agreed to the offer.

Thursday morning I caught the train from Bournemouth; I changed at Clapham Junction for Victoria then took the District Line. The address the receptionist had given was a few minutes' walk from the tube and I was there in plenty of time.

Dr Wright eventually invited me into his consulting room.

"Good afternoon, Vicky, what can I do for you?"

"I used to see myself as transvestite, but I've now decided I am transsexual. I want to start hormone treatment and eventually have surgery."

"I see, suppose you give me your history? We can then discuss why you now consider yourself to be transsexual rather than transvestite. Tell me about your family."

"I'm one of twins, the other is my brother, Peter. We have a sister, Sandra, three years older than us. Both our parents are still alive. Dad is ex-Army and I grew up outside Fareham in Hampshire. I did OK at school, usually in the top third for most subjects."

"What were your favourite subjects?"

"English language and literature, history, geography. I sometimes came top in English literature. Chemistry tended to be my worst subject with maths not far behind."

"How were you at sports?"

"I was pretty rubbish at football, I hated it. I much preferred cross country running but I quite liked hockey. Sailing was my favourite sport though. We did it in senior school as an extra activity during the summer and I joined a sailing club. Peter and I used to race dinghies."

"What other activities did you do?"

"The school had an Army Cadet Unit and I was in the cubs and scouts."

"How did you enjoy those?"

"They were OK but I wasn't as keen as Peter. They were things I did because I was a boy and was expected to want to do them I suppose."

"What about girl or boyfriends?"

"I didn't really have any girlfriends and had no interest in boys. Well . . ."

Dr Wright picked up on my hesitation.

"Go on."

I took a deep breath.

"As David, I had no interest in boyfriends. However, over the last few years, when I dressed as a girl I would often fantasise about being with a man."

"When did you first dress in female clothes?"

"I'm not sure, I remember Sandra dressing me up for a party with her friends. I think Peter had come off his bike. Mum and Dad had driven him to A&E and had asked a neighbour to come round and look after us. I must have been about seven and Sandra would have been ten. I don't know how it came about but I remember wearing one of her party frocks and joining in the biscuits and Corona pop she'd been allowed to take up to her room. I think that would have been the first time."

"What happened after that?"

"I would find Sandra's things in the laundry basket and wear them in my room while doing my homework. I even borrowed a nightie which I wore in bed a few times until I got scared I'd be caught if I overslept. Once we got old enough to be left on our own, I spent more time in my room dressed. I even went for bike rides sometimes, changing behind hedges. It was awkward though as my bike had a crossbar so I had to wear girls' jeans rather than a skirt."

"How did you feel when you were dressed?"

"While I was doing it, it felt right. Afterwards, I knew I shouldn't be doing it. I was a boy and boys shouldn't wear girls' clothes but I couldn't stop. I felt guilty and ashamed."

"You say it felt 'right' being dressed as a girl? Is that how you saw yourself, as a girl."

"I think that's part of the point — we don't 'see' ourselves because we're on the inside looking out. We can't really know how others see us. I can't say I felt I *was* a girl. I had a dangly bit between my legs which meant I was a boy and, apart from dressing, I did my best to behave like one and fit in. Most nights, though, I'd pray that, if there was a God, He'd turn me into a girl while I slept and I'd wake up with the right bits. It didn't happen of course."

Dr Wright smiled when I told him this. I imagined many of his patients said the same.

"Well, anyway, I took every opportunity to dress. By the time I was fifteen, Peter was well into girls and off on dates and Sandra was engaged. She got married when I was sixteen. I remember wishing I was one of the bridesmaids. Of course, it was out of the question and I wouldn't have dared mention it. By then I'd acquired a few things of my own. They were usually from items donated to the scouts for jumble sales. The vast majority of donations were useless but there was an occasional item that was useable."

"How did you feel when you were dressed?" I'd already answered this but assumed he was seeing if my responses were consistent.

"It just felt right."

"Were you sexually aroused?"

"No, not at all. Some of the materials felt much nicer than male equivalents but it wasn't about sexual gratification."

"Did you masturbate while dressed?"

"A few times. I'd fantasise about being a real female and having a boyfriend and making love. But that wasn't why I dressed."

"How did that make you feel?"

"It was strange. I was a boy fantasising about sex with another male. But it didn't seem like it was gay because I was a female in the fantasy. I had no interest in guys when I've been presenting as a male."

I wasn't sure whether what I was saying made any sense to Dr Wright — I wasn't sure it made sense to me; but this was how I felt.

"Did you have any interest in girls at this stage?"

"Yes, but not as girlfriends. It was more about how they behaved and dressed. How they spoke and the gestures they used, not because I fancied them. It was the same with film and pop stars. At school, other boys would say how they liked them but I wished I *was* them."

"And how did you see yourself?"

"I'd looked on the internet and had found information about transvestites and transsexuals. It never occurred to me I might be transsexual. All the reports on the internet, in newspapers and on television about transsexuals implied to be TS, you had to have known all your life you were 'in the wrong body' and that didn't apply to me. I *wanted* to be a girl – but had identified as a boy."

"Have you told anyone about your feelings? Your parents or siblings, colleagues?"

"God no. I couldn't possibly tell them. They'd think I was like Dame Edna or a drag artist; they'd see me as a pervert, I'd be so ashamed."

"Are you working at the moment?"

"Yes, at a Council Leisure Centre in Brixton."

"Don't you think they'd be supportive?"

"I daren't take the risk. In any case, while I thought I was TV, I didn't need to tell anyone. I could do it in secret — which is what I've been doing for several years after all."

"So what's changed? What makes you now think you are transsexual?"

I told him how I'd met Roger, how we'd spent several weekends together then two weeks.

"After living completely as female, I realised I couldn't go back to living as a guy. I feel I've been living a role as a male and can't do it anymore. I realise being TV isn't enough. Those two weeks as Vicky, in particular, have released a force I can't now ignore."

I took another deep breath. The next bit wasn't going to be easy to relate and might make Dr Wright question my sanity. But it was essential for me to be totally honest with him. Just thinking about it brought back the feeling of utter despair I'd felt at the time.

"At the end of the two weeks, I couldn't face being male but I didn't see how I could transition to female. I thought I'd lose everything: my job, family, home, everything. In the past, cross-dressing had acted as a kind of safety valve for my feminine side – but it was no longer enough. I decided to kill myself and took an overdose."

I looked for Dr Wright to react but he sat there on the edge of his seat, fountain pen in hand ready to take notes. Did he think I was unstable?

"Obviously it didn't work. Roger had found a note I'd left and he'd guessed I'd make the attempt where we'd first met. He found me and got me to hospital. When I came round, he asked me to move in with him and offered me a job, he owns a yachting company. It doesn't solve everything. I still need to come out to family and friends but at least I can see a future worth fighting for."

"Do you have any support?"

"Roger, of course, and friends I've made at a club we go to."

"How about your family? Have you told them yet? Are they aware of your overdose."

"No they aren't aware of it or of my decision to transition."

"How do you think they'll take it?"

"I honestly don't know. Judging from comments Dad has made about gay people, I think it may disgust him. Mum won't go against him in public even if she'd support me privately. I have to face to possibility they'll all reject me."

The thought of losing the family made me well up. Dr Wright offered me a box of tissues and I wiped the tears from my eyes.

"The trouble is, I can't go on living a lie, pretending to be something I'm not. I can't face the rest of my life trying to be a man. It's not what I am," I sobbed.

"So what are you?"

"Physically, I have a male body but I don't feel right as a man. It's as though I'm playing a part, doing things people expect men to do. I don't think like a man. I feel much more natural presenting and being accepted as a female. I came across a Cogiati test on the internet, where they give you multiple choice questions and you then score the results."

"Yes, I'm familiar with the test — it's not a diagnostic tool but can be useful."

"Well, as you know then, it shows significant differences between typical responses for men and for women. My score was well into the female range, not even in the overlap area. I also did a test showing which parts of the brain are used more than others. Again, my results showed a balanced use of all four quadrants typical of female scores rather than one quadrant dominant. I know it's a cliché, but I feel like I have a female brain in a male body."

"Are you sure you're not letting those results influence your decision? As I said, they aren't diagnostic tools."

"No, I'd already decided I needed to transition before doing the tests but I thought it was interesting to see they confirmed how I felt."

"OK, so, you are now in a relationship with Roger?"

"Yes."

"How do you see that relationship?"

"He sees me as female and treats me as one. That's how I feel when I'm with him so I'd say it's a heterosexual relationship. When we make love, I imagine he's penetrating my vagina and it feels right. Others may not see it that way, but that doesn't matter. Frankly, I don't care what labels others may put on our relationship. It's right for us and that's all that matters to Roger and me."

Dr Wright made some additional notes on his pad, put down his fountain pen then said:

"Well, Vicky, from what you've told me, your symptoms are consistent with being transsexual."

Just hearing those words lifted a huge weight off my shoulders.

"In view of your suicide attempt, I want to wait until your next appointment before prescribing hormones as they can impact on moods. I want you to have blood tests first in any case. I'll write to your GP organising the tests and provide other letters to allow you to change your documents. All being well, your GP should be able to provide NHS prescriptions for hormones. Make another appointment with Cassie, my receptionist, to see me again in three months' time.

He gave me a letter to carry at all times that was my 'get out of jail' document:

*'TO WHOM IT MAY CONCERN*

*This confirms that Miss Victoria Williamson is having treatment for Male to Female Transsexualism.*

*Wearing women's clothes and taking female hormones is part of this process and is quite appropriate.'*

My nerves tingled when I read it.

It was a dream come true. It truly was. I was on my way and it felt like I'd been released from a prison. A prison I'd created for myself. I was *free*, free to be myself or, more accurately, free to accept who I really was.

I realised the road ahead would be difficult. I was thankful I had Roger's support. There had been other patients in the waiting room who were rejected by their families and friends and had lost their jobs. Some had been living in denial for 20, 30, 40 even 50 years. I was fortunate to be transitioning in my early 20s.

For as long as I remembered, I'd fantasised about falling asleep and waking up with a female body; being offered a pill that would do the same job. Even of having an accident that seriously damaged my genitals giving me the opportunity to tell the surgeon to remove what was left. The fantasies never, ever, included being cured of wanting to change. Now my wildest dreams might come true.

It would probably take a little over a year before I could have surgery. I'd have expected that year to seem like another jail sentence but it didn't. Of course I looked forward to it; and dreaded it at the same time. It would make a huge difference when making love with Roger. It would also mean bikinis fitted much better. But it really wasn't as important as the step I had just taken.

I'd suppressed my feelings all my life. As I'd told Dr Wright, I'd done 'boy' things to bury them — joining the scouts and the army cadets and taking up sailing. Those feelings had simmered below the surface though and, whenever I got the opportunity, I would dress en femme. I would have described it before as cross-dressing but that no longer seemed accurate. Now I saw it as having been dressing as my true gender and my male persona had been a character I'd played.

I phoned Roger from Victoria once I knew which train I'd be on and he was waiting for me at the barrier once more. I ran to him and flung my arms around his neck. He held me to him and span me around — my feet off the ground.

"How did it go then?" asked Roger.

"Great. Dr Wright confirmed the diagnosis of transsexualism. He said he would probably prescribe hormones next time," I replied.

"So what affect should the hormones have? And are there any side effects?" he asked.

"They should give me a feminised body, softer skin, subtler outline and breasts. I'm less likely to have erections." I shuddered at the thought of having an erection. "I need to be careful about damage to the heart and the liver — which is why I have to have regular blood tests."

"We'd better get you set up with a GP down here then. You won't want to be traipsing up to London for appointments."

"I have to see the specialist every three months so he can monitor my progress."

Having decided to transition, I changed my name by deed poll the next day to Victoria Williamson. That meant I could notify the various authorities and the bank of my new status as soon as I got the letters the specialist had promised me.

Saturday morning, Roger and I drove into town to the jewellers where I chose an engagement ring with a central diamond and two sapphires. Having Roger place it on my finger made me feel like a million dollars. Sadly, I wouldn't be able to wear it full time until I moved down in two weeks.

Two weeks.

Fourteen days.

Three hundred and thirty six hours.

How would I cope?

## Chapter 5.   Back to Work
### Monday 30<sup>th</sup> June 03

I reluctantly returned to London on the Sunday afternoon. On Monday morning, I knocked on Andrea's office door and asked if she was free. When she waved me to come in, I closed the door behind me — something we rarely did.

"I hope you're well rested after your holiday and your accident, David, there's a pile of work waiting for you." Andrea must have seen my face and noticed I was holding an envelope.

"Is something up?" she asked.

"Yes. I'm leaving. This is my letter of resignation."

"Oh. I see. This seems rather sudden. What happened on holiday? Did you meet someone by any chance? You know what holiday romances can be like. Is this anything to do with your accident?"

"Yes I did meet someone — but it's a lot more than that. And it wasn't an accident I had."

"Well, she must be special as I thought you enjoyed your work and had a bright future here."

I was tempted to let her think it was a girl I'd met but decided to tell her the full story. I took a deep breath then blurted out: "*He **is** very special and I'm the 'she'*. I've been hiding something for years and only just accepted it. I'm transsexual and plan to transition."

"Wow. Now that is a bombshell. I'd never have guessed. Do you want to talk about it? Look, let's get a coffee and we can have a chat. Stay here. I'll be back in a few minutes."

Andrea returned with two mugs of coffee. We sat together round her little conference table rather than facing each other across her desk. I told her my 'accident' had been attempted suicide because I could no longer face living as a guy.

"I can't imagine how much courage it took for you to tell me the truth David. I'm humbled you felt you could open up to me. Thank you for that. You know if you'd wanted to go through the change here, I'd support you 100% don't you? And let me say now if things don't work out, I'd have you back in a flash either as David or ..."

"Vicky," I said.

"Or as Vicky. I can't promise you'd have the same position. I'll need to replace you. But you know we're rarely at full establishment so there's almost certain to be a vacancy."

"Thanks, that's good to know, though I'm sure it won't be necessary."

"Well, there's no point me trying to persuade you to stay under the circumstances. So I wish you the best of luck. The other staff will need to know about your resignation but not about anything else, unless you choose to tell them. There is one final thing though. If you and your young man get married then I expect an invitation."

She stood up and gave me a hug. "God, you are brave and I suspect you'll need to be."

The following days sped by at work — but the evenings dragged. As soon as I got back to my dismal bedsit, I'd get changed. Roger and I would then spend an hour or so chatting on the phone. That, at least, provided some relief.

Friday lunch time, having made up the hours earlier in the week, I jumped on a train to Bournemouth, my heart racing with anticipation.

Returning, so very grudgingly, on Sunday evening. The trains were quiet at these times so I was able to change in the loos. Going down, I would go straight into the toilets re-emerging after a stop to give the impression I had joined the train there.

The specialist's letters arrived ten days after I saw him. One was for my GP giving his diagnosis of my condition and recommended treatment including hormones. Seeing it in black and white — well, black on vellum — brought home I was truly on my way.

The second are to the Passport Office giving my details and confirming I was under his care: *'for the treatment of Male to Female Transsexualism. She lives exclusively in female role and intends to continue doing this permanently. She has changed her name legally. I would support her application for a new passport in her female name and gender status'*

The third, similar letter, to the DVLA, supported changing my driving licence.

## Chapter 6.  Last Day
### Friday 11<sup>th</sup> July

I invited my colleagues to leaving drinks at a pub near the centre at lunch time on my last Friday. Later that evening, Andrea and Vicky were going out for a farewell meal.

By now I'd donated my male wardrobe to charity shops or thrown it away — apart from the shoes, shirt and trousers I wore to work on my last day. I would ceremonially burn them later. I had, it's true, a pair of trousers, a shirt and a pair of Cuban heel ankle boots which could pass as male attire if a dire emergency occurred —but they'd all come from the women's section. There had been no point keeping male clothes as a back-up plan. I'd already decided living as a guy wasn't possible so I had to make it work as Vicky. And I bloody well would.

Once the others returned to the office after lunch time drinks on Friday, I went to my appointment at the Helen of Troy salon for the works: hair, nail extensions, facial including having my eyebrows shaped, ears pierced and legs waxed. My hair was long enough for the stylist to create a more feminine, feathered look. I had it lightened a little and highlights added. No more wigs for me. I relished the whole experience, it was so different to a gents barbers.

Andrea was already waiting for me in the Italian restaurant we'd chosen. I was apprehensive as I walked through the door. Not because I was concerned about any problems with the restaurant. Nor, after several meals at the one in Bournemouth, was I concerned about the menu. It was really important Andrea approved of Vicky. I'd brought my purple dress back from Roger's last weekend for this evening to look my best.

Even as I walked up to the table, she kept looking towards the door; still waiting for me to enter. At the last minute she looked at me and did a double take.

"Vicky?" she asked incredulously, "God, I didn't recognise you. I really didn't know what to expect — but you look fabulous. It's incredible and your whole face is just glowing. This truly is the real 'you' isn't it?"

"Yes it is — maybe you thought I'd look like Kenny Everett in drag or Danny La Rue?"

She laughed. "Not quite, well, yes," she admitted, "but you look so good, I'm jealous! Hang on a minute what's that on your finger. Show me."

She held my hand while she examined my engagement ring.

"That's so beautiful; the sapphires match your eyes. I can't get over the change in you; how you had to hide your true self all these years. It must have been horrible pretending to be something you weren't. I can't begin to understand how that felt — but I'm so pleased you can be your true self from now on."

## Chapter 7.   New Life
### Saturday 12<sup>th</sup> July 03

The next morning, I strapped my last suitcase on the back of my Vespa motor scooter. I then dropped my flat keys at the landlord's office.

Although the forecast was for a hot day I was wearing overalls and my crash helmet. It wasn't obvious, therefore, I was a very different person to the one that had rented the flat. Until I had to remove a glove to sign a receipt for the refund of my deposit. Then my scarlet nails stared them in the face.

By then I couldn't care less what they thought, it was none of their damned business.

With a top speed of less than 44 mph downhill with a following wind, I wanted to avoid motorways. So, I kept to the A roads. I expected it to take at least four hours, allowing for breaks. As much as I wanted to see Roger, I wasn't going to rush and risk an accident.

By the time I reached the outskirts of London, the sun was beating down from a clear sky. I was overheating, so I removed my overalls and let the wind generated by my speed cool me as I continued down the road to Bournemouth and my new life.

# Chapter 8.   Coming Out
## Monday 14th July 03

I'd asked Roger not to tell the other staff we were together or about my history. I wanted them to get to know me as Vicky, the new girl; not Vicky the boss' fiancée or Vicky the tranny. We wouldn't lie about it and if it came up in conversation then we'd deal with it. We just weren't going to make an issue of it ourselves.

That lasted until morning coffee break when Patty, one of the girls, asked about my engagement ring! I told them Roger and I were together and planned to marry. I said we'd met when I came to Bournemouth on holiday — but not about my history.

There was one important group I really needed to tell my news but had been putting off. That was my parents, sister and brother.

If I'd thought it through earlier, I might have seen them as David and explained face to face. I could still visit them as David but that now felt like a betrayal of Vicky. It wouldn't be easy any longer with my new hair style and colour, my shaped eyebrows, pierced ears, nail extensions. No. It was no longer an option to visit them as David.

Mum and Dad were in their early-fifties. They still had conservative attitudes, with a small 'c', especially towards gay issues and, by association, trans. Sandra, my sister, was three years older than me. She was married with two children, Katie, three years old and Oliver, one.

Peter was my twin brother, but we were very different. While I had joined the scouts and Army Cadet Force to appear to fit in, he'd been enthusiastic. He'd quickly progressed through the qualifications and ranks eventually becoming a Queen's Scout and Troop Leader and a Sergeant in the ACF.

Peter played cricket for the school, I'd kept score.

He revelled in long distance running. I was happier finding something to sketch or paint.

Sailing was the exception. Although competitive, it rarely involved physical contact or even relies mainly on strength. It was as much, if not more, about tactics and finesse in how you set up and handled the boat and that's where I'd scored over him.

He'd dated girls almost as soon as he was into long trousers — having no problem chatting them up. I'd had one fumbling experience and one solitary date for a youth club disco.

When he said he fancied attractive girls we saw, I was wishing I WAS her.

I'd come in for merciless ragging at his hands over the years because of what he saw as my shyness. Now perhaps he would understand. Or would he?

How should I tell them all? Should I phone them? Should I write a letter? Or email?

Shit. This wasn't going to be easy. Not easy? That was an understatement.

I could write an email and copy it to all of them. That way I could take time to include everything I needed to. But that would be cold and I wouldn't be able to judge the tone of any reply.

Should I make it a joke? 'Hey, Sandra, remember when you had me dress up in your things for that party with your friends? Well guess what.'

Or 'Mum, you've been on at me to get a girlfriend. Well, I've got good news and not so good news for you. I'm getting married but I'll be the one in the wedding dress.'

Shit. Double shit.

A phone call then?

I asked Roger how he thought I should handle it. For once he was at a loss. His own parents, Barbara and James had been quite matter of fact about the latest development as he'd previously had boy and girlfriends. They lived in Malta now enjoying the Mediterranean sun in their retirement.

We asked our friends at the Blue Peach if they'd had to face the same problems. A few had. Sadly the reactions they'd had from their families wasn't encouraging. It didn't seem to matter how they had broached the subject.

As I was sitting in the lounge, on the Monday evening, pondering what to do, my mobile rang. It was Mum. I put down my glass of wine to take the call.

"Hello darling. I phoned you at work earlier today to check you were still coming down this weekend. They told me you had resigned. So what are you doing now? Where are you?"

I swallowed hard. I'd quite forgotten I'd planned to spend next weekend with them.

"Yes, that's right. I've left the leisure centre. I've got a new job in Bournemouth with a chandler cum yacht agency and sailing hire place. I met someone while down here and the job fell into my lap, so I took it."

I took a sip of wine while she continued.

"That's marvellous, dear. Sounds like you've hit it lucky there. So where are you living? What's your new address? Now you're down there and with your fortune changing, maybe you'll find a nice girl to settle down with."

"I'm not sure how to put this Mum, can you sit down please."

Roger sat next to me and put his hand reassuringly on my leg.

"Why, David? What's up? You're not ill are you?"

"Not in the sense you mean Mum, though I am having some medical treatment. I didn't want to do this over the phone. I'd rather have done it face to face. But now you're on, I need to tell you something that may come as a shock."

"You're not going to tell us you are gay are you? We've suspected you might be for years."

Obviously they'd picked up on signals I must have been giving out without realising it. At least my news wouldn't be a complete surprise.

"No, I'm not gay but it's similar. I've recently seen a specialist who has confirmed I'm transsexual. I'm going to live the rest of my life as female."

"Pardon? What did you say?"

"I said I'm transsexual and I'm going to live the rest of my life as female."

"You mean like that one on the telly a few weeks ago? When I watched the programme, there were bits that made me think of you. Are you absolutely sure about this David? Looks like a very difficult road, darling."

"Yes Mum, I am certain. I think I've known it's what I've needed to do for a long time. It came to a head about three weeks ago."

"Well, I hope you know what you are doing. It will be strange thinking of you as a young woman rather than as one of my boys. But you are still my child and I love you regardless. But how does that affect your new job. Do they know? Do they mind?"

"That's the other part of the story Mum. My boss met me as Vicky, that's my name now. We've fallen in love and I now live with him. His name is Roger."

"You don't do things by halves do you, love? Are you sure you're not rushing things? So when do we get to meet Roger? And Vicky, of course. I do hope you don't look like Dame Edna Everedge."

"No Mum, I don't look like that. I'll talk to Roger and see when we can come over, and I'll call you back."

I slumped back into the sofa relieved Mum's reaction had been as positive as I could have hoped.

Roger looked at me. "Well?"

"She thought I was going to tell them I was gay. But seems to have accepted I'm trans. She wants to know when we can go and see them."

"Sooner the better, where are they?"

"Near Fareham."

"That's only about an hour from here, we can go over next weekend if you like."

"I'll phone her back and check."

I picked my mobile up to ring her but was pre-empted by an incoming call from Sandra.

"Hello, I think you have something to tell me," she said.

"Mum's already said something I take it."

"She certainly has. Not that she needed to tell me. I've been waiting for you to say something for years. Did you really think I wouldn't notice some of my things had been moved and some of my make-up had been used whenever the family was out and left you at home?"

"But you never said anything."

"What could I say? What would have happened if I'd mentioned it? Would you have admitted it or denied it?"

"Deny it, I suppose."

"So there was no point in saying anything was there? And it might have caused a rift between us."

I felt guilty and embarrassed. I mumbled "Thanks, and I'm sorry if I messed up any of your stuff."

"Forget it. But don't be surprised if I scrounge things from you in future."

I could hardly object to that. "Anytime. But I don't have much you're likely to want at the moment."

"Then that needs to be remedied. We'll arrange a shopping trip and a girls' night out! I think I'm going to enjoy having a sister as well as a brother instead of two pesky brothers. And, little sister, I expect female solidarity from you in future. No more ganging up on me with Peter. Now when do I get to meet Vicky and this guy that's swept you off your feet?"

"I was about to phone Mum and suggest this weekend when your call came through."

I couldn't believe the way the conversation had gone. No recriminations, just loving support.

"I'm not too sure how Peter will take it but I'm on your side," she continued, "I think little Katie will love having an auntie and Oliver will never have known any difference. I know you have to call Mum back so I'll let you go now. Ring me back as soon as you can. And call Peter."

Mum said next weekend would be fine for us to come over we would have a barbecue. She would invite Sandra and her family and Peter. She said she'd told Dad my news but he didn't want to speak right now as he needed to get his head around it.

Three down. One to go.

I smoked a cigarette to steel my nerves and called Peter.

"Yes."

"It's Dave," I said.

"I can see that, but it's not Dave any longer is it?"

"Well, no. It's Vicky from now on."

"Yeah. Right. So Sandra told me. You've got to be out of your f*ing mind. What the hell do you think you're doing? And now you're shacked up with some pouf as well. What do you think my friends will think? Did you stop and wonder about that? Did you? Did you consider that they'll now wonder if I'm the same as you? Well, don't expect me to support you. I don't want to hear your excuses. This is your problem. I don't see why I should have to make any adjustments to suit you."

"Peter, I'm sorry you feel that way. I really am, but I have to live my life the best I can. I'll do my best not to embarrass you. Perhaps someday you'll be able to understand."

"I doubt it. Got to go." Peter terminated the call.

I'd known there was a risk of losing family, but it still hurt that my closest sibling had rejected me and in such a homophobic manner. However, Sandra's support was far more than I could have hoped for.

## Chapter 9.    Meet the Family
## Sunday 20<sup>th</sup> July 03

I tried on almost everything I owned deciding what to wear to meet the family. T-shirt, jeans and trainers minimised the visual change – but was that what I wanted to achieve? The purple dress Roger had bought me the day we met certainly made a statement. It was my favourite — but would that be too much of a culture shock for Mum and Dad? A skirt and blouse would be a compromise. But if I chose that route, which skirt and which blouse? By the time I'd finished trying on different outfits, I'd covered our bed in discarded clothes. Then there was the question of make-up: toned down or full treatment? Jeans and t-shirt would demand it be toned down, a dressier approach would mean the works.

There was little point in fudging the issue. I wanted to be seen and accepted as female so rejected the androgynous look of jeans and t-shirt. I settled on my purple dress. It had brought me luck as it had led to me falling in love with Roger and making the move to Bournemouth. I felt fabulously feminine wearing it and knew it made me look that way.

At two o'clock we pulled up outside Mum & Dad's house. Sandra's car was already there but there was no sign of Peter's motorbike. I assumed he'd carried out his threat of avoiding me. The garden was looking as lovely as ever. My parents put a lot of effort into their roses and keeping the lawn nicely trimmed. The latter having being one of my jobs when I was still at home.

Roger looked at me as we sat there and put his hand on mine. "Are you OK?"

Not really, I thought, but I said "Yes," as I leant across to kiss him. "Come on."

I opened the car door and took Roger's arm as he came round to my side.

I was worried about how Dad would react. Mum had said he needed to get his head around it. That wasn't surprising. It was a huge change and it had taken me years to accept it myself.

The front door opened as we walked up the garden path. Mum stood there. She had a look of surprise and, I think, relief on her face that I didn't look like Dame Edna. Mum and Sandra gave me warm hugs when I walked through the door and kissed Roger on the cheeks.

Roger said "Lovely to meet you Mrs Williamson, these are for you," handing Mum some flowers we'd brought.

She replied "Thank you, they're gorgeous, but please call me Joan."

We walked into the lounge. Dad offered me his hand to shake as usual. Then did the same for Roger as they stepped through the French windows into the garden where they'd set up the barbecue.

Ian, Sandra's husband, just waved at us from the chair on the lawn and said "Hi."

I was about to walk into the garden to have a chat with Dad when Sandra grabbed my arm.

"Where do you think you're going, lady? You're one of the women now — not a male to be waited on any longer. Come on we have work to do in the kitchen. We'll leave the men to get the barbecue going."

Considering how many times I'd joked with her in the past about a woman's place being at the kitchen sink, I deserved the remark.

As I followed Mum and Sandra into the kitchen, I heard Dad asking Roger what he'd like to drink. What he thought of Southampton's chances in the forthcoming football season and insisting he call him Dougie.

"That dress is fabulous and really suits you — give us a twirl," instructed Sandra. "In fact, Vicky, you look great."

"You certainly do," agreed Mum.

"Not like a drag act then?" I asked.

"Not at all, thanks goodness," Mum replied.

Mum and Sandra insisted on seeing my engagement ring.

"So when are you planning to marry?" asked Sandra.

"We can't unfortunately. I'm still legally male and can't marry another male."

"Didn't I hear the government is looking at changing the law on trans people? How would that affect you?"

"Yes, the Gender Recognition Bill, or Gerbill as we call it. They announced it at the beginning of the month which would mean I can be legally recognised as female. If it passes. Then we would be able to get married."

"You don't sound convinced it will pass."

"I'm not. There is still too much opposition to it. They haven't actually introduced it yet. People like the Chingford Skinhead, Norman Tebbutt, have made speeches condemning the idea. Some churches, especially the Evangelical Alliance, are totally opposed."

"Didn't I also hear of another bill allowing same sex couples to register a partnership?"

"Yes, there is that option. But Roger and I don't consider we are the same gender. So while that's a possibility it doesn't seem right for us. In any case, that's facing similar opposition to the Gender Recognition Bill. It seems either will take a long time to come in to effect."

"Hopefully the Gerbill, did you call it? will pass and you can marry; if that's what you want."

"It is what we want; so I do hope it passes, but we aren't holding our breath. In the meantime, we're thinking of organising a 'commitment' ceremony. We'll make the same sort of promises in front of family and friends. But it won't have any legal significance. Now, what can I do to help?"

"Put an apron on first to protect that dress, which I may want to borrow sometime, sis. Then chop up some of the celery for the salad."

Smoke drifted across the kitchen window as the men began to light the charcoal. It looked like it would be a while before the coals were ready to cook the meat. Once the salads were all prepared and taken out to the long table set up in the garden Sandra, Mum and I joined the guys.

Little Katie looked at me from behind her Mum's legs — not sure what to make of me. Sandra took her hand and said gently, "This is your Aunty Vicky who used to be your Uncle David."

"Is she a lady now instead of a man then?" asked Katie.

"Yes, darling,"

"Oh. Can I have a drink of orange juice please?"

As she drank her juice, Katie came and climbed on my lap.

"Aunty Vicky, can you play ball with me later?"

"If you like," I told her as I slipped my fingers through her hair. I felt a tear forming in the corner of my eye at the simple acceptance of my three year old niece."

Eventually, the burgers, sausages, steaks and some vegetarian kebabs were ready.

"I'm sorry Peter isn't here," Mum said as we sat down at the table. "It seems he had to attend some meeting or other today." We both recognised it was a white lie but I let it pass.

"Who wants wine? Joan? Sandra? Roger? Ian? Da... sorry, Vicky?" asked dad, stumbling over my name.

Serving dishes were passed up and down the table and we filled our plates. Before we started to eat, Dad tapped the side of his wine glass with his fork. Having attracted everyone's attention, he stood up.

"Today is a very special day. On Monday Da – sorry I mean Vicky, dropped a bombshell on us by announcing she was changing sex. I know it didn't come as much of a surprise to Sandra but it did to me. I won't pretend I wasn't stunned or that I understand it. But that doesn't matter. Da.., sorry I will get used to it. VICKY is the one who has to decide what is right for her and we'll support her 100%. Seeing him sorry HER with Roger it's obvious they care deeply about each other. I'm sure he'll be good for Vicky — I got it right that time. Now please raise your glasses and toast Vicky and Roger and their future together."

I burst into tears at his words and ran into the house and up the stairs.

Sandra followed me into the bathroom.

"Are you OK? I bet your emotions are up and down at the moment with all the changes you're going through. And if you haven't been nervous about today well, let me tell you, I bloody well have been. Dad's words were lovely though weren't they?"

I smiled as I looked at her "Yes they were perfect. I bet I look a state — and I haven't even started on hormones yet."

"God help you when you do then!" She gave me a hug, held my head in her hands and kissed my forehead. "But, you know what? I do believe you will be fine."

I looked in the mirror and saw the mess my mascara had made.

"Use waterproof mascara next time, Sis."

"Now you tell me! Now leave me to have a pee. I'll be down in a minute."

When I went back into the garden. I walked over to Dad and gave him a kiss on the cheek. He stood up and kissed me back, something he would never have done with David.

"I hope I didn't upset you, love."

"No Dad, quite the opposite. What you said was perfect and I really appreciate it and the welcome you've given Roger."

"Ay, well he's not such a bad type. I hadn't realised he was a sailor. He's asked Ian and me if we want to crew with you for the first weekend of Cowes Week."

"That's great — some of the old crew back together again."

# Chapter 10.  Taking Stock
## Thursday 31st July 03

My salary at the end of July was nearly three hundred pounds more than at the Leisure Centre; and my outgoings would be more than halved; though not by as much as I'd expected.

I hadn't appreciated how much more I'd be spending on my hair, nails, make-up, skin care, perfume and clothes. Gone were the six pound trips to the barbers every three months, now it would be forty pounds every six weeks. My nails needed doing every three weeks, another twenty pounds each time. Roger had already bought me some clothes but I needed to expand my wardrobe. It was no longer a case of wearing the same few skirts and tops for everything as I'd done before transition. Now I needed a selection of outfits for work, for meals out and for clubs. As for shoes, a couple of pairs of trainers and two pairs of black shoes had sufficed for David. Now I needed at least a couple of pairs of medium heels for work and higher heels for going out. And sometimes a pair in a shop window would scream 'Buy Me.'

I would have about five hundred per month for my transition fund. Electrolysis would cost about a thousand over the next year. Consultant's fees and fares to and from his office another six hundred. Based on a referral for surgery after a year then another couple of months before the surgeon could fit me in, took me to about August next year. But I'd probably wait until the end of the sailing season in late September. That gave me the quieter winter months to recuperate from the op, which gave me enough time to save up for the surgery.

Although I knew some girls had Gender Reassignment Surgery, Breast Augmentation and Facial Feminization Surgery in a single session, I'd decided I was content with my face and, as my breasts would continue to develop for a year or so after GRS, I'd leave BA until I saw the eventual results of the hormones.

I was really thrilled how things were working out.

# Chapter 11.  Cowes Week
## 1st – 9th August 03

Ten o'clock Friday morning we gathered at the marina; we loaded our kit and the provisions for the next couple of days on a trolley; then wheeled it down the pontoons to our berth. 'Summer Dreams', our Sunfast 37 yacht, bobbed gently on the water; the fenders between the hull and the pontoon were doing their job; preventing damage as the wash from passing boats pitched the yacht towards the jetty.

I'd done my Day Skipper course and exam and had taken part in some Cowes Week races in a similar yacht out of Chichester so was familiar with the class. Around the marina, waves lapped against the shore and halyards slapped against masts; I'd always found the sound soothing when sleeping on board, despite the fact the lines should be secured to prevent wear and tear.

I took hold of the shroud and swung each leg in turn over the guard rail. Dad followed me onto the side deck. I went below. Ian unloaded the trolley and passed the kit and supplies to Dad in the cockpit, Dad then passed them down to me in the galley. I stowed the food in the cool box or cupboards and our individual gear in our cabins.

Roger and I had the starboard side aft cabin. Dad and Ian had opted to share the fore cabin with the spare sails; Charles, one of Roger's business contacts and his girlfriend, Tanya had the port aft cabin. The saloon sofas also converted into berths but we didn't need them this weekend.

Two nights ago, Roger handed me two charts covering the Solent and the Isle of Wight and the Needles Channel to Bill of Portland and a tidal stream atlas.

"Ok – let's see if you can remember your Yachtmaster theory training. Prepare a passage plan from Poole to the River Medina," he'd instructed.

I'd enjoyed this aspect of the training. I looked up the high water at Portsmouth, the 'standard port' for this area. It would be at 0756 British Summer Time. I calculated how far we'd get each hour and the effect of the tide; easy in this case as it was heading in the same direction for most of the trip; so would increase our speed over the ground.

"If we leave Poole Harbour by 11 am, we will pick up the flood tide. That will carry us past the Needles and through the race off Hurst Castle. It might be choppy through the race as the wind will be against the current," I told him after I'd done the calculations.

"Sounds good to me, what time do you expect to get to Cowes?"

"Allowing for some boat handling practice en route, about 4pm," I'd said. "That should be perfect for getting up to the Folly Inn and finding a mooring."

"Excellent. How do you feel about sharing a bed with me with your dad and brother in law a few feet away?"

"They accepted Sandra and Peter having their partners to stay under the same roof without being married. OK so our position is different; but they know we live together so there's no point in pretending otherwise. I'm certainly not going to sleep in a different cabin."

"I should hope not," Roger had added, sealing the remark with a kiss that lingered.

"I'm more concerned about them slipping up over my name or pronouns and revealing I'm trans," I'd admitted.

"I know you're not ashamed of being trans, so why are you anxious about that happening?"

"Of course I'm not ashamed of it or going to lie about it. But nor is it something I should have to reveal to all and sundry, it's not any concern of theirs. But I am concerned it might affect your business with Charles."

"If it comes out, he and his girlfriend can either accept it or not. If they have a problem with it, he can take his business elsewhere, you're much more important."

I'd kissed him for his support.

Roger had taken my passage plan and put it with the charts into his navigation bag without verifying my calculations.

"Aren't you going to check my calculations?" I'd asked.

"Do I need to?"

"I don't think so."

"That's good enough for me. You should know how I work by now. Give someone a job to do and let them get on with it. If they need help — then they know they can ask for it. It sometimes leads to errors but we can usually sort it out and they learn more that way than if I checked everything first. In this case, I don't imagine you will have made an error."

Roger's approach, using mistakes as learning opportunities rather than reasons to blame someone, made sense and explained why we had such a good team around us.

Food and kit stowed, I checked the engine and the electrical and radio systems. I asked Ian to make sure the water tank was full. I also confirmed where the life jackets and harnesses were. Everything seemed to be fine, as I'd expected, so I went back up on deck and took the cover off the mainsail.

We now only needed the final members of the crew to arrive.

I then saw Roger greeting Charles and Tanya at the entrance to the pontoons. I watched as he pointed out Summer Dreams. I saw Tanya stamp her foot and drop her bag and shake her head vehemently. Even from across the pontoons I made out her scream of "No Way!"

Charles seemed to be trying to persuade her but she kept shaking her head. In the end, as Tanya walked away, Charles shook Roger's hand and turned to follow his girlfriend.

Roger then came down the pontoon alone.

"It seems Tanya had been expecting a motor yacht. She planned to spend time sunbathing on the deck and watching the other boats; not taking part in the races. She's flatly refused to come, so she and Charles have gone off to a hotel instead," he explained.

"What a shame," I replied.

"OK madam skipper, Take her out please," Roger said to me. I stuck my tongue out at him, started the motor and asked Dad to stand by the stern and Ian to take the bow.

We'd already taken in the springs so I told them to release the bow and stern lines. We reversed out of our berth and set course to leave the marina. Dad and Ian pulled in the fenders and stowed them under the cockpit seating as we followed the channel to the entrance to Poole harbour.

Clear of the entrance, we put the bow into the wind hoisted the mainsail then unfurled the foresail. We switched off the engine and turned back onto course. Dad and Ian were in the cockpit to handle the foresail. Roger watched us from the steps down to the cabin.

I asked Ian to trim the genoa and he looked a bit confused.

"The foresail is the genoa," I told him. "If the foresail overlaps the main sail, it's called a genoa or gennie. If it doesn't it's called a jib."

"I see," said Ian as he wound the sheet around the winch and used the winch handle to pull in the rope. "I've only ever heard them called jibs before."

"That's yachting for you. Lots of different names for simple things. Like ropes having different names depending on what they are used for. Halyard if it pulls a sail up; sheet if it pulls the sail in; shrouds to hold up the mast, though they are usually steel on yachts."

I wanted to see how the boat handled so, once it settled on course and had built up speed, I called "Ready about."

"Ready," said Ian, preparing to release the genoa sheet from the winch.

"Ready," said Dad, taking hold of the line on the other side.

"Ready," said Roger.

"Lee-oh!" I called and turned into the wind. As the bow passed through the wind and the boom swung across, Ian released his line. Dad wound his line round the winch on the other side then pulled in. Ian had crossed over and put the winch handle in place and was winding the genoa sheet in. Summer Dreams settled onto her new tack. We built up speed again then tacked once more back onto our original course.

"Nice tacks, well done crew," said Roger.

"Anyone for bacon sandwiches?" he asked. We all said yes to the traditional sailing meal when under way.

An hour later and the wind had backed, as forecast, and coming over our port quarter. It was now perfect for the spinnaker, the large billowing sail, from the front of the boat.

Ian passed the spinnaker bag up from the fore cabin then joined me on the fore deck.

"Have you handled spinnakers before?" I asked Ian, as the only previous time we'd sailed together had been in the Med and the chartered yacht hadn't had a spinnaker.

"No, so you'll have to show me exactly what I need to do."

"Ok – well as you can see there are three corners of the sail poking out of the bag. One is green, one red and one is green and red."

"OK — presumably that indicates which rope is attached where."

"Correct. Care to hazard a guess which goes where?"

"Well, based on starboard being the green light side of the boat and port being red, I'd guess the starboard sheet goes to the green corner; the port sheet to the red corner which means the halyard goes to the green and red; which makes sense as the port and starboard sides meet at the top."

"Spot on; and it's important to remember everything goes outside of all other ropes, sails and shrouds on the boat so it can fly freely."

"So how did you learn to handle spinnakers?" Ian asked me.

"Peter and I had one on the Fireball dinghy we shared."

"Isn't that a high performance racing dinghy?"

"It certainly is. Lots of sail area and light weight. They skim across the surface, what we call planing, rather than cutting through the waves. The large sail area means the crew often has to get out on a trapeze to balance the force of the wind."

"How does that work?"

"There's a wire from about three quarters of the way up the mast. The crew hooks the end of it onto a harness they wear; then stand on the edge of the deck and lean out."

"Sounds hairy!"

"It can be and if the wind drops suddenly, you need to be able to bend your legs to balance or even come off the trapeze or you can end up in the water."

"I think I'll stick to cruisers!" Ian concluded.

I thought back to the hundreds of races Peter and I had done together; often three on a Sunday and one or two on Wednesday evenings over several years. It was a pity he wasn't with us. Sailing had been our one common interest. But, he'd been unable to accept my change.

Lines attached we hoisted the spinnaker; while Roger and Dad released the genoa and furled it from the cockpit. I clicked the end of the spinnaker pole over the port line pushed it out so I could click the other end onto a fitting on the front of the mast. This took a bit of effort. I wondered if I'd still be able to cope with it when the hormones started to affect my muscles.

I adjusted the position of the spinnaker pole then secured the lines controlling the height and fore and aft position and took the other sheet in my hand. We needed to play this so the front of the spinnaker was on the edge of curling in, tightening it as it started to do so, until it stopped then easing it again. It was concentrated work but the key to getting maximum speed.

We were able to keep the spinnaker up as we sailed along the north coast of the Isle of Wight, passing Alum Bay and Yarmouth and made excellent time. I was able to give Ian some practice at handling the spinnaker as well.

As we sighted Cowes, we dropped the spinnaker and stowed it again ready to use in the race if the winds and our course permitted.

Off the entrance to the River Medina, we headed into the wind again; started the engine and dropped the main sail; furled the genoa then turned up river. Inside the entrance we passed the East Cowes to Southampton Ferry to port and crossed over the chains of the floating bridge ferry. We wound past crowded moorings and marinas eventually coming into sight of the Folly Inn's pontoons in the middle of the river. We were directed by the berthing master to a space and tied up. With everything secured and work done for the day, we sat in the cockpit with our sundowners — in my case a glass of the Cava, which we had planned to use for Buck's Fizzes in the morning for the guests.

We then picked up our wash kit and went ashore by water taxi to use the showers and toilets at the Folly before joining the crush for meals.

The menu, written up on a blackboard, offered a good range of traditional dishes all guaranteed to satisfy the hungriest of sailors. I'd learned not to underestimate the portion sizes so I skipped the starter and chose the Hunter's Chicken. Roger settled on the Slow-Cooked Pork Belly. Dad chose the Beef and Ale pie and Ian the Mixed Grill. If we had any space left for deserts, I planned to have the Eton Mess sundae. IF I had any space left!

By the time we'd placed our orders, bought drinks from the bar and made our way through the crowd back to our table and sat down, the waitresses were bringing our meals from the kitchen.

In the corner of the restaurant, a group was playing. The commotion of a hundred or more voices talking from all angles gave the place a huge buzz of anticipation. Odd words or phrases would stand out as tall sailing stories reverberated around the restaurant:

"I called 'Starboard' but he held his course."

"Then the idiot dropped the winch handle overboard."

"She just wouldn't sail closer to the wind."

"We finished 12th on the water but were penalised for being over the line at the start."

And was that Ellen MacArthur and Ben Ainslie at the table across the room? They were certainly involved in the event and the Folly Inn was a favourite with yachties.

I looked around. No one was taking any notice of me – even though I wasn't wearing any make-up and I was wearing androgynous clothes. I was simply one of the crowd. If anyone had told me when I was last here two years ago I'd be back as a female with a fiancé and with Dad and my Brother in Law all totally accepting me as Vicky I'd have thought they were mad.

Appetites slated, we walked back to the jetty for the water taxi to our pontoon. As we queued on the landing stage under the full moon with the light reflecting on the river, I snuggled into Roger's rugged arms. My mind wandered as he wrapped his jacket around me to protect me from the cool breeze off the water.

"A penny for them," he said breaking into my thoughts.

"I was reflecting how my whole life has changed in the last couple of months and how lucky I am nearly everyone that matters has accepted me."

"So no regrets?"

"Only that Peter has rejected me – but that's his decision," I sighed.

"And his loss," added Roger, "but perhaps he will eventually come to terms with it."

"I hope so, I really don't want it to cause problems within the family for either of us. But it wasn't only the rejection, it was the homophobic and transphobic words he used. I didn't imagine he could be so bigoted."

"Perhaps he was lashing out — people do tend to use words they know will hurt the most when they are upset."

"I suppose so — but it's no less upsetting even so."

It didn't take long for the water taxi to arrive and we were soon back on board Summer Dreams for a few drinks before settling down for the night and an early start the next morning.

The Saturday morning's race was delayed until lunch time due to a lack of wind but we finished just inside the top ten in our class when it did fill in — so were reasonably content.

Roger had a call from the guests that had been due to join us at Poole. Charles' girlfriend, Tanya, had submitted, reluctantly, and only after an expensive present, to join us for a day's sailing on the Monday. There was no way she was going to sleep on board. They would meet us at a marina on the Hamble on the Monday morning.

After racing on Sunday, we sailed up Southampton Water and into the Hamble. We moored off the 'Jolly Sailor' pub where we enjoyed an excellent meal. As an avid fan of the 'Howards Way' TV series about sailing (I'd always wanted to be Lynne Howard) I particularly enjoyed visiting an iconic feature of the set.

We made our way down the river the next morning to Hamble Point Marina; joining the bustling fleet of other yachts heading out to take part in or watch the racing, to pick up our two passengers. Unsurprisingly, they weren't waiting for us when we arrived so we tied up on a visitors' berth at the end of a pontoon. I knew Roger was negotiating with Charles — definitely *not* Charlie or, heaven forbid, Chaz — to supply parts for a range of luxury power boats so we had to be patient.

Eventually we saw Charles and Tanya sauntering down the jetty from the controlled entrance.

"Better put a step on the pontoon for Lady Muck. And undo the access guardrail," I suggested.

Roger gave me a conspiratorial smile and nodded his head. "Probably wise," he agreed.

"Sorry to keep you waiting," boomed Charles. "Permission to come aboard?"

"Good morning Charles. Good morning Tanya. Welcome aboard. We're in good time," replied Roger in the most affable manner he could.

Tanya and Charles stepped down into the cockpit. As Ian and Dad prepared to cast us off. I offered our guests a Buck's Fizz. Tanya took a sip then shuddered. "Is that made with freshly squeezed oranges and champagne?" she demanded.

"Sorry, no. We don't really have the facility to make fresh orange juice on board so it's from a carton and we use Cava."

"Yes, you can tell." She handed the glass back to me. "Put my bag somewhere safe." She commanded. Roger could see my hackles rising but shook his head slightly, pleading with me to be patient.

I gave her my sweetest smile. "My pleasure, Ms Wood. Gucci isn't it?" I gushed. Even I recognised the double G logo. Roger rolled his eyes.

Charles was at the helm as we cruised down the river and out into Southampton Water again. Roger asked me to take the helm and hold us head to wind while they hoisted the mainsail.

Charles looked askance at me and I heard him mutter "Are you sure she can handle it?" to Roger.

"Vicky is actually better qualified than anyone on board except me," replied Roger. "She has her Coastal Skipper and has already passed the Yachtmaster theory. She only needs a couple more long passages in command to take her practical, which she will walk. No need to worry on her score."

"Yes, but a woman in charge . . . " Charles let the thought hang there.

It was ironic. If Charles had known me as David, he'd have had no issue with me being in command. He might even have admired me for getting my qualifications at such an early age. But I was now experiencing sexism. I almost felt sorry for Tanya. Almost.

I don't think anyone was unhappy when we returned to the Hamble that evening to drop off our guests except, perhaps, Charles who seemed oblivious to the atmosphere Tanya was creating. It could be he was used to it.

---###---

We weren't taking part in any more of the Cowes Week races; we'd planned to head over to France to complete the long passage and night passage requirements for my Yachtmaster qualification.

So, on Tuesday afternoon, we left the Hamble; made our way down to the Needles then turned south with me as skipper. Our destination was Ouistreham on the Normandy coast.

We split into two watches at eight pm, Roger with Dad and Ian with me. Ian and I were on the first watch until midnight and again from four until eight. As we left the Needles astern it was beginning to get dark.

"Can you switch on the navigation lights please?" I asked Ian. "Then check we are showing green forward on the starboard side, red on the port side and white from the stern."

Ian did as I asked. "Yes lights are on and showing correctly."

"Thanks. We'll be crossing the main shipping channels before long so we need to keep a good look out for large vessels. They don't always maintain a good watch. Theoretically they should give way to us but we'll still lose any argument if they do run us down; and it has happened!"

"Good point," he laughed nervously.

Just before ten, Ian called my attention to some lights. "They are about thirty degrees off our port bow. Looks to me like two white lights and a green one. The left hand white light as we see it is higher than the right hand one."

I saw them for myself when I looked in the direction he'd indicated.

"Well spotted. It's a ship over fifty metres in length crossing from port to starboard. Keep an eye on the lights and let me know if they stay on a constant bearing from us. If they do, it would mean we were on a collision course. I think it's much more likely to pass well ahead of us, so the lights will move across our bows."

"OK."

"But still keep an eye out for any other lights at the same time, the shipping lanes can be very busy."

Just before midnight, Ian caught sight of another light some distance off our port bow.

"There's a white light ahead and to port," he said.

"Keep watching it. A single white light means it's either at anchor which isn't likely in the middle of the channel or we are seeing the stern of whatever it is. It may not be easy to know if we are gaining on it, if indeed we are, until we get a lot closer; or it may disappear if it's pulling away from us."

"OK skipper," Ian replied.

"It may well gradually move across our bows if our courses are crossing and we are overtaking it. We need to keep watch in case we get close to their stern.

Clouds were obscuring the moon making it a dark night. But I could now make out the light myself.

I kept watching it as it wasn't behaving as I'd expect. The bearing to it was moving from left to right rather quicker than I'd expect if we were seeing the stern light and our courses were crossing.

Shit! It was only about sixty metres away crossing us almost at right angles. I sounded the horn, swung the wheel to starboard to try to avoid being T-boned and yelled "hold on" to our crew. The other boat passed down our port side about two metres away as I saw the helmsman coming up into his cockpit from below.

When he saw me, he yelled "Sorry."

"Get your sodding navigation lights sorted out, you're only showing a white light all round," I yelled in a most unladylike manner.

Roger and Dad came up from below. I turned the wheel back to port and we passed behind the offending yacht as we resumed our course.

"What happened?" asked Roger.

"We nearly got run down by another yacht not showing correct lights and with its helm down below. It nearly hit us amidships," I told him.

"Panic over. Well done, nice reactions and avoidance. Are you OK?" Roger said.

"I'm fine," I assured him.

"OK, well it's time for a change of watch anyway so go and get some rest."

Fifteen minutes later, I was in my sleeping bag and asleep.

Sunrise the next morning was a little after five thirty but the sky would start to lighten shortly after our next watch started. I was up again in good time to wash and dress and make a cup of coffee for everyone before Ian and I took over from Dad and Roger at four.

There had been no more scares during the night. We had made good time and were now only about forty miles from Ouistreham.

The wind was on our starboard quarter. So after breakfast of bacon sandwiches at seven, we hoisted the spinnaker and started to surf down the waves under a clearing blue sky that promised a glorious day.

As we entered the mouth of the Orne river, we passed the Brittany Ferries terminal to our starboard with its queues of vehicles for Portsmouth. There would be British holidaymakers heading home to London, Bristol, Birmingham and all points north and lorries, that may have been delivering British products to the French market, now loaded with French cheeses and wine for UK supermarkets. There might even be continental holidaymakers visiting the Lake District or Dartmoor or Oxford.

We kept to starboard and entered the canal lock to moor at the yacht club on the side of the canal. Having secured the boat, we took a stroll into the town.

"I think there's a boulangerie next to the Phare restaurant on the Place de General Charles de Gaulle," I mentioned to Roger. "At least, there was last time I was here two years ago."

"Croissants certainly would make a welcome change for breakfast from bacon butties."

"Especially with some Normandy butter and preserves. I think there's a charcouterie round the corner, so we can also get some nice ham for lunch as well to have with some baguettes."

"Good idea. Are you happy organising that? I don't want you thinking we are dumping the catering on you because you're the only woman on board."

I reflected on what Roger had said and realised it was a win-win for me. If they *had* left the catering to me because I was the only woman in the group, that was confirmation of how they perceived me and I couldn't take offence at that.

We booked a table at the restaurant for the evening and decided to have a drink in the bar before returning to the boat. Back at the yacht club, we made use of the showers before dinner.

Next morning, after breakfasting on fresh croissants and with baguettes and ham ready to make for lunch, we prepared to get under way.

The wind was from the north, driving breaking waves onto the coast as we motored through the canal lock to the open sea.

"Thank goodness we have roller reefing on the foresail," I told Roger. "Last time I was here, we had similar conditions but I had to go up to the bow and swop the jib for a storm jib. The waves were crashing over me as the bows lifted about eight feet then dropped again. I was totally submerged each time. Fortunately, I was well secured with my harness of course."

"Lovely," replied Roger.

"Actually, I didn't really mind it. My kit shrugged off most of the water."

Our passage home was slow as we beat into the wind for the first few hours. Gradually the wind veered more easterly and eased slightly so we could unreef the sail and bring the full genoa into action and settle onto a reach. As night fell, the clouds started to clear and the stars began to appear. The beam from a lighthouse miles off to the east regularly cut into the black sky.

For a while, Roger and I were sitting together in the cockpit, steering by the Pole Star as the bow periodically cut into a wave and sent spray over us. The boat was nicely balanced so it took the lightest of touches on the wheel. Roger's arm was around my shoulder and he stole (we stole) the occasional kiss.

"This is utterly magical," I remarked, "steering by the stars; the other constellations appearing and disappearing as the clouds scud across the sky; that lighthouse off to starboard; the spray from the waves hitting us — mind you, you do make a very good shelter from the spray."

"Is that all I'm good for?" he joked.

"I wouldn't say it's *all* you're good for. I can think of a few other things as well."

I snuggled into his arms as our lips met again.

I went below at ten for a rest while Ian came up into the cockpit to join Roger for their watch. Dad and I would take over from them in four hours.

Later, as we sat together in the cockpit when we did our watch, Dad turned to me. "I need to say something to you and I'd appreciate it if you wouldn't interrupt."

'Was this going to be good or bad?' I wondered. "OK, Dad."

"It's just four weeks since you told us what you intended doing and we met you as Vicky and Roger for the first time."

He paused — then continued, "I have to say I was very dubious about the whole thing. I wondered if you were making a huge mistake and had been persuaded to do something you'd regret later. I also wondered if you were rushing into things with Roger."

As he paused again, I was nervous where this might be going. I held my breath.

"Well, I have to tell you now I realise I was wrong. Totally wrong."

I breathed again and looked him straight in the face. I saw tears gathering at the corners of his eyes.

"Must be the wind," he said as he wiped them away.

Then he continued. "Being with you and Roger for the last few days, it's obvious you are far happier now than I've ever seen you. I look at you and I just see my daughter Vicky. I even struggle to visualise you as anything else — and I'm glad that's the case. My only regret is that Peter can't accept you, at least at the moment."

"Thanks Dad. That means so much to me," I replied, with a lump in my throat, "I'm sad too that Peter is struggling with it; but I have to remember it took me twenty years to accept what I am, so I can't expect everyone else to accept it instantly. Hopefully he'll come round eventually. If not then I still have you, Mum and Sandra and I hope none of you fall out with Peter over me."

"That's up to Peter. We certainly won't put up with him bad mouthing you. But what I wanted to say is your Mum and I feel guilty about not picking up on your situation when you were younger and doing something about it."

"Don't be," I told him. "If you'd asked me anything I don't suppose I'd have admitted it in any case. I wouldn't have been able to say anything."

"We wondered if it was something we'd done that caused you to be as you are; but I think we treated you and Peter the same, I don't think we had favourites."

"Dad, you didn't cause this — it was in me when I was born. Carol Holt, the nurse who looked after me when I was in hospital, explained it's to do with the flow of testosterone in the womb and the effect it has on the foetus. It could be Peter got some of my share but, do you know what? I'm really happy the way I am. I know there are going to be problems, but Roger and I will face them and get through them together."

"And you can count on our support too. One hundred per cent," said Dad, "and Sandra is really chuffed at have a sister after all the years of putting up with two brothers."

Dad put his arm around my shoulders and kissed me on the forehead which really surprised me. He wasn't usually so affectionate. While his words had meant a lot, that gesture really did show he now truly saw me as his daughter.

The sun started to rise, burning off the early morning mist as the Isle of Wight emerged on the horizon off our port bow. The wind was now a steady force five, driving us along at a little over six knots. Another couple of hours and we'd be passing the Nab Tower then Bembridge Ledge before entering the Solent. As we approached them, we'd be closing on the routes taken by the cross-channel ferries from the French ports, including the ones from Ouistreham, and would need to keep a good watch for them.

A few minutes before six o'clock, I heard the kettle whistling. Roger stuck his head up the companionway and asked if we wanted a coffee.

"Looks like it's going to be another lovely day," he said passing us steaming mugs and looking around.

The coffee hit the spot. "I needed that," commented Dad.

"Me too." I added.

As we approached Cowes, the fleets were forming for more race starts so we hove too and kept well clear while we watched them.

By lunch time, we were tied up again on a pontoon at the Folly Inn. After more than twenty four hours at sea, I needed a shower, not least to get the salt water out of my hair. We all grabbed our wash bags and towels and called up the water taxi to take us ashore. Suitably refreshed, we had lunch in the restaurant before dropping our wash kit back at Summer Dreams and catching the water bus into Cowes.

We wandered around the narrow bustling streets, in and out of quaint, and not so quaint, shops. I particularly liked a picture of three yachts racing. It was about thirty inches by eighteen.

"That would go well in the hall, Roger."

"It certainly would. Let's get it." He took it to the till and started to get out his credit card.

"Let me pay for it please," I told him.

"No, it's OK, I'll get it."

"Roger, I *want* to buy it. It's the first thing I've bought for our home so please let me get it."

He looked at me and realised how important this step was. He tilted his head in submission and let me pay instead.

"I'll let you carry it though," I conceded with a grin.

On Saturday evening, we sailed out of the estuary for the traditional end of Cowes week firework display. It felt as though you could step from one boat to another right across the entrance to the Medina. As always the fireworks were spectacular; the official display being supplemented by many of the watching fleet firing off outdated flares.

As the last of the fireworks faded, we set sail back to Poole. The overnight sail would be yet another passage to add to my log book. I'd already done the minimum needed for my Yachtmaster but it wouldn't do any harm to have exceeded those required.

It had been an excellent week with some great sailing — if challenging at times. Dad's remarks on the way back from Ouistreham had been a real highpoint for me.

Life settled into a routine over the following few weeks. Later that month I took my Yachtmaster practical exam. As Roger had predicted, I passed with flying colours.

Once I'd been paid again, I met Sandra for lunch and some retail therapy.

# Chapter 12.  Back to Earls Court
## 26<sup>th</sup> Sept 03

As the fourth Friday in September approached, I started to become nervous about my next appointment with Dr Nicholas Wright. Would he prescribe hormones for me this time? I'd had the blood tests he'd required; they'd been fine so there shouldn't be any medical reasons to delay.

Emotionally I was a million miles from where I'd been before my first visit, which had been soon after my suicide attempt.

I was really enjoying my job. I'd have loved it even if Roger and I hadn't been involved. I quickly picked up the technical side of the chandlery and, because of my sailing experience, held my own in any conversation or negotiation.

After a few weeks Roger said "I've been watching you work. You've been effectively leading the admin and the shop team. How would you like to be Operations Managers responsible for everything other than training?"

"Are you sure I'm up to it?"

"What do you think?"

"I think so — but what will the others think? Will they assume I'm getting the promotion because I'm your girlfriend?"

"Doesn't really matter if they do. I want you to take the job because I know you're right for it and you've earned it. It will also mean a significant increase in your salary of course to reflect the increased responsibilities."

As a result of the pay rise, my transition fund was well on target.

The other staff might have been resentful over my promotion but, apart from Sophie Bradshaw, they weren't. She'd been sullen with me ever since I arrived. It seems she'd had her eyes on Roger herself. Well, hands off girl. He's mine.

The forecast was for another sunny day. I wore a pastel yellow and sky blue floral short sleeved blouse and royal blue knee length A line skirt. Navy sandals with a one inch heel and a matching handbag completed my outfit. My hair was done in a ponytail — now quite a bit longer than when I'd first seen Dr Wright. Roger was meeting me after my appointment and we were spending the weekend in London.

I took my seat and lit a cigarette — something I was doing less and less these days, but I needed it this morning to calm my nerves. This was a crucial meeting with Dr Wright. It was important to me he prescribed hormones today and I could think of little else just then. The other girls at the support group had assured me he would. I didn't see why he wouldn't but there was always that niggle at the back of my mind.

When the refreshment trolley came round, I bought a coffee and settled back to listen to music on my iPod and tried to read the new copy of Yachts and Yachting — but my mind kept returning to the possibility Dr Wright would find some reason to withhold hormones. I stared out of the window as the train sped through the English countryside. The fields were parched from the long hot summer; our own garden at home had suffered from the hosepipe ban, the lawn covered in brown patches.

Would Dr Wright think I was ready for hormones or not? Would he have found some other medical reason to delay? Would he want to allow more time since my stupid attempt to kill myself? Would he be worried Roger and I might split up at some time and leave me in a worse state than before? Maybe he'd think I'd rushed into moving down to live with Roger? Or all my eggs were in one basket living and working with Roger. If we did split up I would be left without a job or a home. But we weren't going to split up if I had anything to do with it.

Before I realised it, the fields and woods had given way to suburban houses and we were approaching Clapham Junction where I needed to change for Victoria then the underground to Earls Court. I emerged on Warwick Road and turned left for the few minutes' walk down to

Nicholas Wright's basement offices. His receptionist greeted me and told me to take a seat.

"There might be a few minutes wait as he's running a bit behind schedule this morning," Cassie told me.

"No problem," I said "is there a loo I can use?"

"Yes — through the black door over there on the right," she replied.

When I came back and took my seat, the person next to me asked it was my first appointment.

"Second," I answered.

"It's my fourth today. I'm praying he's going to refer me for surgery. Who are you thinking of using? I'm Beverley Harris, Bev to my friends."

"I'm Vicky Williamson, I really haven't got around to thinking about who to use," I told her.

"Well, I had been thinking of King, but he may be retiring. I think there's a Mr Singer taking over from him. Then there's Fry in Leicester or several in Thailand. The USA and Canadian surgeons are outside my budget." She then proceeded to give me her views of the pros and cons of each of them.

"I'm probably a year off surgery yet so plenty of time to think about that. One step at a time, I'm hoping to be prescribed hormones today." At that, she was called into Nicholas' office. I started to think, despite my protestations, I would need to look into potential surgeons if today went to plan.

Half an hour later Bev came out of the private sanctum. She gave me a thumbs-up and wished me luck as she crossed to the reception desk to settle up with Cassie.

Nicholas' door opened again a few minutes later.

"Come on in Vicky, take a seat," he invited indicating the chair I should use. He then sat down again in his own chair, swivelling to face me.

"How have things been since we last met?" he asked, as he picked up his black fountain pen ready to take notes on his pad.

"I don't really think they could be much better," I told him.

"That sounds promising. Last time, just before you saw me, you'd been admitted to hospital following a self-harm incident. Have there been any further similar instances?"

"No, None at all."

"So what has been going on for you? You said last time you were going to leave your job in London and move down to Bournemouth where you were going to work with your boyfriend and move in with him. How did that pan out?"

"Very well. I am now living and working with Roger. I'm Operations Manager for his company. We are officially engaged and plan to have a commitment ceremony where we will effectively get married even if it's not legally recognised."

"Well, if the Gender Recognition Bill passes through parliament, you might be able to get married legally."

"Have you heard how that's going? All I see are rumours and reports of campaigns against it."

"I think it will pass. It has to for the government to satisfy last year's European Court of Human Rights ruling. The question will be in the detail. Would you go for that option if you could?"

"Definitely. We simply don't want to plan on it then be disappointed."

"How significant would that disappointment be to you?"

I wondered if his question was a trap. Was he concerned I'd be tempted to do something stupid?

"If we were planning on a proper wedding, it would be a blow but not crucial. We are happy enough to go with the ceremony we already have planned. Being legally married would be a bonus."

"How about when you resigned from your previous job? How did that go?"

"I was completely open with Andrea, my boss, including about trying to kill myself. She said she'd welcome me back at any time if things don't work out; but I know that won't be necessary. We had a very nice dinner together before I moved to Bournemouth. I didn't tell other colleagues anything except I'd been offered a job down there that involved sailing."

"And how are things at work?"

"Fine, the other staff know I'm Roger's fiancée – but I haven't mentioned I'm transsexual. They may suspect something but nobody has asked any questions."

"Have you said anything to your family?"

"Yes — they know I'm now Vicky and living and working with Roger."

"What was their reaction?"

"Mum thought I was going to tell them I was gay. Dad struggled at first but is fine with it now. My sister, Sandra, had already guessed. I used her things when I was alone in the house and she'd noticed. We now have a fabulous relationship as sisters. Katie, her daughter, told me last week she likes me a lot more as Aunty Vicky than as Uncle David. The only difficulty is my twin brother Peter. He was very abusive when I told him and we haven't seen each other since then."

"How do you feel about that?"

"Sad, but it's his decision. I have to be me and if he can't accept that then so be it."

"Do you have any other support in Bournemouth? I think you mentioned there was a group there."

"There is and I've started attending. Carol Holt, the nurse who looked after me in hospital, came with me the first time. I think I told you she used to work at Charing Cross and is quite a regular at the group."

"Well, Vicky, you seem to have transitioned socially very well. You present totally comfortably as female. You have good support around you — far more than many of my patients I have to say. In that respect you are very fortunate. Your blood tests were fine so I am very happy to prescribe you hormones if that's what you want."

I could have kissed him. But I didn't. I just said it was what I wanted.

"Come back and see me in another three months. Cassie will make the appointment for you."

As I left Nicholas' office, I saw Roger sitting in reception.

I touched my forefinger to my thumb giving the scuba "OK" signal as I walked over to him. I gave him a quick kiss on the lips. I could see the other girls waiting for appointments were jealous.

Cassie was waiting for me to book my next appointment, tapping her fingers on her desk and smiling. I approached her desk, settled my account and arranged my next date. As Cassie handed me a receipt, she pulled it back as I was about to take hold of it.

"If you ever get tired of Roger, will you please pass him on to me?" she asked with a wink. "He's lovely, you lucky girl."

"Will you still be around in eighty or ninety years' time? Because I don't plan to give him up anytime soon."

"I can dream, can't I?" she insisted.

I laughed as I put my bank card and receipt back in my purse.

"I need a chemist," I told Roger waving the prescription at him.

Roger had parked his car on the Square so we left it there while we found chemist on Earls Court Road and I had my prescription filled.

We then drove to the Royal Garden Hotel on Kensington High Road. We dropped the MGB in the basement car park; took the lift to reception; and registered as Mr and Mrs Dalton. It felt fabulous hearing Roger give that as our names; though I did feel a bit of a fraud as we weren't actually married. On the other hand, it didn't feel at all inappropriate to be female.

Formalities completed, we walked over to the lifts to the right of the reception desk and were whisked to the eighth floor. Our room overlooked Kensington Gardens. We could see the Post Office tower in the distance and the Royal Albert Hall off to the right.

Our plan was to have an early pre-theatre dinner in the hotel's Park Terrace restaurant then take a cab to the theatre for Les Miserables. First things first though. I needed a shower. I then handed Roger the Estraderm patch and asked him to stick it to my right buttock. Having obliged, he kissed it.

"I'm looking forward to the results" he whispered.

"So am I but bear in mind I'll be going through a teenage girl's puberty so be prepared for me getting moody," I warned him.

"I hadn't thought about that. Oh shit!"

# Chapter 13. Commitment Ceremony
## 18<sup>th</sup> Oct 03

"So, Vicky, what are we going to do about us?"

I felt as though someone had punched me in the stomach. "Wwwwwhat do you mean?" I stuttered – dreading he might want to end our relationship. I wouldn't have blamed him if he had. Despite his constant declarations of love, I found it so difficult to believe I'd really won his heart — how could I have been so lucky?

"Well, there's still no sign of this new bill the government keeps promising. So are we going to wait for it so we can get married? Or are we going to have our own ceremony?"

The relief flooded my emotions and I couldn't stop the tears flowing down my face.

"Hey, is getting hitched to me such a horrible thought?" he asked as he wiped away the tears.

"I thought for a horrible moment you were going to say it was all over. I couldn't bear that."

"You silly girl. Haven't I told you a hundred times how much I love you? Why do you find that so hard to believe?"

"I don't know. I suppose it's I don't believe I deserve you. I know the hormones are messing with my emotions; but I warned you that would happen," I replied lifting my eyes, looking into his face and giving a wry smile.

"Yes you did — and you weren't wrong. But back to my question. Are we going to wait for this Gender Recognition Bill or do our own thing?"

Despite his reassurances, I still wanted a formal celebration of our relationship as soon as possible. Even when the government introduced the bill, it would take a couple of years before it came into effect and another few months after that to organise a full blown wedding.

"I still want the full wedding with all the trimmings when we can; but let's do our own thing as soon as possible please."

"By full wedding, are you thinking bridesmaids, best man, church ceremony, ushers, photographer, wedding breakfast?"

"Well, not a church, perhaps somewhere with a similar ambiance — not a registry office."

"And what about our own ceremony? Do you have anything in mind for that?"

"Let's make it small, just immediate family and friends."

We kept the guest list tight but still ended up with 20, including my former boss, Andrea. We didn't need anyone to officiate but we asked a DJ from the Blue Peach to act as Master of Ceremonies.

If it had only been friends attending, we would have held it at the Blue Peach but we also wanted family members present so we looked for somewhere a bit more salubrious. We considered several venues and settled on the Priory Room at the Beach View Hotel.

Having agreed the date and organised the venue, I got together with Sandra and Mum for their advice on what dress to wear.

It was at times like these I was particularly conscious I hadn't had the benefit of growing up as a girl. Whilst most young women learned so much from imitating their mums and older sisters, my experimentation had always been in total secrecy. Or so I'd thought.

"I'm not sure what to wear," I told them. "I want it to be special. But I also want a full legal wedding as soon as possible once the law changes and I want that to be even more special. Does that make sense?"

"Of course it does," said Mum

"OK, so you want to keep the full bridal gown and bridesmaids for the legal wedding?" asked Sandra.

"Yes."

"But you need a dress that looks bridal but not a full gown? Why not have a look at bridesmaids' dresses? They should fit the bill."

It was an obvious solution but I'd been too overwhelmed by the event to think of it.

We looked through a dozen or more websites to draw up a shortlist of five stores that had suitable stock. Just looking at the various options was all my birthdays and Christmases rolled into one. It really began to register I was getting 'married'. Who cared if the law would take a couple of years to catch up? *I really was getting married!* And it was with the support of most of the family. Remembering Peter wouldn't be there brought me down again.

"What's up darling?" asked Mum as I sat there with a tear rolling down my cheek.

"I was thinking it's sad Peter won't be there with us," I said sorrowfully then decided to lighten the mood. "But, come on, let's call the stores and see if we can set up appointments for next week."

One establishment proved somewhat snotty.

"Oh no, we have any appointments *that* soon. *Our* brides plan much further ahead."

Perhaps they thought I was rushing the wedding because I was pregnant. Chance would be a fine thing. Which left us with four to visit.

When little Katie heard it would be 'like a wedding' she asked if she could be a bridesmaid. I explained I wasn't having bridesmaids but she could be my flower girl if she wanted. She jumped up and down with excitement at that.

I lost track of how many dresses I tried on. Some close fitting, others more flared, above the knee, on the knee, calf and full length — and in various colours.

If I'd been excited looking at the ranges on the websites, trying the dresses on and seeing myself in the mirrors was unbelievable — in most cases. When I tried a shocking pink knee length sheath which the sales consultant insisted would be perfect, both Mum and Sandra shook their heads in horror and struggled not to laugh as I emerged from the changing cubicle. When I saw my reflection, I had to agree with their judgement. I looked like a Raspberry Mivvi ice lolly.

Nevertheless, with that exception, I found it difficult to believe the young woman I saw in the mirror was me.

I still had lingering doubts about how others might perceive me. The hormone treatment had hardly had any time to affect me other than emotionally; so I still expected to see some masculinity in my features. Yet I didn't think I was showing any such signs; and the sales consultants seemed to simply accept me as being female. Fortunately, I'd never had a strong jawline or an Adam's Apple and had never had noticeable body hair.

As much as I enjoyed trying on the dresses; feeling the different materials against my body and the swirl of skirts as I moved, I was flagging by the end of each day. At times, I wondered if I'd ever find something that was perfect; some had been 'nice'; others had been almost there but there was always something not quite right.

In the end it was a final choice of two, fortunately both in the same store. The winner, by a whisker, was a cocktail style. It was slightly below the knee with an off the shoulder lace bodice and sleeves and a multi layered flared skirt in navy. The store also had a matching version for children which we bought for Katie to wear.

Then I had to find shoes. Fortunately, it didn't take as long to find a pair of three inch heel sandals also in navy.

I took Mum and Sandra out for a dinner the second evening to thank them for their help and support.

"I've really had a lot of fun. I never imagined I'd be involved in planning the female side of another wedding after Sandra's," Mum declared.

"Well, I did occasionally dream of helping a sister plan her wedding; even if she was still my brother at the time," laughed Sandra.

I'd been conditioned to hide my emotions for nearly twenty years but the hormones and my female puberty were winning the battle and there was another tear in my eye, as I replied, "Well, I hope there will be proper wedding in a couple of years — and I'll want you to be my maid of honour."

We had our Hen and Stag nights a week before the ceremony as we were having dinner with our parents on the Friday evening.

My hen party, comprising Sandra, several of the girls from the office, Carol Holt and Jacqui and Karen from the group, had a meal at a Thai restaurant then back to the Blue Peach for a 'bop'. I don't think there was anything Freudian in choosing a Thai restaurant with the country's reputation for gender surgery. But who knows? I was dreading the others organising a male stripper for me but, thankfully, they saved me that embarrassment.

I don't know where Roger's stag group ended up and, to be honest, I'm not sure I want to know.

Gradually, the "to do" list I'd created in Excel was ticked off and the weekend of the celebration finally arrived. It was just as well, as my nerves were getting pretty ragged by then.

Which was crazy.

Roger and I already lived together. Everyone that mattered knew we loved each other and the ceremony had no legal basis. But it still mattered to us. We wanted to declare our love and commitment to each other in front of our friends and family.

To think, I planned to go through all of this again in a few years for the legal wedding. I must be mad. Ironically, I needed letters from two psychiatrists to confirm I wasn't, in order to have surgery.

Barbara and James, Roger's parents, came over from Malta on the Friday for the dinner with my parents, Roger and me.

Like my own father, James had been in the forces. In his case it had been the RAF. When he'd left the service in 1985, James had taken his gratuity and built the company Roger now owned. He'd made some very shrewd investments during the 1980s which had enabled him to pass on the business and take early retirement.

We met Barbara and James for drinks an hour before dinner. My mum and dad were giving me time alone first with Roger's parents. It was the first time we'd met face to face although we had spoken a few times on the phone and on Skype. They'd welcomed me warmly when Roger had told them about me — which had surprised me at the time as they were older than my own parents and I expected older people to be less understanding. It showed how you should never judge.

Both greeted me with a hug and kiss. Barbara handed me a gift "Just a little something from Malta," she said. It was a lovely lace shawl.

They then showed me an email Roger had sent to them after the first week of our holiday together.

*"Mum and Dad, hold on to your hats. I've met someone I plan to spend the rest of my life with. You'll love her too when you meet her. Her name is Vicky. She is gorgeous, and she makes me laugh. She's been stopping with me this week and we've done all the usual touristy stuff. I need to be careful not to scare her off so it's a case of softly, softly. But you know how determined I can be so she doesn't stand a chance."*

I looked at Roger and, for once, I was speechless. He had the grace to blush. I was surprised he had been so forthcoming and prepared to tell his parents at such an early stage. Roger was usually quite reserved; he could show he cared; and he was my rock, someone I could rely on utterly. But he didn't often show his feelings to other people so sometimes seemed cold if you didn't know him.

"Did you really know after that first week together?" I asked.

"No, it was after the first weekend. That's why I was so glad to see you walking down the platform the following week."

I shook my head in amazement. How on earth did someone like him fall for someone like me and so quickly?

He pulled me into his arms and kissed my lips.

"I love you," I told him.

"I know," he replied.

At that moment, I saw Mum and Dad at the entrance to the bar. They came over and I introduced them to Roger's parents.

The dinner was even more relaxed than I could have dreamed. The food and drink was fabulous and the service superb which boded well for tomorrow's ceremony.

There had always been the risk the two groups of parents wouldn't get on. But they shared the experience of forces life — moving around from posting to posting and they swopped stories. They even found they'd been stationed at the same time in the late seventies at SHAPE, the NATO military headquarters near Brussels. Dad was in Motor Transport; James had worked in the office of SACEUR, the Supreme Commander Europe. The chances were they'd passed each other in the corridors at HQ, at Church, around the swimming pool or in the queue at the American run cinema.

I enjoyed hearing them relate their stories. I'd had no personal desire to join up but I appreciated how important such tales were to service personnel and how the banter built a rapport. I was delighted our two sets of parents were well on their way to becoming firm friends.

There were also a few anecdotes about Roger and me which caused a few blushes. Thankfully no one produced any naked baby pictures.

"Do you remember when we lived at Wittering and your cousin Stephen came to visit us one Easter? You took him over to the other side of the airfield to show him the Hunter they used for firefighting practice. You came off your bike in the middle of the airfield. Only you could manage that," James reminded Roger. "You staggered home then collapsed in the kitchen, half your face scrapped away from contact with the runway and complaining about your back. We had to call an ambulance to take you to Peterborough General Hospital. To make matters worse, the C.O. found your bike abandoned on the runway."

"Thanks Dad. And can I remind you of the time you put up a huge crate in the garden as a tool shed and were painting it black. You were standing on a chair, I think. One of the legs sank into the lawn and you toppled over and ended up with paint all over you."

I sat there open mouthed at the thought of the scene trying hard not to laugh in case it offended James. Barbara confirmed it had indeed happened.

"It took hours to get all the paint off James, especially out of his hair."

Fortunately, James acknowledged the funny side as well and we all laughed.

I was very relieved to escape with no revelations about seriously embarrassing moments; or relate incidents that would have been boyish.

By the time we had eaten and had coffees, it was gone ten. We adjourned to the bar for a nightcap. Although it wasn't actually a wedding, Roger was not allowed to see me the next morning until the ceremony so he was to spend the night at home while I stayed at the hotel.

As I lay in bed that night, I reflected on the last few months. Was it really only five months since that day on the beach and only three months since I moved in with Roger.

But it was a lifetime.

I struggled to believe how much had changed. David, a secretive transvestite with no friends and an uncertain future had morphed into

Vicky, a young woman already on the path to correcting the flawed body she'd been born with, about to get married in the morning. Unbelievable.

It was a wonder I fell asleep as my mind churned over what might have happened and how close I'd come to throwing everything away. But, amazingly, I did sleep. I may have dreamt that night but I didn't remember anything.

The next morning, I woke up alone in a bed for the first time for several months. I'd automatically reached for Roger for a morning kiss — then remembered where I was and why.

The butterflies in my stomach suddenly all took flight. I was sure it wouldn't help calm them but I made myself a coffee while I dressed. Then I had a light breakfast, reflecting that Roger would probably be having full English at home. At least he wouldn't have a hangover from a stag do. Unless he'd gone to the Blue Peach instead of straight home after dinner.

I took a taxi to the salon where I was meeting Sandra and Katie to have our hair and nails done and, for me, a facial. Then it would be back to the hotel to dress and have full bridal make-up.

Just before four, Sandra, Katie and I took the lift to the ground floor. As we made our way through the lobby to the Priory Room, there were comments of "Doesn't she look lovely?" and "Beautiful." And a few "Good Lucks." It made me feel fabulous.

My heart gave a flutter when I saw Roger standing at the entrance to the room. He looked so handsome in a three piece grey suit with sky blue shirt and Royal Ocean Racing Club tie.

We'd decided we would walk in together rather than the bride entering on her father's arm. We smiled and had a quick kiss, at which Katie giggled. Then our friends and family turned to look at us as the music announced our entrance.

We'd based the ceremony on a civil wedding; starting with us coming down the aisle together to Wet Wet Wet's 'Love is all around.' It had been an inspired choice by Roger as I felt the support of all our guests. When we got to the front of the room, I turned and gave Katie my bouquet.

The MC then welcomed everyone and reminded them why we were there.

This was followed by U2's 'Beautiful Day', which seemed perfect for the occasion.

Roger and I then made our declarations of love and promises to each other.

The Beatles 'All you need is love' then followed before we exchanged rings.

One of Mum's favourite songs, Elvis' 'I can't help falling in love with you' which had made a comeback, wound up the ceremony. Then we walked into the adjacent room for the sit down buffet to 'Get the Party started' by pink!

Dad gave a short speech when we had eaten and our MC read out a few cards and messages from friends and relations who couldn't be with us. There was, sadly, nothing from Peter. Mum, Dad and Sandra didn't even keep up the pretence he was unable to attend.

During the buffet, the staff converted the room used for the ceremony into a disco. Then, while we went outside for some photographs, they slid back the dividing panels and rearranged some of the furniture so we could move from tables to dance floor and back.

More of our friends from the Blue Peach joined us for an evening disco. Roger led me to the dance floor as the first notes of 'Bridge over Troubled Water' played. It had been the smoochy number we'd danced to back at the Bella Rosa restaurant. I needed to pinch myself to confirm I wasn't dreaming.

During the evening, I persuaded Dad to join me for a dance, at the end of which James asked if he could have the pleasure of the next one. Later, as I sat down, giving my feet a temporary respite and enjoying a glass of Cava, I reflected the day had gone perfectly and I couldn't have been happier. I twisted the ring Roger had placed on my finger round and round. I was now Mrs Vicky Dalton.

Folks were still dancing at midnight when Roger and I said goodnight and retired to our bed.

## Chapter 14. Backlash

### Nov 03

The nights were closing in, the weather was becoming colder and business was getting quieter as October turned into November and November was about to give way to December. Roger and I were working on the business plan and where our priorities should lie. It was tempting to focus on things that interested us personally but we had decided to bid for a schools contract. This was to provide training on weekday afternoons for children from 9 years old.

It would require an investment in suitable boats, probably a mixture of Optimists, Picos and Toppers, plus an additional rescue boat and a minimum of four members of staff available at any time. All of the staff would need to be CRB cleared before working with the kids. That shouldn't be a problem. None of us had a criminal record and there was a system for trans individuals to be cleared without their former name appearing on the clearance certificate.

Roger and I had really gelled at work as well as personally. We bounced ideas off each other and the final result was always far more effective than either of us would have come up with individually. Generally Roger had the strategic vision while I was good at looking at the details and seeing ideas through to reality; by which time Roger was onto the next idea.

We put the finishing touches to the bid document one Thursday evening at home; then called it a night and headed for bed.

By now the hormones were having their desired effect and my breasts were filling out and I didn't need any extra help to fill a B cup. The nipples were incredibly sensitive which made lovemaking rather noisy as I squirmed and cried out as Roger gave them plenty of attention.

The next evening, I attended the support group. We had recently renamed it 'T-Time'. The main topic of conversation was the introduction, finally, of the Gender Recognition Bill. It was already nicknamed the Gerbil. Now it would get interesting.

The Evangelical Alliance and the right wing of the Tory party including the Chingford Skinhead, Norman Tebbit, led powerful lobbies against it. We could only hope our allies would defeat their objections without too many significant compromises.

As we left the club that night, there was a gang of young men and women walking past who jeered at us.

"Christ – will you look at that," said one pointing to Yvonne, one of the older members, who struggled to look feminine.

"Do you take it up the bum?" taunted one of the females. The bottle, from which she'd been drinking a moment before, was waving in the air as she barely managed to stand upright on her four inch stilettos.

They gathered around us and became threatening. The intimidation became jostling and I don't mind admitting I was scared. One of them threw a punch and Karen, the smallest of our group, fell to the floor with blood flooding from her nose. At that, Jacqui, one of older members, stepped forward. To look at, you might not have considered her to be much of a threat — but you'd be mistaken. She'd grown up on a rough estate in South Manchester and had joined the army at 16.

Emboldened by Karen's fall, the same individual swung at Jacqui. In a blink of an eye, Jacqui grabbed his arm, twisted it behind his back then stamped hard on the back of his calf. As he fell to the floor, she kicked him between the legs — making me wince. She then dropped onto his back, her knee digging into his kidneys. She took hold of his hair, lifted his head off the ground then slammed it back down. As she rolled him on his back, his face was covered in blood. Jacqui now pulled back her right arm and started to give him a straight finger jab to the throat but stopped millimetres from his larynx. The look she gave him at that point was terrifying. It had been over in about fifteen seconds.

"Don't be fooled by the frock darling. I've eaten far tougher people than you for breakfast. Now run along to mummy before I really hurt you. And don't even think about trying to get revenge. I have ways of finding you that you wouldn't imagine."

I don't think I'd ever heard anyone speak in such an icy tone. It sent a shiver down *my* spine, so I don't know what it did to him.

The attacker's friends had stepped away when Jacqui launched her defence. Now the one on the ground stood up and held his hands in the air in surrender and backed off.

"God, Jacqui, how did you do that?" I asked her.

"Speed, Aggression, Surprise," she said coldly. It sounded like a mantra.

"Where on earth did you learn how to do it?"

"I could tell you, but I doubt you'd believe me," was all she would say as she stood there apparently without a hair out of place and smoothed her skirt down.

"Damn," she exclaimed. "I've broken a nail."

"Remind me never to get on the wrong side of you," said Laura, one of our other members.

I was concerned one of the girls in the gang had been Sophie who worked for us. She hadn't taken part in the jeering, she'd stayed on the edge of the group looking rather embarrassed as she'd clearly recognised me. I was quite certain she would have made the connection between me and the other more obvious trans members of our group.

We checked Karen was OK. Her nose was a mess but not broken. I drove her to our office by the quayside. She used the loo to tidy up and get changed before driving herself home. I phoned Roger to let him know I'd be later than usual but he was still concerned when I got home.

We realised Sophie might well start rumours at work. I'd now been there four months. It was plenty of time for the staff to get to know me, so now seemed the right time to come out to the others and pre-empt any false stories. I shouldn't have had to reveal my history. It wasn't anyone else's business. But I'd prefer to tell the other staff myself rather than look as though I was hiding something I was ashamed of.

As we cuddled in bed that night I looked at Roger and said "Thank you."

"What for?"

"For loving me, for being you, for saving my life."

"My pleasure — do I get a reward?"

"Anytime," I whispered as I reached for his penis.

Next morning, we arrived at the office before anyone else, as usual, and produced a notice for the chandlery door saying we'd be opening half an hour later than usual 'for staff training'.

We gathered everyone in the main office. I announced quite simply I was transsexual. I was going through the transition process and planned to have surgery. I said if anyone had questions, they could ask them now or come and see me privately. Nobody seemed at all concerned with the news. It was an anti-climax which left me feeling somewhat deflated. Usually when we make such an announcement, people raise questions about which toilets the trans person would use — but I'd been using the ladies for months and there had been no problems so why should there be in future?

Although she didn't say anything, I was still concerned about Sophie. It was a relief when she handed in her notice the following Friday, having phoned in sick on the Thursday. But if I thought that was the last we'd heard of her, I was mistaken.

A week later it was time for my third appointment with Nicholas Wright in London. There wasn't much to report. The hormones were having their desired effect. I felt comfortable with what I was doing and my personal life was great. I hadn't heard from Peter but the rest of the family had accepted me and it was difficult to see how things could be much better.

Nicholas made a few more notes in my file.

"I'd expect to refer you for the second psychiatric consultation and a surgeon after our next appointment. Have you had any thoughts about who you'd want to see?"

"I've been thinking of the team at Leicester as my first choice," I told him.

"That's a good option. I'd be happy to write to them."

As I took the train home, I hummed the Carpenters' 'Top of the World.' "Everything I want the world to be is now comin' true especially for me." That certainly seemed to be the case.

Then we hit problems.

The Bournemouth Bugle, came out the next week with a front page headline: 'Sex Change Sailing Instructor bids for Schools Contract.' It was the usual rabble rousing misinformation but might damage our chances of winning the contract. The article raised concerns about the likelihood of our company and me in particular recruiting youngsters, who were too young to understand, into a gay or trans lifestyle.

There was only one likely source of the report: Sophie.

I offered to resign from the business — or, at least, from the instructing team planned for the schools' work. But Roger wouldn't think of it. "We'll fight this together and if we win, great, if we don't then we'll still survive."

How could I not love this guy?

When we arrived home that evening we saw immediately some kind person had broken a window. Someone had also scratched 'tranny' in the paintwork on the front door. When we opened the door we found they'd posted dog shit through the letterbox. Fortunately it had only landed on the doormat.

The newspaper report had stirred up trouble for us personally as well as for the business. Roger reported the vandalism to the police. They weren't particularly interested and only went through the motions.

"I doubt if we'll find any witnesses and without being able to identify who might have done the damage, there's not much we can do," said one of the officers.

"So you're not even going to investigate?" I asked.

"There isn't anything to go on."

"So we have to put up with broken windows and having tranny scratched on the door?"

He shrugged his shoulders. "Well I suppose they do have a point as you are a tranny."

My hackles started to rise. "I am *not* a tranny. I am transsexual but even if I had been a tranny that doesn't justify vandalism."

"Well, as I say, there's not much we can do. We'll make a note of it and keep an eye on the area when passing."

Their attitude annoyed me as much as the vandalism. Once the police had left, Roger phoned a glazier to replace the window. He then got paint from the garage and covered up the scratch marks on the door while I prepared our dinner.

We called in a Public Relations Consultant and outlined the situation. She advised against responding to the newspaper article saying it would only extend the coverage. Instead, she wrote a briefing paper for members of the council's equality committee and local school governors and organised an open meeting where they could come and ask questions.

It was a nervous period while we waited for the outcome of the bids. The arguments around the abolition of Clause 28 had held sway and parliament was now considering the Gender Recognition Bill and a Civil Partnership Bill. But we were fighting a local authority that had a significant conservative majority. The Tories had fought to keep the clause and many were fighting the new legislation.

We had more trouble at the house. Another broken window, eggs thrown at other windows and the front door. After our previous experience with the local police, we didn't bother reporting the incidents. We did, however, set up security cameras which seemed to deter further problems.

It was mid-February before we heard the outcome of our bid. We hadn't won the contract. It had gone to another sailing school. It was a disappointment but not a huge surprise. Our contact at the council assured us the newspaper article had not influenced the decision — but he'd have said that whether or not it was true.

In the meantime, the Gerbil was making progress. Numerous amendments had been tabled mainly over marriages, the possibility of it creating same sex marriages and the rights of ministers and registrars to refuse to perform the ceremonies; how to define sex and why it wasn't possible to change a person's sex or gender; or competing in sport; or sharing private facilities; if one could be recognised in a different gender without having had surgery. Thankfully, despite of the efforts of various well known politicians and bishops the bill seemed to be on track.

# Chapter 15. Final Appointment
## March 04

I couldn't believe it was time for my fourth session with Dr Wright — but I was back on a train for London.

As Roger had predicted, apart from the council contract, we hadn't lost business because of the newspaper revelations. Most of our customers weren't from the Bournemouth area so wouldn't have seen the local rag. We had put our expansion plans on hold but business was still up on the previous year. I smiled to think a few people had come into the chandlers hoping to glimpse the sex change 'freak' and had bought something. So, if anything, we made a bit more money. I was very relieved at the outcome.

Ironically, we heard the sailing school that had won the contract was struggling to find qualified staff to cover the extra work. There were rumours they might have to hand the contract back or subcontract some of the training. Roger and I had discussed whether to offer to help them but felt the long game was to let them fail then pick up the pieces.

I was delighted when, as expected, Nicholas Wright referred me to a second psychiatrist and my choice of surgeon. They both operated from a private hospital on the edge of Leicester. I had appointments with them for the same Thursday afternoon in the middle of May. I could have gone earlier but there wasn't much point. I would complete my twelve month's Real Life Experience on 12th July. However, I didn't want my surgery until the end of the sailing season; I was aiming for mid-September. It meant a slightly longer wait than necessary but I'd still be well ahead of the dates expected through the NHS.

Of course I wanted my body to match how I felt. I longed to be able to make love with Roger like any other woman. But we'd have the rest of our lives together. I was surprised there was no longer a sense of urgency but glad I wasn't obsessed with having surgery like some of my friends. I'm sure it was because I was in control; while most of them were subject to the apparent whims of the GICs.

# Chapter 16. Fry & Khan
## 10<sup>th</sup> June 2004

It was a 350 mile round trip from Bournemouth to the hospital in Leicester for my appointments with the surgeon, Mr Fry, and the second psychiatrist Dr Khan.

Driving there and back in a day would be a challenge in the MGB, so we booked a hotel near Stratford upon Avon for two nights. We could then go to the theatre on the Friday. Whichever way my appointments at the hospital went, we had something to celebrate as the Gender Recognition Bill had completed its passage through parliament and now only needed Royal Assent to become law — so Roger and I would be able marry as soon as I obtained a Gender Recognition Certificate.

For the first six months, applications would be limited to those who had been living in role for more than six years (and I hadn't). So, it would be October next year before the panel would consider my application. In case there were any hiccups in my application we were tentatively thinking of a Christmas wedding. Perhaps a snowy scene would add a touch of magic to the photographs and make it very different to our commitment ceremony.

When I'd told Dr Wright I wouldn't be devastated if we weren't able to have a proper wedding and we'd be happy with our own commitment ceremony, it had been true — but it didn't stop the excitement at the thought of being able to legally marry.

We checked into our hotel on the way to Leicester as it might be late by the time we finished at the hospital. I was due to see Dr Khan at six thirty then Mr Fry an hour later. I didn't think I had anything to worry about with either appointment but it didn't stop me being nervous.

The directions took us off the M1 and round to the eastern side of the city. There we found a modern looking three storey building with car parking at the front, close to the reception. Friendly staff greeted us when I told them who I was there to see. They offered us coffee and showed us to a comfortable waiting area.

Promptly at half past six, the door to Dr Khan's office opened.

"Vicky Dalton?"

"That's me. Is it OK for Roger to come in with me?"

"Certainly. Take a seat. I understand you are looking for a second referral for GRS?" His manner seemed somewhat curt but maybe he'd had a long day. I hoped it wasn't a reaction to me.

"Yes Doctor Khan, as I think you know, I've been seeing Dr Wright for a year."

"Yes, I have his letter. Tell me your history please."

I related my background and current situation. He took notes but I couldn't tell from his expression how he was reacting to my story.

"So you've been living and working full time for more than a year now?"

"Yes doctor."

"And you've been on hormones for most of that time."

"For about nine months."

"And you've been having regular blood tests?"

"Oh yes."

He sat back in his chair and put his hands together the finger tips touching. He looked straight at me and the hint of a smile appeared. That smile gave me hope.

"Based on what you've told me, I'm happy to refer you for surgery. Who do you plan to use?"

"I'm thinking of Mr Fry."

"Good choice," he responded. "When are you seeing him?"

"I have an appointment with him at seven-thirty."

"Fine, you can tell him I'll confirm my assessment to him in writing. And best of luck to you." He stood up and offered me his hand to shake.

"Thank you Doctor Khan."

I could have skipped out of his office. One down, one to go. I hadn't been particularly concerned about Dr Khan, but it was always possible Mr Fry would find some medical reason why I couldn't undergo surgery.

When we entered Mr Fry's consulting room, he asked if I understood what the proposed surgery involved. I said I thought I did but he explained the procedure to eliminate any doubts.

His approach was matter of fact. But, I suppose, that was the best way to deal with the subject. He needed to ensure patients understood the risks without giving too much cause for anxiety. Not that the risks would put many of us off by the time we got to this point. Any dangers would be no more relevant to us than the chance of being in an accident on the way to the hospital.

"You will have your own private room, of course, with en suite facilities. You should register at nine am on the Friday morning. Once they've settled you in, the nurse will give you a dose of Picolax to clear out your system and a second dose later in the day. When you take the doses, I advise you not to be more than a few feet from the toilets."

That sounded unpleasant but it was important the bowels be clear in case of any damage and potential infections.

"We will prep you early on the Saturday morning and take you to the operating theatre. The surgery takes around five to six hours."

He picked up a laminated diagram showing the procedure to illustrate his explanation. I knew the principles but this made it much clearer.

"It involves removing the testicles and the inside of the penis. We reposition part of the tip as a clitoris and redirect the urethra. We create a cavity and invert the penile skin to create the neo-vagina. Then we use the scrotum to create labia."

Roger was holding my hand and I felt his nails digging into my palm. I glanced at him. His face had gone pale and he had crossed his legs. Poor chap; no doubt he was imagining it happening to his own equipment whereas I was focussed on the outcome rather than appendages I was more than happy to lose.

"We keep you in the recovery room until we are satisfied you've stabilised and come round from the anaesthetic. We then bring you back to your own room."

"OK," I replied — there seemed to be nothing anything else to say.

I could only imagine how it would be after surgery. I thought it might compare with giving birth — painful, but more than compensated for by the outcome and a sense of satisfaction and achievement afterwards.

"You will have a pack inserted into the neo-vagina to prevent it healing up. That will typically remain in place for five days. During that time you must remain in bed and limited to lifting your head and shoulders up slightly. This avoids pressure on the site of the operation."

That didn't sound too comfortable, but OK, I would have to endure it.

"For the first few days we allow only water by mouth. You may gradually flavour it with fruit cordial then have tea or coffee with a little milk. You won't be permitted solid food until about day five."

Oh well, that should help my diet.

"Once we remove the pack and catheter, you can get out of bed. You will be quite weak at that stage so will need to take it easy. Do you have any questions about the procedure?"

I didn't. I wasn't looking forward to the process of the surgery and recovery. Instead, I focussed on the end result and that would make it all worthwhile, or so I hoped.

"Right can you undress from the waist down and lie on the couch for me please so I can see what I have to work with?"

I did as he asked. I thought I'd be embarrassed as Dr Fry was the only man, other than Roger, who had touched my penis but Dr Fry had seen them hundreds of times before and was completely professional.

"That looks fine. Well, if you are happy to proceed, I'm happy to undertake the surgery. All I need now is a report from a second psychiatrist."

My smile felt like it stretched from ear to ear at the news.

"I saw Dr Khan before you, Mr Fry. He said he would provide the second report," I told him as I pulled up my knickers and straightened my dress.

"Oh well, that's fine. Did you want to sort out a date now for surgery?"

"Yes please. I was thinking mid-late September. We run a sailing business. I was looking for it to be after the season dies down and I can recuperate during the winter."

"I can do 18th September if that suits you?"

"That would be perfect." *I had a date for surgery!* It really was going to happen.

"Good. I will write and confirm the arrangements. We will expect the fees to be paid by the time you are admitted. Is that OK?"

"No problem," I told him. I already had more than enough in my transition account.

"I hooked my arm through Roger's as we walked out of the hospital. If I hadn't been holding on to him, I'm sure I'd have floated away I was so euphoric.

Our dinner that evening was a double celebration. I hope we didn't disturb the residents in adjoining rooms too much when we continued the celebrations in bed.

84

# Chapter 17. Mayday, Mayday, Mayday

A couple of weeks after my trip to Leicester, we took Summer Dreams down the coast to Salcombe. On our return trip we were battling into a south-easterly force seven. Summer Dreams was well maintained and Roger and I were both experienced, so the ride was exhilarating rather than scary as we crashed through the waves; spray, and sometimes solid water, hitting us as we sat in the cockpit. It reminded me of my transition journey. I realised my life wouldn't be as straightforward as it might have been if I hadn't been trans. There would be difficulties ahead — but I now had the support I needed. I knew where I was going, and what was involved in getting there. I felt confident I would overcome whatever fate threw at me.

Then the radio burst into life.

"Mayday, Mayday, Mayday."

My stomach tightened and a lump formed in my throat as I heard those words. Words no sailor wants to hear or transmit. I cleared my head and went into autopilot mode and focussed on what we could do to help. I picked up a pencil ready to take notes and sat at the chart table next to the radio.

"This is Excalibur, Excalibur, Excalibur.

"Mayday, Excalibur.

"Our position is five-zero degrees one-two decimal five minutes north, three degrees three-zero decimal nine minutes west."

I wrote down the location.

"We are a Sadler thirty-two Bermuda rigged yacht, white hull, white sails with number two two."

I knew the type. The first time I'd done the Round the Island Race had been in a Sadler thirty-two.

"There are three, repeat figures three, crew still on board." That 'still on board' hit me.

"We broached and one crew has been lost overboard. Our mast has been broken and we cannot restart the engine. We are swamped but not sinking. Over."

I could imagine the chaos on board Excalibur and the crew's shock at losing one of their number over the side.

Checking our position on the Sat Nav, I saw we were about three miles from Excalibur.

Roger was on the helm but listening to the message as well.

"Steer zero-four-three magnetic." I told him. He was already starting the engine.

I considered replying to Excalibur but waited until the Coastguard had responded, as the first priority would be to get help on the way to search for the missing crew.

When the coastguard failed to respond after two minutes, I transmitted a 'Mayday Relay' call. The coastguard came back immediately and Excalibur responded. But, once again, it was apparent the coastguard couldn't hear them. Excalibur's main radio aerial had probably been at the top of the mast, now lost overboard. They were likely to now be using a hand-held radio. I offered to act as a relay for messages from Excalibur to the coastguard. I advised we were heading for Excalibur and should be with them in about half an hour.

They accepted our offer with alacrity and I felt gratified we could assist rather than listen helplessly to messages which were likely to become ever more hopeless unless the missing crew was found quickly.

The coastguard scrambled the Search and Rescue helicopter from Newquay and two lifeboats from Salcombe to search for Excalibur's missing crewmember and attend the stricken yacht. We would probably be first on the scene followed shortly afterwards by the fast Atlantic 85 lifeboat. The helicopter from Newquay was expected about ten to fifteen minutes later and the larger Tamar class lifeboat from Salcombe ten to fifteen minutes later still.

I asked the Coastguard to work out a likely position for the missing crew member based on Excalibur's position when they were lost overboard and prevailing tidal streams. I suggested we approach Excalibur along the potential path they'd have drifted. It wouldn't add significantly to our transit time but we might get lucky. If so, it might make the difference between survival and recovering a body.

I imagined what it would be like to be the missing crew or if the missing person had been Roger. Apart from the cold and the discomfort of being tossed around by the waves with spray stinging exposed flesh, it would be frightening knowing how difficult it would be to find you so the chances were you wouldn't make it. They'd know survival times would depend on what they were wearing and water temperature. It might be as little as half an hour even for someone reasonably fit and unlikely to be longer than two to three hours unless wearing a full immersion suit.

The coastguard agreed with our suggestion and gave us a waypoint to head for. They complimented us on our suggestion which gave me a brief warm glow. I'd feel a lot better, though, if we were to find the missing person.

I joined Roger on deck and we dropped the mainsail and furled the jib and motored towards Excalibur. Roger watched the sea to port while I watched it to starboard.

Visibility from deck level on our yacht wasn't good. We could easily have passed within ten yards of the missing person and not seen them if there was a crest of a wave between us.

Unsurprisingly, we saw nothing of the missing crew before reaching the stricken yacht.

As we reached them, Roger called out:

"Ahoy Excalibur. Do you need anything? Are any of you injured?"

"We're fine — a few scratches and bruises from the knock-down. Good to see you. Thanks for your help."

"No problem. I don't think there is any point us passing you a line, do you?"

"No. We're in no immediate danger of going aground and with all due respect I don't think you'd have much success trying to tow us in these conditions."

"Totally agree. We'll take position upwind of you to try and give you a bit of shelter from the wind and driving rain. It might make you more comfortable."

"Cheers. Anything would help."

The first of the lifeboats was now approaching.

As the missing crew was the priority, the Atlantic 85 lifeboat advised they would carry out a standard search pattern from Excalibur's position when they broached. They asked us to remain with Excalibur and continue acting as relay. As our mast was still upright, we'd also be a focal point to find Excalibur again.

The thwack thwack thwack of rotor blades told us the Sea King rescue helicopter had reached us. It was a comforting sound which meant the search would be much more effective now. We heard them speaking to the two lifeboats to agree a search plan. A call to Excalibur checking there was no immediate danger to them. Finally to us, asking if we were happy to continue our role, which, of course, we were.

I was very thankful for the full wet-weather gear I was wearing which shrugged off the worst of the weather. I took the opportunity to make coffee for Roger and me. I then thought about the crew on the other yacht and imagined them shivering from their own immersion during the knock-down.

I called them on the radio.

"Excalibur, Summer Dreams, do you have any way of making a hot drink?"

"Summer Dreams, Excalibur. Negative. The cooker is out of action. Over."

"Would you prefer coffee or soup? Over."

"Soup would be great, thanks. Over."

I heated a large can of tomato soup and found our biggest flask. Taking the filled flask on deck, I secured it to a fender for buoyancy and attached a light rope.

Roger gingerly took Summer Dreams to about ten yards from Excalibur. I coiled the line and prepared to throw it over to them.

"Ready?" I called to them.

"Ready," they confirmed.

I threw half the coiled line — allowing the rest to be drawn off my hand. One of the other crew caught hold it. I lowered the fender and flask over the side into the water before I let go and watched as they pulled it over. Roger was already reversing us away from Excalibur to give ourselves more sea room.

I heard a very warm "Thanks, Mate" from the other crew. Hmm, mate is usually male. But, I don't suppose it was obvious I was female in my sailing gear. And my voice had dropped an octave when I'd shouted to them. Oh well, I'd forgive them misgendering me under the circumstances and just waved.

The lifeboats continued their search patterns while the helicopter used its infra-red camera to see if it could pick up any signs of body heat.

Time was running out. If they didn't find the missing person in the next thirty to forty-five minutes, their chances of survival would be very slim. My hopes for a good outcome were dwindling and I thought about the missing crew's family and friends.

Then the Sea King reported a possible sighting. It hovered about a mile away from us, lifting my spirits and giving us some hope. The Atlantic lifeboat sped over to the sighting to investigate more closely. We caught sight of them occasionally while we were both on the crests of waves. But we soon lost them as they or we dropped into troughs. The waves were about three to four metres from trough to crest. The wind had dropped slightly from the earlier force seven but was still whipping the tops of the waves into a stinging spray.

It was a false alarm and another few vital minutes had slid away. I realised it would soon be a matter of recovering a body rather than saving a life. A depressing thought.

Then the Sea King identified another possible sighting and the Atlantic lifeboat investigated once more.

The radio burst into life again.

"This is Atlantic eight-five, we have recovered missing crew. He is hypothermic and has a superficial head wound but otherwise fine. Over."

I felt a huge sense of relief at the news, and hugged Roger. It felt great to have helped save someone's life and I felt another lump in my throat.

"Atlantic eight-five from Excalibur. Thank you and all of those involved. Thanks. Out."

The open Atlantic lifeboat rendezvoused with the larger Tamar to transfer the casualty. They would be much more comfortable in the enclosed cabin. They then headed back to Salcombe while the Tamar took Excalibur in tow and headed for Dartmouth. The helicopter had also headed back to its base at Newquay. We were about to resume our course back home to Poole. Then the radio called again.

"Summer Dreams, Excalibur. Thanks for all your help. I think we owe you dinner, oh and a fender and a flask, if you'd like to join us in Dartmouth." The lifeboat would have to return to Salcombe as soon as it had dropped off the casualty and Excalibur.

Roger and I looked at each other. We'd be a day later than planned getting home but that wouldn't matter. We accepted the offer and arranged to meet at a restaurant near the quay. It would be great to get together with the guys from Excalibur having shared an emotional few hours. It's rare, thank God, you help save someone's life and spend what had seemed like an eternity hoping against hope for a happy outcome while dreading it wouldn't be.

Four hours later, having moored and cleaned ourselves up, we were strolling along the quay. We entered the Ferry Restaurant. Two of the Excalibur crew greeted us with hugs and, in my case, kisses. They immediately thrust large glasses of wine into our hands.

"I'm Ben, this is Craig. The boss Ray has gone with PeeWee, the idiot who fell in the drink, to the hospital. They needed to see if there was anything between his ears. Turns out he had a slight scratch to the forehead but nothing else and they'll be with us in half an hour."

"That's good to hear. So where were you heading?"

"We're all part of the same Territorial Army unit and we'd been on passage from Guernsey back here to Dartmouth. We got hit by a freak wave. PeeWee was hooking on his safety line at the time and got washed overboard as we broached."

"PeeWee?" I asked.

"His initials are PW — hence PeeWee."

"I get you. That was bad luck, getting hit as he was hooking on."

"Yeah, it's not as though he's an inexperienced sailor. Anyway, when we broached, the sail went under the water. When the boat tried to right itself, the strain was too much for the shrouds which gave way. Then the mast broke."

"We were fortunate you were around and able to relay our Mayday," said Ben ruefully. "If you hadn't got the message through when you did, I don't think PeeWee would have survived. He owes you big time."

"He doesn't owe us anything — we did what any other sailors would have done," I insisted.

Ben looked at me sheepishly. "Look, I hope this doesn't come across as rude, especially under the circumstances. But when we were out there and you were in wet-weather gear and shouting to us, I thought you were a guy which is why I called you mate. But now, well I can see you're female and a very attractive one. So, I'm sorry if I insulted you."

"Stop digging Ben," said Craig, "you're embarrassing her."

"No, I'm not embarrassed. In fact I'm transsexual and I know my voice drops a couple of octaves when I shout. So there you go." I rarely revealed my background like this on first meeting; but after what we'd all been through earlier, it hardly seemed to matter.

"Well Vicky. Fair play to you. As far as I'm concerned, you're female and if your husband wasn't sitting there, I'd be more than happy to ask you out. And I tell you what — you showed bags of guts out there today. I'd welcome you on my team any time." He leant over and gave me a kiss on the cheek.

"I second that," said Craig who leant over from the other side to give me a kiss.

"'Scuse me guys — but that's my wife you're coming on to," protested Roger light-heartedly. I'm sure he realised having two macho guys acknowledging me as female was very affirming.

"Ah, skipper, PeeWee, come and meet our rescuers. This is Vicky and this is Roger."

With my back to the door, I hadn't realised the rest of Excalibur's crew had come into the restaurant.

I looked up and said "hello," to Ray. I then turned to my other side to welcome PeeWee when I realised whose face was partly hidden by a Zapa moustache. I couldn't believe what I was seeing.

"Peter?"

"Do I know you?" He looked confused — then something triggered a memory.

"Oh Shit fuck bugger. David? Is it you?"

"What's the problem," asked Garry, "do you two know each other?"

"Well, yes. Peter's my twin brother. But we haven't spoken since I told him I was transsexual," I said, standing up to face Peter.

"Is that true PeeWee? Not that I'm doubting you Vicky," said Craig. "Why? Oh, I get it, you think we'd have taken the piss. Well we would have done but you should have been able to take it. Fuck me. The crap we have to go through on selection, a bit of banter would have been nothing. And, you know what? I reckon Vicky showed a hell of a lot of balls out there today — no offence. I told her I'd be happy for her to be on my team anytime and I meant it."

"I suppose you thought we'd think you were the same did you? So fucking what? Why should you care what others think. Except whether you can do the job and you've shown that. But this also shows you can be a total dickhead," added Ben.

Peter held his hands up in surrender.

"OK. Yes, I worried about what others might think and all of you are right, that was wrong."

"Too effing right, you git," contributed Ray.

"Yeah, well, out there in the water today I had time to think about a lot of things and what was and wasn't important."

"PeeWee thinking. Now that's a first," said Ben.

"It wouldn't matter, in any case, now you arseholes know."

It seemed Peter had matured a lot in the year we'd not seen each other.

He held his arms out and I stepped closer. He hugged me and kissed me on the forehead. "Can you forgive me for all the hurtful things I said?"

"Of course. This is Roger by the way."

"I owe you an apology too, Roger — I said some shitty things about you as well."

He held his hand out to Roger for him to shake.

Roger had no hesitation taking Peter's outstretched hand. I thought there might be a typical alpha male contest as they shook hands. But, perhaps, both were confident in their own skins and didn't need to compete.

Peter continued, "The last nine months' training and selection have changed me. I've learned to be a lot more self-sufficient so I no longer care as much about what other people think. Now, come on, who's having what to drink? Beers all round — or would you prefer something else, Vicky?"

That single short question swept away the sadness of the last year. We were back where we'd been before I'd told him I was trans.

Over the meal I brought Pete (as he now preferred to be called, — we both had to get used to using different names for each other) up to speed with what had been happening with Roger and me. He told me he'd joined the TA 'Artists' Rifles' based at Duke of York's Barracks, Chelsea, soon after my revelations.

"Did you say you'd had to go through a lot of selection and training? It sounds a lot more than I'd expect for the TA," I asked him.

"Ah well, it's not a run of the mill TA unit, The Artist's Rifles are 21st Regiment SAS Reserves. We train almost to the same level as the regulars."

"Are you talking about the lot that stormed the Iranian Embassy and the book Bravo Two-Zero? David Stirling's outfit?" Roger asked incredulously.

"Well those are the regulars, we're the reserves but selection and training is still tough."

I found it difficult to believe my brother was now part of an elite Special Forces unit. But it was probably the level of training and fitness he'd gained that had helped him to survive long enough to be rescued. As we'd hugged, his body had felt much firmer than I remembered from when we'd played together and he'd wrestled me. I also saw a much more self-assured and mature individual. I felt proud of my little brother (I'm older by 32 minutes).

I shook my head and said "You've changed a lot since last year."

"I've changed? What about you?"

"Ah, yes, you have a point there."

As we waited for our main courses, Pete said. "By the way, the rest of the family know I'm in the TA but not that it's the SAS reserves. I told them it was the Artists' Rifles'. It sounds a bit less hazardous. I suspect Dad has made the connection but keeps it to himself."

He then asked "Can I borrow your phone to ring Mum and Dad and Sandra? Mine got damaged in the water."

I dialled the number and put it on speaker. When Mum picked up and said "Hello, Vicky" he interrupted and said "It's not Vicky — it's Pete using Vicky's phone."

"Why are you using Vicky's phone. Is she all right? How are you involved?"

"I'm fine Mum," I interrupted.

"So, what's going on?" she demanded to know.

"Slow down, Mum. I had an accident earlier today and Vicky was part of the team that rescued me. I'm OK and having dinner with Roger and Vicky and some of the unit. I thought you'd want to know everything is good again with Vicky and me and Roger."

Mum was dumbfounded. There was a pause as she took the information on board then she managed to say. "Oh, I am *so* glad, it wasn't right the two of you not talking."

"Well, no need to worry any more, Mum," I interjected. "We'll give you the details when we see you next time but we also want to ring Sandra."

Sandra was also delighted to hear the news and said she would organise a barbecue to celebrate.

"Oh Christ," said Pete "I've just thought, it's now two females against one male sibling. You and Sandra are going to give me shit aren't you?"

I smiled and nodded my head.

# Chapter 18. Surgery
## 18th September

The Gender Recognition Act received its Royal Assent on 1st July 2004 and we had a party at the Blue Peach to celebrate. We already knew the earliest I could obtain legal recognition would be the following October; but, at least, it would now happen. In the meantime, there was surgery to look forward to, if that's the right term.

We have to stop taking hormones six weeks before the op to minimise the risk of deep vein thrombosis during surgery.

The brain has receptors for the hormones it expects based on gender. If they aren't present, the body reacts. For women going through menopause, this can include night sweats. I'd experienced similar symptoms as a teenager but these had disappeared once I was on HRT. Now they were back with a vengeance soaking my nightdresses, pillowcases and sheets; showing how my brain craved oestrogen. I also felt awkward in my body in a way that I couldn't explain. It was the dysphoria returning. I'd be glad to lose the testosterone my body was still producing and which was flowing through my system unfettered by oestrogen.

Finally, the day arrived for me to go in to hospital. We'd travelled up the night before and stopped in a hotel as check in was nine am.

My room was on the side of the hospital with views out over a grassy bank. Between the bed and the window was an easy chair for guests. The en suite facilities were to the left of the bed; there was a television and telephone — in fact pretty much as you'd find in many hotels. The monitoring instruments made it clear, however, this was a hospital, not a hotel.

If I'd thought Mr Fry had exaggerated the potency of Picolax, I soon found out he hadn't. I stayed within easy reach of my en suite facilities for an hour after each of the two doses.

Mr Fry visited me just before tea was due on the Friday.

"Hello Vicky, how are you feeling?"

"Fine thanks."

"Any concerns?"

"Not really. In fact, I'm surprised I don't feel particularly excited or nervous; simply resigned to whatever happens. If it all goes well, then that's brilliant. If something goes wrong, and I don't make it then at least I'll have died doing something that was important to me."

I felt Roger's hand squeeze mine and saw his eyes cloud over.

"Don't worry, darling," I told him. "I'm confident that won't happen. Mr Fry has a great reputation."

"Thank you Vicky, we have no intention of losing you. You are a fit young woman and there is no reason to expect any problems. So don't worry Roger."

"There is one thing though," I added. "The only thing that does concern me is if something was to go wrong and I was to end up as a vegetable. I really don't want that to happen. So I'm telling both of you, if it does, then I don't want to be resuscitated."

Mr Fry laid his hand on my shoulder and gave it a squeeze. "I understand exactly Vicky, don't worry that won't happen."

Looking over at Roger, I said "I want your word too, Roger."

"But.."

"No, darling, no buts. There's no point in you being tied to me if I'm being kept alive by machines and unable to communicate. You have to be able to move on — and I want your promise to do that."

"But...."

"I said no buts, Roger. Look it's not going to happen in any case. But I have to know I'm not going to spend years in a coma with you feeling trapped. Now give me your word, darling."

I saw the tear forming in his eye as he leant across and kissed me. "OK Vicky, I promise." It made a change for me to take the stronger role in our relationship but I had nothing to lose. I'd either get where I wanted to be or wouldn't be around to worry; while Roger was facing the possibility, however remote, of losing me.

I recognised there was likely to be pain after surgery, but that would diminish afterwards. I'd simply have to put up with what was left after painkillers had done their work. A push button hanging above my bed would provide doses of morphine if the pain became too much.

Saturday morning, they prepped me for theatre then wheeled me along the corridor to the lift. The ceiling lights flashed as I passed under each in turn. Then there was a bang as the trolley struck the door to the operating theatre ante-room. The last I remembered was counting down from ten as they applied the anaesthetic.

Then I was back in my bed. I was very groggy as I came round again. Roger's gorgeous face was the first thing I focused on.

"Hi darling, welcome back."

I was confused. Perhaps the anaesthetic was still having an effect but I wasn't in any pain at all. Did that mean they hadn't done the op? Then I realised there was lots of padding around my groin — known as the 'teddy bear'.

Roger leant over and kissed me. "It all went fine Vicky. Mr Fry was very pleased with everything."

He'd done it. Fabulous. I gave a quick prayer of thanks even though I didn't believe in God.

The nurse came in at that point.

"Hi Vicky, I'm Glynis, How are you feeling? Are you in any pain?"

"It's uncomfortable but there's no actual pain. May I have some water please?"

"Of course. I'm afraid that's all you're allowed for the next couple of days as we have to keep your bowels clear in case they need to do any more work. Here you are."

I took a sip from the cup she passed me; it was like those you give to toddlers with a lid and spout.

"By day three, you can have cordial then tea on day four. I'm afraid you can't have any solid food until Mr Fry removes the pack."

"That's fine. I don't care."

All I needed was sitting next to me and everything I'd wanted had been done. The anaesthetic had numbed my emotions as well as the pain. Instead of the elation I might have expected, I just felt totally content.

Looking around my room, I was amazed to see so many cards and bunches of flowers. But the best sight was Roger. I couldn't believe how lucky I'd been to meet him.

"Who are all the flowers and cards from?" I asked him.

He stepped over to the window ledge.

"The girls at T-Time, the office, the Blue Peach, your mum and dad, my mum and dad, Sandra, Pete and Andrea. Oh and me. Some of them have sent individual cards including this from Katie.

Katie's card was handmade. It had a picture of me on the front and a multi-coloured message 'get well soon, I love you Aunty Vicky' inside.

Roger stayed with me until the fifth day after surgery when they removed the pack from inside the neo-vagina. The nurses asked him to leave the room while that was done.

"Good morning Vicky. Everything looks to be healing splendidly so we are going to remove the pack this morning," Mr Fry told me.

"*Ouch!*" I cried as he tried to extract it.

"Oh, I'm sorry Vicky, one of the stitches is still in place."

Until now, whenever the nurses had asked me how much pain I was in on a scale of one to ten, my reply had always been "I'm not." But that had made my eyes water.

Once he had removed the overlooked stitch, the pack came out easily.

The following day, they removed the catheter so I was now free to use the en suite toilet. The first time, during the night, it was fine. But the second time I sat on the loo, I hadn't the faintest idea what to do. How do I urinate? What muscles do I use? I was on the verge of panicking when I thought 'calm down, you did it during the night so let nature take over'. I stood back up then sat down again and relaxed. Thankfully it worked. But no one tells you these things in advance!

One thing they had warned about, however, is the helicopter effect.

Instead of going down when you wee, the urine sprays out sideways like the rotors of a helicopter. Chances are, it shoots through the gap between the seat and the toilet bowl and unerringly finds anything down around your ankles! I soon learned to stuff paper into the gap to avoid having wet knickers.

Apart from shortening the times taken to get to surgery, one of the advantages I'd anticipated with going private was having an appetising menu rather than NHS food. But the first meal I ordered tasted horrible. My tongue was coated — possibly in salt from the forced detox of nothing but water. Everything tasted vile and even seemed to burn my mouth. Those appetising lamb chops were evil. Anything sweet was turned sour. Tea was just about tolerable. It was so unfair.

Roger returned on the Friday afternoon ready for me to leave on the Saturday. Instead of the MGB, he had a sporty version of the Toyota Corolla. I was very grateful he had. The MGB would have been too firm a ride for me, even with a rubber ring to sit on. On the way home, I found the only disadvantage of having had the op. I desperately needed the loo. Pre-op, it would have been a simple matter of nipping behind a convenient bush next to a lay-bye. Not any longer.

I joked the red Corolla was a girly car for Roger even in the T-Sport version. He looked across at me, smiled and said "Perfect for you then."

"What did you say?" I asked.

"This is for you. I'm keeping the MGB. It actually makes sense in lots of ways. Unless you don't want it of course."

On line I used Firebird as my ID on some forums. It had been developed from my old CB handle of Fireball (based on the dinghies Peter and I used to sail). After transition, 'balls' no longer seemed appropriate so I'd changed it to Firebird. A sporty red Corolla was perfect and the nickname was transferred to her.

# Chapter 19. Recuperation

## Sept –Dec 04

The first few weeks following surgery were tedious. I was given a Patients' Guide. It stated I must not lift anything heavy for several weeks or drive a car for four to five weeks. So Firebird sat forlornly on the drive unless Roger was taking me somewhere. I couldn't return to work or go swimming for six weeks. It also suggested it would be three months before I should have penetrative sex. In the meantime, I had to dilate up to three times a day for twenty to thirty minutes using a set of different sized tools to maintain the vaginal depth. As each session involved preparation and cleaning up afterwards, this important process took up nearly half the day for the first few weeks. I could, and did, however, fantasise as I dilated, imagining a different item penetrating me. I couldn't wait for the real thing.

I became familiar with daytime television schedules. After watching so many quizzes, I reckoned I could compete on Mastermind, well at least Weakest Link. And I comfort ate; usually Danish biscuits, which undid the good work of my forced diet in hospital.

I wasn't good at just resting and Roger had cause to rebuke me for trying to do too much too soon. I regretted having planned surgery for September. If it had been in the spring, I could, at least, have sat in the garden or pottered around outside. But the boredom was a small price to pay for what I now had.

Once I could drive and start swimming again, I took advantage of the local pool. It was such a relief to wear a swimming costume and not have to worry about a bulge between my legs.

I thought back to the odd occasions when I'd gone swimming in the past. I'd worn a skirted costume and control panties underneath to keep things under control. Getting changed, I'd had to wait until there was an individual cubicle free which drew attention as most of the other swimmers were happy to change in the communal area. After swimming, I'd had to be very careful leaving the showers and, again, wait for a free cubicle or take my things into a toilet. I'd also worried about the risk of my towel slipping and being exposed and causing an uproar. Now I could stand naked in the communal area with no problem. Everyone else saw me as just one of the girls. That simple act was so liberating and I took my time applying body lotion all over.

I continued to attend the T-Time group meetings. It was apparent several of the other members were envious I was now post-op. Many of them would take years to get to the same point. Most were transvestite so had no intention of undergoing surgery. But it didn't stop some of them fantasising over having a vagina.

I was there one evening when Laura sat down with us.

"God did I have a bastard of a date last night." She said as she plonked her drink on the table and slumped into a chair.

"This guy contacted me on T-dateline. He invited me to his place for a coffee. When I got there he was wearing a dressing gown when he opened the door. I thought it was because I was earlier than I'd said I'd be. But he took me into his lounge and sat down on the settee. There wasn't anywhere else to sit, so I joined him after taking off my jacket. He didn't even offer to take it or get me a drink; the television was on in the corner and he was using a laptop to chat to other contacts on the web."

She paused to take a drink and light a cigarette, then continued:

"His knee nudged mine. I thought he might slide his arm behind me and pull me closer for a snog. Instead he undid his dressing gown, threw it open and said 'well, there it is, what do you think?'"

"I was tempted to say it looked like a penis, only smaller. But I was still hoping for some action so I took hold and fondled it. I hoped he'd get the message and reciprocate but he leaned back and left me to it. God, talk about frustrating. He then put his hand behind my head and pushed me down onto it. After a few minutes I told him it wasn't working for me and he just said 'you want it in you don't you'. Well, of course I did. I paid a lot of money for my designer vagina and I still haven't used it properly. The only things I've had up me are those damned dilators. He got up, stood in front of me and pulled me to the edge of the seat. Then he pulled my knickers to one side and was about to stick his cock in me when I told him to put a condom on first, which he did. He then fumbled around but still couldn't get it in me."

She took another drink.

"OK, so I'm desperate but this wasn't doing anything for me so I ended up wanking him off then leaving. Where do these guys come from?"

"Well, I guess that's what you have to expect from that sort of website. They're only on there for the sex," I reminded her.

"I don't have a problem with them wanting sex. That's what I want too. But they guarantee the earth in their profiles, claiming to know how to treat a lady. How your pleasure is their first priority and promise you the time of your life. Then they don't even switch off the television or stop chatting to others on the web. As for foreplay, they don't even know the word. It's all right for you, you lucky bitch, you've got Roger."

Well, yes, I had Roger but we still had to wait a few more weeks so Laura might still get there before me.

"So are you taking your profile off the website?" I asked

"No. I'm hoping if I kiss enough frogs one might turn out OK. But that guy last night was a total toad. Anyway, what have the rest of you been up to?"

"I finally agreed a date for me to transition at work," announced Suzanne. "They are still unhappy about me using the ladies until I have surgery and want me to use the disabled loo instead."

"That's outrageous," exclaimed Hilary who has a reputation for pushing as hard as she could when it came to trans rights.

"As far as I am aware, there is no law about which loos to use only around public decency," I said.

"In fact the disabled loo is more convenient for me so I don't actually mind despite it being a matter of principle. If it means I get a smoother ride in other areas then it's a compromise I don't mind making."

"Even so, Suzanne, it's so wrong for them to ban you from the ladies," Hilary insisted.

Marilyn tutted as two of the transvestite members of the group approached the bar.

"Just look at those two, they're part of the reason for Suzanne's company's stance," she remarked. "They look ridiculous. Miniskirts up to their crotches, far too much padding in their bras, five inch heels on thigh high boots and their wigs! Where did they get those wigs? A joke shop? Why do all the trannies think they should be blonde? As for their make-up they must have applied it with a trowel. Yet their five o'clock shadow still shows through. They piss me off; they play at being women and give transsexuals a bad name."

"Oh come on Marilyn. They are entitled to dress as they like. Just because they go over the top is no reason to despise them," Karen pointed out.

"Karen, if you'd been through all I have, to get where I am, you'd see I'm right. In fact, I'd expect you to recognise the problems trannies like them cause us. It's the impression they give that leads to attacks like the one on you. That and the general increase in anti-social behaviour because of uncontrolled immigration. Foreigners don't understand British values," Marilyn continued.

"That's absurd," Karen responded. "The group that attacked us were locals, heck, one of them worked for Roger and Vicky."

"Yes, but why did they start taking the piss? Because they thought Yvonne looked ridiculous. She doesn't look in the least convincing. Then anyone with her gets tarred with the same brush. People round here see trannies like those two leave the premises and lump the rest of us in with them. I transitioned in 1973. We had to fight for recognition by the NHS. If we didn't wear skirts for our appointments, they didn't take us seriously. There were no laws protecting us. We could get fired, thrown out of our accommodation or refused admission to any establishment that didn't want to serve us — in fact we can still get thrown out of a lot of places just for being trans. We had to work hard to pass as female including speech therapy, electrolysis and in those days it was all needle electrolysis and painful. There were no sources of advice or information like the internet so we had to do it the hard way, watching how women behaved and copying them."

"So, are you saying before anyone is allowed to go out in public, they should have to learn to pass as women?"

"Not quite — but before they mix with the general public they should at least make an effort to look female not parodies of women. If they want to come to a club like this and dress while in here, fine. It doesn't matter as much but if they are going out in the street then they should think about how it impacts on real transsexuals. I think we need a separate group for transsexuals or have separate evenings for us. In fact, it needs to be at a different venue as I think being associated with gays also causes us problems. I mean we are totally different to gays. We're not always looking for sex or hopping from one bed to another."

"Chance would be a fine thing," remarked Laura.

Marilyn gave Laura a withering look.

"Yes, well, Laura, we're not all sex mad."

"And some of us aren't past it!" retorted Laura as she stood up and walked over to the bar.

"Tart," whispered Marilyn under her breath. "But what can you expect from a half-breed?"

"What did you say?" I asked sharply.

"Laura is mixed race, didn't you know?"

"And what difference does that make?" I demanded.

"Oh come on. You can't expect her to behave like a real Englishwoman if she's a mongrel, can you? I've got nothing against her background but it's a fact of life she isn't like you or me. And that explains her promiscuity. I mean you and I wouldn't behave like she does, would we?"

I couldn't believe what I was hearing.

"Look," Marilyn continued. "Foreigners are different to us. Stands to reason. The English have been a civilised race for centuries while most of the immigrants come from peoples that were still running around in loin cloths and enslaving and eating each other until we made them part of the empire. Unfortunately, too many of them think England owes them the right to come over here and they are entitled to housing and benefits. And it's often those from African and Asian countries that are most transphobic. We need to control immigration a lot more and only admit those we need or who respect our way of life and get rid of all illegal immigrants. We should tattoo anyone caught trying to enter illegally and permanently ban them from applying for legal entry. Those that do come in should have to prove they can support themselves and not be a drain on the country."

"What, even refugees?"

"How can anyone claim to be a refugee arriving in England? They have to have crossed several other European countries where they could have claimed asylum. But those countries want to push them on their way out over their borders to their neighbours. So much for EU cooperation. The sooner we are out of that cesspool the better."

Marilyn's extreme right wing views were hardly a secret within the group and she had a few cronies that shared them.

"Marilyn, the group constitution respects everyone's rights to hold different political views. But, as chair, can I remind you it also requires we all treat each other with respect? I have to say some of your comments this evening have come very close to crossing the line," I said.

"I beg your pardon? Just because I resent those trannies making my life more difficult or calling Laura a tart, you're saying I'm breaking the club rules? Well, fuck you. You can take the group and stuff it where the sun doesn't shine."

With that, she stormed out of the club.

"What do you make of that, Vicky?" asked Karen.

"You'd think being the target of discrimination would make you more sensitive to others' differences but she is just not a pleasant person. She moans about others giving trans a bad name but she probably causes even more problems. Just shows being trans doesn't make you a nice person," I replied.

# Chapter 20. Paris
## 17th – 20th December 2004

Roger allowed me to gradually return to work; two short days from 10 am to 3 pm to start with; then by an extra short day each week 'til I was back to a full week. Then extending the hours each day to full time over another three weeks. I was back to full time early in December.

A couple of weeks before Christmas, we caught a flight from Southampton to Paris for the weekend. Our hotel was near Porte de St Cloud, convenient for the Metro for sightseeing. Tonight, we were having a romantic dinner then an early night. Tomorrow would be three months since surgery. We didn't think it would be a problem to make love one day early. I couldn't wait.

After a fabulous meal, which I think both of us rushed, and an excellent bottle of champagne, we took a taxi back to the hotel. In the room, Roger picked up the telephone and called room service.

"Bonsoir, ici Roger Dalton chambre deux cents vingt-deux, nous voulons une bouteille de champagne s'il vous plaît. Oui, le Veuve Clicquot. Oui, toute de suite s'il vous plais. Merci bien."

"It will be straight up."

"I'll get changed while we wait." I said.

I took the sexy white nightdress and negligée I'd bought specially for tonight into the bathroom, brushing my teeth while in there. I wasn't going to go back into the bedroom until room service had delivered the champagne so I stayed where I was, the frustration building.

Eventually, there was a knock on the door and I heard Roger thanking the waiter.

As I walked into the room, Roger had opened the bottle and was pouring a glass each, he then turned to me.

"Darling, you look absolutely gorgeous. Here," he said, handing me a glass, "to us."

"To us, darling," I replied

"Sod the champagne," he said. "Come here"

He then took me in his arms and I undid his shirt buttons and trousers while kissing. He lifted me up and laid me on the bed. I opened my legs for him to get between. He lubricated the entrance to my vagina then positioned his penis and gently inserted it. As I'd been warned, it hurt a bit and I winced but despite that, it felt so fabulous. I wrapped my legs round his and held him tight. It felt so right to be facing him and being able to kiss while making love.

I lost my virginity for the second time.

"Are you OK darling?"

"Oh yes, yes, *yes!*" I assured him.

He then picked up the pace. After a few minutes I felt a tension building in my shoulders. It spread to my arms and down to my groin and I started to spasm as the orgasm hit. I then felt Roger coming. Spent, we just lay there.

"That was incredible," I managed to say as I eventually caught my breath. "I've never felt anything like that before."

Roger couldn't say anything. His mouth was around my right breast — his tongue flicking my nipple, my hands holding him there.

As I lay back, my thoughts returned, once more, to last May and all that had happened since then. I couldn't believe how incredibly lucky I had been.

After a late breakfast on the Saturday, we bought Paris Visite passes for public transport at the Metro station and went sightseeing. It was a clear crisp day with a bright azure sky that wouldn't have been out of place on the Mediterranean coast. I'd never been to Paris before. Well, apart from sailing visits to channel ports, I'd never been outside England before so it was all very exciting. We took the Metro to the Trocadero and walked through the gardens and across the bridge to the Eifel Tower. The view of the Tower from the Place de Trocadero, with nothing to impede the panorama, was impressive. Standing underneath the structure it was fantastic.

Inevitably, we decided to go to the top. We looked at the snaking queues for the lift, then at each other.

"Are you game?" Roger asked.

"Of course," I replied and we headed for the much shorter line for tickets via the 704 stairs to the second stage. I was thankful my trips to the swimming pool had rebuilt my stamina for the climb.

Winding up through the tower's structure was an experience but the wind whipped through the girders making us glad we'd wrapped up warm. We eventually reached the second level where we took the lift to the top. The view was spectacular with virtually all of Paris visible.

Once we'd had our fill of the view from the top, we joined the queue to return to the ground. Back on terra firma, we took a bus to the Notre Dame before an early dinner then back to the hotel for an early night and ......

As it was pouring with rain on Sunday morning, we decided against our original plans to explore the Bois de Boulogne or take the open bus ride around Paris. We opted instead for the Bateau Mouche river boat. By the time the cruise had finished, the rain had eased so we visited the Christmas market on the Champs Elysees. We picked up gifts that caught our eyes for the family from the colourful stalls. Then it was back to the hotel to change before going out to dinner and cabaret in Pigalle.

It was a magical weekend and I had several occasions to mentally thank Mr Fry for his work and not only mentally. We sent him and Dr Wright postcards telling them what a fabulously satisfying time we were having. I was certain they'd read between the lines.

Sadly, Monday morning came round and it was time to return home. We vowed we'd be back before too long. Perhaps in the spring.

## Chapter 21. Christmas 2004
### 24th – 26th December 2004

We took the staff out for a Christmas dinner on the Wednesday evening before Christmas then closed the office until Monday 3rd January. In theory the Monday was a bank holiday but we gave everyone the choice of having the Thursday and Friday off before Christmas (and the whole of Christmas week) in exchange for working on the Monday. As this gave them eleven days off, some took the opportunity to go skiing.

Roger and I drove over to my parent's on Christmas Eve in my Toyota. It was just as well we were in my car as it was packed with presents for everyone as well as some bottles of wine and our suitcase. It would have been impossible to fit all of that in the MGB.

Mum and Dad had decorated the house as they had when we were children; a holly wreath on the front door; the hall, living and dining rooms had streamers from the corners of the ceiling into the central light fitting; symmetrically placed pendants hanging between the streamers; tinsel around each of the paintings on the walls; Christmas cards on ribbons suspended either side of the roaring log fire. There was a real tree in its usual corner decorated with many of the ornaments I remembered: little Santa Clauses, gold and silver bells, purple, red and green balls, candles in tiny holders that would have been lit at one time but were now replaced with lights that flashed on and off. Tiny Christmas crackers and chocolates hung from the needle covered boughs. Silver, purple, red and green tinsel wrapped around the branches and an angel looking down from the top of the tree.

Remembering my childhood created mixed feelings. It was lovely remembering the happy times we'd share; but it was a boyhood, not the memories of a young girl.

The presents I'd received had been typical boys' toys: trainsets, Airfix models to make; or camping equipment to use with the scouts. To be honest, I'd been happy with most of the items. I hadn't craved dolls like some trans friends. The only gift I had really resented, though, was a football from my Uncle Henry. I never enjoyed playing football — even kick-arounds. I didn't mind cricket and quite enjoyed hockey. Perhaps my dislike of football was because boys were expected to like the game and something in my mind was already saying I was different.

This year, as usual, small gifts were piled around the base of the tree — ready to be shared out after tea on Christmas day.

The burning pine logs on the fire gave out a scent I loved. It spoke of stability, of everything being right in the world — at least this corner of it. One aroma that would be missing this year was cigar or pipe smoke. Dad had traditionally had a cigar on Christmas day instead of his usual pipe but had given up smoking after a health scare last year. Pete and I had joined him in smoking cigars instead of cigarettes after Christmas dinner but Pete had stopped smoking as part of his keep fit drive to meet the demanding standards the TA selection process had imposed.

I'd also stopped smoking following surgery. To be honest, it had never been my intention to give up completely. I had stopped thirty six hours before surgery to minimise the risk of a reaction to the anaesthetic and potential damage to the surgeon's work if I started coughing violently. I'd taken a fresh pack of cigarettes into hospital with me and there would have been nothing to stop me starting up again but I hadn't felt the need for another cigarette. I was much more relaxed now I had the body I'd always wanted. Roger had followed suit so none of the immediate family now smoked.

Mum and I spent a couple of hours preparing all the vegetables for Christmas dinner. There would be ten of us with Sandra and her family coming over after church and Pete bringing his girlfriend, Kerry.

"I hope the turkey will be big enough for everyone," she said nervously.

"It's fourteen pounds so it should be sufficient. We've got the joint of pork as well not to mention the pigs in blankets," I reminded her. It felt totally natural to be discussing 'women's work' with Mum even if it was stereotyping.

By the time we'd finished preparing the vegetables, Mum and I were ready for a quick and easy dinner. We'd peeled extra potatoes which I put on to boil while I poached some smoked haddock in milk with some chives. While that simmered, I cut up some tomatoes. I put haddock into the bottom of a casserole dish, covered it with the sliced tomatoes then a cheese sauce made with the milk used to poach the haddock. I spread the mashed potatoes on top and grated mature cheddar cheese onto the potato. Twenty minutes in the oven and it was ready to serve. Judging by the way the dish was cleared, it may have been simple but very successful.

We then settled down to watch television. Given the options we agreed on BBC 2 with University Challenge Special followed by the film Chocolat rather than Eastenders and Outtakes on BBC1 or Mr Bean and Celebrity Who Wants to be a Millionaire on ITV. A large Tia Maria on the rocks and cuddling Roger made it a perfect evening for me.

University Challenge became competitive between us all. Thankfully, being a celebrity edition, the questions weren't as challenging as the usual student versions.

Christmas morning, I put the turkey in the oven while Mum made cups of tea or coffee for everyone. We then gathered in the lounge to exchange presents. Roger and I had bought Dad a set of wood turning tools as he'd set up a hobby workshop in the garden. We gave Mum a bottle of Yves St Laurent Y perfume which was her favourite. I gave Roger a sat nav for the car. Mum and Dad gave me drop earrings with sapphires and Roger a sailing kit bag to replace one Dad had noticed was well past its best. When I opened Roger's present it was clear there had been collusion as it was a matching sapphire necklace and bracelet.

Gifts exchanged, Dad prepared a full breakfast for everyone while we got dressed.

Sandra's family's arrival was announced by four year old Katie charging in, climbing onto my lap, giving me a kiss.

"Merry Christmas Aunty Vicky Santa came and left me a trampoline but we couldn't get it in the car so we've had to leave it at home and this Annabell doll look Aunty Vicky her eyes close when she goes to sleep."

It came out as a single sentence without a pause to breathe.

"Well, darling, I think he may have left some things here for you as well. Let's see shall we?"

Katie's eyes popped out on stalks as Roger carried a large parcel over for her to unwrap. Once the paper had been strewn over the lounge floor it revealed a pram for her new doll.

"Oh thank you Aunty Vicky and Uncle Roger." She rewarded each of us with a kiss.

By the time we'd all exchanged gifts and tidied up the resultant mess, we needed to put the joint of pork into the second oven. Preparing dinner for ten would need careful management of the various ingredients if they were all to be ready at two o'clock as planned.

Pete and Kerry arrived in her car about twelve thirty. This was the first time any of us had met Kerry as their relationship had developed since the summer. She wore a ruby dress with boat neckline and pleated skirt. Pete's Zapa moustache seemed even bushier than it had been in May. His reticence over my changes had clearly been overcome when he gave me a hug and kiss the same as Sandra. Kerry seemed puzzled when we went into the lounge and Dad offered everyone a drink.

"Something wrong, Kerry?" I asked.

"Well, Pete said one of his sisters used to be his brother, David wasn't it? Is there another one of you?"

"No, only Pete, Sandra and me. I used to be David."

Kerry pushed my arm and said: "Oh please don't mess around, I don't want to make an awful mistake and upset people."

"I'm not messing around. I was David but now I'm Vicky."

She stood there open mouthed.

"Really? But you look ...." Her remark tailed off. "I mean, you look like any other woman." She finished.

"What did you expect? A Drag Queen?"

"Putting your foot in it are you babe?" asked Pete.

"Looks like it. I'm so sorry," she said. "I didn't mean to be rude."

"It's fine," I assured her.

"How did you and Pete meet?" asked Sandra. I excused myself to put the potatoes on to par boil ready to roast.

Our planning worked out perfectly. All the food brought to the table at two o'clock — without having been sitting around going cold.

We pulled the crackers; read out the daft jokes; placed silly hats on heads and recovered the little toys from wherever they'd flown when the crackers had been pulled. Dad carved the turkey, as was his traditional right, Pete did duty on the roast pork. We stocked our plates from the serving dishes and charged our glasses; passed around the cranberry jelly and apple sauce; drew in deep breaths then took up our knives and forks to attack the feast that faced us, for which we ought to be very grateful.

I looked around the table. Mum on the end to my left, Pete opposite me with Katie next to him then Ian and Kerry. Dad at the head of the table, then Roger, Sandra, little Oliver in his high chair between Sandra and me. I hadn't dare dream such a tableau could exist. The thought that I'd nearly thrown everything away nineteen months ago when I'd sat in the sand dunes and taken all those pills brought a lump to my throat. Now here I was, the entire family supportive of my transition — even Pete who'd struggled with it at first. My body now pretty much matched how I felt, at least externally. Roger and I were married as far as we were concerned; in twelve months we'd be able to make that a legally recognised union once I'd received my gender recognition.

Pete was looking across the table at me, possibly noticing I'd been pensive. He raised his glass and I picked mine up to share a toast. Katie raised her glass of orange juice and clinked her glass against ours. At the other end of the table, Roger raised his glass and I blew him a kiss.

At three, we retired to the lounge to watch the Queen's Christmas message. An opportunity for our main course to settle before tackling the Christmas pudding with a choice of brandy butter, crème fraiche, clotted cream or ice cream.

The tradition in our house was to exchange small 'tree gifts' after tea — but as it was nearly four by the time we'd finished dinner, it was unlikely anyone would want anything further to eat until well past Katie and Oliver's bed times. So, for once, we distributed the presents once we'd cleared the table and everything had been put into the dishwasher or hand washed and put away.

The tree gifts tended to be joke or small items. Kerry was somewhat bemused by our tradition — Roger had become familiar with it last year.

We then got together in teams of two for a game of Trivial Pursuit. Pete and I took on Ian and Mum, Sandra and Dad and Kerry and Roger. Katie joined Pete and me to play. At the end of the game, our team won. Once Sandra and her family had left to get Katie and Oliver to bed, the others claimed they'd let us win because Katie was in our team. Pete and I were not convinced.

It had been the best Christmas I could ever remember.

On Boxing Day, Mum's brother, Henry, sister Margaret and their families arrived for the afternoon. I'd sent out a 'round robin' letter the previous year with Christmas cards so they knew what I'd been planning but this was the first time I'd seen them since my transition.

I wasn't surprised when Uncle Nigel didn't know how to react to me though Aunty Margaret and cousin Claire both gave me a hug.

But it was Uncle Henry's response that disappointed me. He seemed to refuse to even acknowledge me. An approach his wife, Veronica, and their son Kevin followed. They talked to everyone except Roger or me. They also made quite an issue over having been to midnight mass on Christmas Eve and again on Christmas Day and commenting on how important they thought it was to keep to traditional family values and teachings. It was obvious they were having a go at me. I certainly wasn't going to let their bigoted views upset me. They were dinosaurs and their time had passed.

Uncle Nigel accepted a cup of tea from me and, as I took a chair next to his, he asked "How are you now? All sorted out down there?" his head nodding towards my crotch.

"Nigel!" his wife admonished. "Sorry Vicky."

I laughed it off, it was hardly the worst thing someone had ever asked.

"Yes Uncle Nigel, it's all fine now, thank you."

# Chapter 22.  A New Challenge
## 15<sup>th</sup> January 2005

Roger and I were at the Blue Peach one Saturday when Denise Clarke, a lesbian, asked if she could have a private word with me. We found a quiet booth on the ground floor and she asked me what I'd like to drink. I was intrigued why she wanted to chat but had to wait until she'd been to the bar. She put a glass of Chardonnay on the table in front of me and sat down.

"Are you aware I'm a Prison Officer?" she asked.

I hadn't been but we didn't pry into each other's private lives at the Blue Peach.

"We've had a new prisoner arrive who says she is transsexual and has been undergoing treatment. She's only seventeen and has had a rough life which led to her being where she is. She is asking if it's possible to find someone who would befriend and visit her; someone who knows what it's like to be trans and who is about her own age. I wondered if you knew of anyone who might be suitable and willing to help?"

"Most of the group are considerably older. The only ones near her age are Karen and myself. What would it involve?"

"Be someone she can talk to about how she is feeling, someone who knows what it's like to be trans. We have counsellors but frankly, they'd struggle to understand her circumstances."

"I see. It's a hell of a responsibility. Would this be as a representative of the prison service or totally independent?"

"It would be as an outsider. No responsibility to the prison at all. Well, I say none but if she was to tell you she planned to escape or self-harm you'd need to let us know about that."

"Can I think about it and talk it through with Roger? What's she in prison for — or can't I ask that? Would I be putting myself at risk?

"Of course you should talk to Roger about it. I don't think it would impact on your reputation, you'd effectively be in the same position as a prison visitor. They're usually seen as do-gooders, though I appreciate you being trans may be seen differently. She's doing three and a half years for drug offences. She was in the local press a couple of months ago so I'm not disclosing confidential information. In any case, she has given me permission to pass on relevant details to anyone I think might help. I'll give you her name if you decide to see her."

"Where is she being held?" Obviously I needed to know what would be involved in visiting.

Denise hesitated before replying, "I'm not sure if I can tell you where she is without breaking prison service rules even though I haven't yet mentioned her name, but I work at Elmwood Young Offenders Institution."

A nod is as good as a wink to a blind man on a galloping horse as my Dad used to say. Elmwood was only ten miles or so from Bournemouth so distance wasn't a problem.

"Isn't that a male prison?"

"Yes. Legally she is male and hasn't had surgery so has to be held in a male establishment. If she has surgery or gets one of these new Gender Recognition Certificates they might move her to a female prison. We've had some post-op prisoners move to female prisons in the past."

"Jesus. It's a hell of a thing you're asking."

"I realise that Vicky — but I didn't know who else to approach. I feel sorry for the kid. She's had a hell of a life with abuse by her father and step-father. Shit, forget I said that. I shouldn't have mentioned it."

112

"I'll talk to Roger and see what he says — but I'm not making any promises."

As I re-joined Roger, he raised his eyebrows and tilted his head to one side in query. Nestling into his arms and moulding my body to his on the dance floor, I told him I'd explain in the morning.

"So what did Denise want last night?" asked Roger as we loaded the dishwasher with the breakfast dishes. I poured us cups of coffee and suggested we go into the lounge.

"Denise wants me to befriend a trans drug dealer serving three and a half years in Elmwood Prison."

Said like that, it sounded judgemental and with an obvious negative response.

"Denise says the prisoner had a rough time as a kid. She feels sorry for her and wants to help if she can."

"What are you going to say? Sounds like you don't really want to do it."

"I'm not keen, you know what I think about drugs and perhaps she deserves to be locked up."

"But?"

Roger realised despite my reluctance, I was still considering the idea.

"But, I've been so lucky and this is a chance for me to pay something back. Maybe if she sees a positive role model she can turn her life around. Perhaps, too, if no one is prepared to help her, especially from the trans community, she'll feel even more excluded. Maybe I feel guilty about my original reaction. Maybe Karma will bite me if I don't do what I can to help others."

"I don't think you owe anyone anything, but if you want to help then you know I'll support you all the way." I'd have expected nothing less from Roger.

"I've got reservations. Will I be putting myself at risk and could it have a negative reaction for the business?"

"I can't see how it can affect us, so don't worry about that. I assume you'd only meet the individual in the prison visiting areas with prison officers around. Perhaps that's something to talk to Denise about."

# Chapter 23. Mia

When I agreed to at least visit Mia and discuss befriending her, she suggested I read the Pre-Sentence Report prepared by the Probation Service and statements she'd given the police. She arranged for her solicitor to provide me with copies of the documents. (I'm conscious of referring to her as Mia and 'she' — but that's how I see her, although the PSR referred to her using her male name and pronouns.) I collected the papers in person. It gave me a chance to meet her solicitor — in fact it was his suggestion.

Mr Galbraith of Cohen, Parker and Donaldson was happy to see me. Like Denise, he had a soft spot for Mia and was prepared to go above and beyond the demands of his job to help her. We had an off the record chat (with Mia's prior blessing) which provided background that wouldn't be in the documents, then he handed over a dossier.

That evening, after pouring us a glass of wine each, I sat down at the dining room table to look at the documents while Roger watched a film on television in the lounge.

If I'd thought I'd had problems being trans, Mia's story certainly made me think again. I couldn't believe any individual could have survived the life she'd led.

Her mother, Louise, and father, Len, had divorced before Mia was five years old. The papers didn't specify the reason for the divorce but I got the impression both had had affairs. Mia's mother had then had other relationships before marrying Barry, who was significantly younger than her, when Mia/ Martin had been eight. That marriage was also turbulent according to the PSR.

Louise had then died in June 2002. Mia had been 14 and Barry, her step-father, continued to care for her.

I thought back to my childhood. How would I have coped under those circumstances? It brought a lump to my throat and I took another large drink of wine.

Mia had sorted out her mother's effects but had kept some of her clothes and other items. According to the PSR, Mia had 'cross-dressed' since she was about eight using items she found in the laundry basket in the bathroom (I wondered if all trans people did that). By the time she was eleven or twelve, her mother often left her alone in the house during the day when she was off school which gave her further opportunities to dress. That was something else I related to!

114

The family home at the time was an end of terrace council house on the edge of a village north of Christchurch. The property wasn't overlooked and gave Mia the privacy she needed. She was slightly above average in most classes at school, quiet and reserved. She had few friends but with no obvious signs of bullying.

The 'few friends' also resonated. I was beginning to see Mia and I had a great deal in common.

Her step-father, Barry, was a delivery driver. His employers said he was reliable and they'd had no cause to doubt his honesty.

According to the report of Barry's trial, he had come home early one afternoon and found Mia cross-dressed. He had allowed Mia to dress when at home and they lived as father and daughter for some months. Then Barry had seduced Mia and they started an affair. As Mia had been under 16 at the time it started, the police charged him with statutory rape. I was shocked an adult would do that to a child. Perhaps I was being naive.

My wineglass was empty by now. I put my head round the lounge door as an explosion destroyed HMS Hood on the television. Roger was watching 'Sink the Bismark'.

"Do you want a refill?" I asked.

"Yes please, how's it going?"

"Pretty upsetting to be honest."

"Well, take care of your own wellbeing while you're helping others, please darling. I don't want you to get depressed."

I poured out the wine then returned to the papers. I picked up the statement Mia had given the police when they arrested her in June:

*'After the police arrested my step-father, Barry, Social Services contacted my birth father, Len. He agreed to have me live with him and his family. He made it clear the cross-dressing had to stop. When we were alone, he threatened he'd beat it out of me if necessary.*

*'I was heartbroken. Barry and I hadn't been hurting anyone. If we'd waited a few more months, there wouldn't have been any case to answer.'*

It seemed the sex had been consensual rather than forced, even though Mia had been under age. From my reading of the case, Mia had been quite mature for her years. I wondered about the consequences of strict divisions between something being illegal and legal based on age. If it was meant to ensure someone would be mature enough to make an informed decision then it would inevitably err on the side of caution.

Perhaps if the question had been based on the individual's maturity, Mia might have been judged more than able to consent. But that wasn't how the law worked and, as a consequence, two lives had been badly compromised. I focussed again on the statement.

*'Barry had been looking into the Tavistock gender clinic that specialised in young trans people. I had an appointment in November. Now that was out of the question with Len.'*

I could imagine this would have been devastating for Mia. To have been so close to starting treatment, then have that hope taken away from her again. I thought many young trans people, perhaps half of them, would have taken their own lives in such circumstances or tried to do so.

*'Len's wife Rosemary and two children Charlene and Bradley didn't know what to make of me. Neither of them wanted to share a bedroom. This posed a problem as the family home was a three bedroom semi in a Little Avonford, a few miles north of Christchurch. There was no question of me sharing with Charlene; and Bradley refused to share with a shirt-lifter, as he described me. The only option was to convert the dining room, which was rarely used, into a bedroom for me.*

*'Charlene eventually accepted me when we found we had the same tastes in music and she realised I could help her with her make-up and hair and discuss fashions together like any two girls. She realised I was female mentally and offered to let me use some of her things when we were alone in the house providing we kept it totally secret from her father — I never regarded him as my father.*

*'Eventually we were caught out when Len returned unexpectedly one afternoon, he went ballistic at both Charlene and me.*

*'He forced me to have a tattoo to make it more difficult to go out in public as a girl; then forced me to sign up for the army, which he said would make a real man of me. He threatened to make Charlene suffer more if I didn't sign the forms. Charlene was annoyed with me for agreeing to this and pointed out whilst her punishment might be for a few days, going in the army would affect me for much longer.'*

How could anyone force someone to join the services? How did they imagine that would stop them being trans?

*'I decided to leave home so took a coach the next morning to London. Charlene gave me a bag containing some of her clothes I liked wearing. I found a bedsit and a job in London. I visited a trans club where I made money by having sex with some of the men who visited with that in mind. Vince then approached*

*me. He told me he ran a high class escort service and invited me to join his team. I accepted the offer and moved into the house his girls shared. If clients wanted cocaine, E, crack, meth or other drugs, we would deliver it. Vince added it to their bills. I did not actually sell the drugs to the clients, I only delivered them.*

'I was then arrested and charged with supplying class A drugs.'

Shit! That poor girl. And I'd considered rejecting her request for a befriender. I felt ashamed of myself. For the first time since my operation, I felt the need for a cigarette. Fortunately there were none in the house so the craving passed.

"Coffee darling?" asked Roger, whose film had finished. "Are you OK? You look distressed." I walked into the kitchen with him. He filled the filter machine and prepared the mugs for the coffee.

"I'll be fine but this case is harrowing. I can't believe what people have done to her."

"Can you tell me anything about it?"

"I shouldn't. But I'm determined to meet her and see if I can help."

Back in the dining room, I picked up the Pre-Sentence Report written at the end of the trial.

It summarised Mia's background and the sources of information used to produce the report. Compared with Mia's own statement, it was succinct bordering on terse.

It stated Mia's involvement in the supply of Class A drugs was a significant role. She understood of the scale of the operation. She was motivated by financial or other advantage. (Not to supply would cost her bookings). The offence was categorised as Level 3 as she was supplying to the end user. The starting point for a significant role at that level was 4 years 6 months' custody. In mitigation, the report stated Mia had no previous convictions and mentioned her personal circumstances — having had to leave her home due to her father's bullying.

This was all technical stuff based on new rules being introduced nationally later in the year but trialled in a couple of probation areas in 2004.

The writer said Mia had a high risk of reoffending as she had shown no remorse for the offence and was likely to return to her escort lifestyle on release, which would place her in the same position. She was not assessed as a high risk of serious harm. These judgements were justified in the report by quoting something called an OASys assessment.

Throughout the PSR, the writer referred to Mia as Martin and used male pronouns. He also rejected the suggestion Mia was transsexual or she had a medical condition that required long term treatment. He referred to her instead as a she-male or transvestite.

I read: *'Martin Evans has a history of cross-dressing since an early age. When he first moved to London he frequented a club catering for transvestites and men seeking sex with transvestites and she-males/lady boys.'*

The report continued: *'There is no evidence Martin Evans is transsexual. He was not prescribed hormone treatment by any NHS clinic and bought them off the internet. Evans has developed breasts and created an illusion of a feminine body. He appears to be a she-male using the combination of breasts and male genitalia to make a living having sex for money.'*

*'In my view he is a gay transvestite. If awarded a custodial sentence (as recommended) there is no reason to consider a female establishment. He is legally male and even if he had been transsexual he has not yet undergone sex change surgery.'*

My blood boiled when I saw this. If I'd been able to get hold of the officer, I might have ended up sharing a cell with Mia.

When I rang Mia's solicitor to let him know I would see her, he agreed with my view there was significant transphobia influencing the report.

The report recommended a custodial sentence with the term reduced to take account of her guilty plea and the other mitigating circumstances.

The court settled on a sentence of three years six months.

Because she had not had surgery, Mia would be held in a male prison despite living as female for more than two years and, according to Denise, her appearance and behaviour was totally female. She would clearly be at risk in a male establishment despite any attempts by the authorities to keep her safe. The reality was some officers wouldn't be too concerned if she 'got what was coming to her' especially as she'd been on the game.

I put the papers back in their folder, locked them in my briefcase and went into the lounge.

I poured myself a vodka and looked at Roger holding up the bottle as a question.

"Yes please," he said, "bad as that was it?"

"Dreadful. It's disgraceful how she's been treated. Appalling. She's no angel but that's no wonder after what she's been through."

I tossed back the vodka and reached for the bottle for a refill.

Roger knitted his eyebrows and looked at me.

"It must have been bad to affect you like this."

I sat by him and he held me close. Then the tears flowed. My emotions were in turmoil. I felt so sad about Mia's position; angry about the way the authorities had dealt with her, the way she was placed with her birth father and the Probation Officer's dismissive attitude; guilty at my initial reaction to hearing about her. Most of all I felt determined I would, at least, visit her to see if I could be of any help and at least meet her.

If we established a rapport, then we could continue — if I felt I was being manipulated, then I would simply not visit her again.

Roger held me close but even that created ambivalent feelings. Of course I felt loved and lucky to have my life with Roger — but it also contrasted with Mia's situation. Did I deserve all I had? Absolutely not. Did Mia deserve to be where she was? Not at all from what I'd seen.

# Chapter 24.  The Visit
## 27th January 2005

Mia sent me a visiting order for the last Thursday afternoon in January. As I drove up to the prison, I felt quite anxious. I had no idea what I might face or what reactions I might attract.

Parking next to the high windowless concrete walls topped with razor wire, I locked my mobile in the glove compartment, took a deep breath and opened the car door. The path to the entrance led past the vehicle entrance with its double doors, large enough to admit the prison vans. An HM Prisons flag fluttered intermittently from a flagpole. Various notices were secured to the external walls including a warning of the dire consequences of bringing prohibited items into the establishment.

I reached the visitor entrance and, after taking another deep breath, entered the forbidding building.

Inside the foyer were lockers where visitors could leave banned items and a counter behind which stood a prison officer protected by a glass screen from the counter to the ceiling. I said I was there to see Mia Evans and showed her my visiting order.

"You mean Martin Evans," she insisted. She looked me up and down as though I was something she'd scrape off her shoes.

I felt quite vulnerable myself and wasn't in any position to argue so accepted that, within the prison, the service regarded Mia as male and her name was Martin.

The officer directed me to the visitor centre.

The main room was about thirty feet square with tables and chairs securely bolted to the floor; presumably to prevent them being used as weapons. A vending machine was located by one wall and several prison officers stood watching over the scene.

I waited for Mia to join me. She sat down at the table opposite me. She looked as nervous as I felt. I was sure she was suspicious of me.

"Hi Mia, I'm Vicky. Pity we're not meeting under different circumstances."

I passed her some cigarettes and some chocolate and drinks I'd bought from the vending machine.

"Too true. Thanks for coming anyway — and for these," she said pointing to the supplies. "I'm not sure what you can do, if anything, but it's wicked to talk to someone who knows where I'm coming from. The rest in here haven't got a bloody clue, even Miss Clarke, who isn't too bad for a screw."

"I don't know what I can do either – except listen and maybe give you a chance to get things off your chest."

"Yeah, well even that might help. What do you know about my case?"

"I've seen the documents your solicitor sent me. Have to say it seemed the Probation Officer who wrote the Pre-Sentence Report had big problems with trans folks."

"Sure did. I think he was gay and thought transwomen have surgery because we want to have sex with men but won't accept we are queer. Doesn't explain transwomen who are lesbians, but he didn't see that."

"So, how are you being treated in here? Are you having any problems?"

"Could be worse. I get catcalls all the time and told to show other inmates my tits and crude suggestions about how they'd like to shag me. The screws take action most of the time if they see the crap going on but they don't see everything. They do, at least, allocate me private time to shower rather than having to share with the rest of them."

I had no idea how I'd react to such treatment. I'd had a few whistles, but was sure similar instances within a closed environment would be so much more threatening. There would always be the chance of being caught on your own and the threats put into action before anyone could stop it. I changed the subject.

"So, what's happening about your hormone treatment, are you still getting that?"

"Yes, thank God, though it was touch and go for a while. I originally got hormones off the internet. When I worked for Vince, I saw Dr Wright as a private patient. Do you know him?"

"Yes, I saw him myself."

"Oh, cool. Well he prescribed patches for me on my second appointment. The prison doctor contacted him and agreed to continue providing them; thank fuck. I don't know what I'd have done if they hadn't."

The thought of having to come off hormones after starting them made me shudder.

"Well, that's something anyway. Are you going to be able to continue seeing Nicholas Wright while you're in here?"

"I doubt it. I suspect the Governor will think it's too much bloody hassle. I can write to him to keep him up to date and might even be able to phone him. I can't see them spending the time and money to get me up to London though." Mia looked resigned to the situation.

"Hmm probably not. Well, is there anything in particular you're looking for from me?"

"God, I'm not sure. My life so far has been pretty fucked up and I want to sort it out. Not only completing transition and having surgery but having as normal a life as I can afterwards. My plan before I got arrested was to save enough for surgery and to go to Uni and get a degree. Perhaps I can then put my shitty past behind me and have a fresh start. I think it would help to have someone to talk to who has experience of transitioning and who might advise me on what's involved in surgery and other things like Uni." Mia had started to relax in her seat; perhaps she was beginning to trust me.

"Well, I didn't go to university myself but I looked into it so have an idea where to start. I'd have thought the education department here could help too. Do you know if they do A level courses you can get on?"

"Yes they do and I've already started English, French and German. I did well in my GCSEs — so I'm better placed than most in here."

"That sounds encouraging. How long are you in here for?"

121

"I got three and a half bastard years. If I keep my head down, I should be out again in twenty-one months."

"What then?"

"If things work out, I'd be out again in August next year. I'm a bit behind on the courses for sitting A levels that year but I have little else to do in here so can focus on catching up."

"You sound like you know what you want and how to get it. Do you mind me asking how is your life got so fucked up as you described it? I've seen some of the background from your statement and the PSR. But it would be useful to hear it first-hand. Tell me to f-off if you want."

Mia looked at me, her lips squeezed together, then dropped her eyes to the floor and I saw tears well up. She pulled herself together, sat upright again and wiped her eyes with the sleeve of her grey sweatshirt. Taking a deep breath she licked her lips then answered me.

"It sure wasn't fucking planned to end up the way it did. My birth father, Len, walked out on Mum and me when I was five. Mum married Barry when I was eight and things were reasonably OK. I mean there were occasional rows between Mum and Barry, usually over money and Mum having to work part time to make ends meet. Barry was a driver for a fuel supplier delivering central heating oil. I was doing OK at school. I used to dress whenever I got the opportunity when Mum was out at work during the school holidays."

I smiled at the thought of taking advantage of every opportunity to cross dress. I remembered my own experience of doing exactly the same; even if it was only for a few minutes.

"I know what you mean," I confirmed.

Mia looked at me and a faint smile flickered across her face.

"Yeah. I guess you do which is why I wanted someone who had experienced the same."

"Yeah I can see why you'd want that."

"Anyway. Mum then got cancer and died. Which was fucking devastating." Her eyes dropped to the floor again and her shoulders drooped.

"I can imagine." I began to have sympathy for Mia instead of the negative attitude I'd had over the drugs. I got the feeling her urban language was forced; perhaps as a defensive ploy in prison. Neither of us grew up in inner city areas though we'd both moved to them in our late teens. Maybe she was trying to impress me with her hardness.

"Barry continued to look after me, but I became even more withdrawn and had few friends. Well, you know what it's like when you're trying to hide who you really are. You're not comfortable doing boy stuff but can't really mix with the girls."

"Oh Yes!" I knew that situation only too well.

"Barry finished work at the depot at five thirty so it would be quarter to six before he got home. The bus dropped me off about four so I had about an hour and a half each day when I could dress. I'd change as soon as I got home. I'd put on an apron and prepare our dinner ready to cook. Then I'd start my homework. I'd change again later but kept my knickers on under my jeans and finished off the dinner ready for Barry getting home."

"Sounds like a good arrangement."

"It was, until the day Barry came home early and found me still dressed as Mia."

Her eyes looked up and to the side as she remembered that incident.

"Shit!"

"Well, I thought I was in deep trouble but he sat me down and we talked about it. He asked where I'd got the clothes from. I told him they were some of mum's old stuff I'd kept for myself. By this time I'd found out about gender dysphoria on the net. When I saw he wasn't angry, I showed him what I'd found. He was actually far more understanding than I expected him to be. He asked if I thought I was transsexual and I said I was."

"Barry sounds very supportive." I thought Mia had been lucky to have had him.

Then I remembered he was in prison for raping her.

"He was. Barry asked if I had a female name and I said it was Mia. He said if I wanted to dress as Mia rather than Martin when not at school, he had no objections. He suggested, though, we keep the arrangement private — which I was happy to agree to."

"Mmm I can see why he'd suggest that." Not everyone would have agreed with the way Barry supported Mia.

"He then pointed out it was all very well me wearing my mother's old outfits but perhaps I should have some of my own, more appropriate for a fifteen year old girl. The next Saturday, we picked out the most suitable items from my existing cache to wear. We drove over to Southampton to buy some more items and got some tops and miniskirts and other bits and pieces."

"Sounds enough though to start."

"It was. From then on, I changed as soon as I got in and stayed that way. Not having to watch the clock made it easier for me to spend time on my homework. I made up the ground I'd lost since Mum died."

"So it was working out well for you?"

She smiled again.

"It was. Then one Monday, I was preparing dinner when Barry arrived home. He came into the kitchen and said something smelled good. He slipped his arm around my waist and kissed my cheek. It didn't seem inappropriate, just something any father might do to their daughter. It felt quite affirming to me that he saw me as his daughter."

"I can appreciate why you'd feel that."

Mia took a sip from the can of coke.

"After dinner, we sat together on the sofa to watch television. He said I looked much happier as Mia. I said I was and kissed him on his cheek and thanked him for being so supportive. He put his arm around my shoulder. I leant my head on his shoulder just like lots of daughters do with their Dads."

She had a wistful look as she related this period.

"Understandable. I imagine it made you feel secure too." While I felt uncomfortable with Barry's actions, I appreciated why Mia might not have seen them as wrong.

"It did. As I brushed my teeth one evening, wearing a short nightshirt I'd found in Next, I could see Barry watching me in the mirror. He told me I looked sexy and would drive boys wild. I had fantasised about having a boyfriend and it was exciting to hear a man say I was sexy even if he was my step-Dad. I wiped my face and smiled at him and thanked him for the compliment."

"You still didn't see that as inappropriate?"

"No, I didn't think anything. I was just happy he allowed me to be who I was. In bed that night, I took out the vibrator I'd bought. I reached behind me and inserted it and switched it on. Then I slid it in and out as though I was being fucked."

Mia looked at me, perhaps searching for a reaction. I remembered doing the same — maybe most trans people did.

124

She continued: "I hadn't heard Barry on the landing and was surprised when he opened my bedroom door. He was wearing his dressing gown. He asked what the buzzing noise was. When he saw what I was doing, he came and sat on the side of my bed. He reached over and took hold of the vibrator. To my surprise, he slid it in and out. 'You like that don't you?' he said. I said I did. He then took my hand and put it on his prick and I fondled it. Barry then leant closer and kissed my lips. It wasn't a chaste kiss like we'd had before, but one that lingered. I opened my mouth and his tongue probed. I turned to face him and put my arms around his neck. He'd had to let go of the vibrator while I did so but now he lay down beside me, reached behind me and started to thrust deeper with the vibrator while we kissed. I continued to fondle his prick which had become hard. It wasn't a lot thicker than the vibrator."

She looked at me. Was she challenging me to find her story repugnant?

"Go on," I told her." It was vital not to display any judgemental reaction to what she was telling me if I was to get the full story and be able to understand her.

"He removed the vibrator, rolled me on my back and got between my legs, I felt his prick probing and I urged him on with a 'Yes, yes, fuck me please.' We screwed urgently — as though we had only minutes left to live. As soon as he'd come, Barry rolled off me and sat on the edge of the bed with his head in his hands. And said 'I'm so sorry, Mia. I got carried away. I shouldn't have done that to you.'"

She took a deep breath, looked straight at me, then continued:

"If Barry had been my birth Dad. Or if my Mum had still been alive, it would have been wrong. But he wasn't and she wasn't and it didn't seem wrong at all. I told him I wasn't sorry we did it; I knelt behind him on the bed and put my arms around him. I told him he hadn't forced me and I'd wanted to do it as much as he had. I also told him I wanted to do it again and again and again."

Mia stared into my eyes as though she was daring me to criticise her. I kept my face as unemotional as possible. How could I criticise her? I hadn't suffered what she had. And, when I faced difficulties, I'd tried to end my life.

"Are you OK telling me all of this?" I asked her, hoping my question wouldn't seem critical.

"If I'm going to ask you to help me, I think you need to know the truth. I've hidden too much in my life and want stuff out in the open at the moment — at least with you. Anyway, from that night, our relationship changed from step-dad/ stepdaughter to lovers. We knew others wouldn't understand so we had to keep it secret. But it suited us.

"Our affair might have continued for years if it hadn't been for a chance encounter in Southampton. Mrs Wilson, my history teacher had spotted Barry while he waited near the changing rooms in Dorothy Perkins while I tried on some summer dresses. I emerged from the changing rooms and came back to Barry. I told him they fitted fine, kissing him on the lips before I saw Mrs Wilson approaching. She demanded to know why I was dressed as I was and what was going on. It was pointless trying to hide the situation. The kiss I'd given Barry had obviously not been one a child would give a parent and I was dressed as a girl. She reported what she'd seen to Social Services who then investigated. When their enquiries revealed Barry and I had been having an affair while I was still under age, they called in the police."

Mia lit a cigarette and paused.

"Well that really is some story. I can't begin to understand how you'd feel after that."

"Yes, well that's only half of the story."

She took a breath. Bit her lips and crossed her arms. I was no expert on body language but assumed Mia was uncomfortable with what she was about to relate.

"After Barry was arrested, I was placed in care while a more permanent arrangement was put in place. Social Services contacted my birth father, Len, and he agreed I could live with him and his family. He made it clear the cross-dressing had to stop. When we were alone, he threatened he'd beat it out of me if necessary."

"Yes, I saw that in your statement to the police."

How did anyone think you could beat being trans out of a person? I suspect my face reflected my anger with Len.

"Oh yeah, so you know Charlene allowed me to wear some of her clothes. Len found out and forced me to have this ink." She pulled up her sleeve and showed me the tattoo he'd made her have. "And I ended up leaving their place and moving to London where I joined Vince's team."

"Yes." I shook my head at the abuse.

"Charlene and I became friendlier when we found we shared the same taste in music and liked some of the same groups including Girls Aloud, U2 and Britney. I then gave her some tips about make-up and we talked about fashions we liked and she asked whether I thought different outfits suited her. We even discussed underwear and which style would be best under an outfit she was planning to wear on a date that weekend. She then stared at me with a thoughtful look on her face and said 'You think like a girl don't you? You're not a boy in your mind are you?' I told her she was right and I was transgender."

"How did she react?" I felt my face softening.

"She asked if I planned to live permanently as a girl and have surgery. When I said I did, she asked how her dad stopping me from wearing girls' clothes made me feel and if it was a big issue for me. I told her it was massive, it was denying who I really was."

"What did she say to that?"

"She hesitated than said, 'OK, look, I can't go against Dad openly. He'd kill me, but if we are on our own you can use some of my things in the house. Would that help? We'll have to keep it a secret between us.'"

Mia unfolded her arms, a smile flickered across her face and her eyes brightened as she related this episode.

"Wow! How did that make you feel?"

"I couldn't believe what I was hearing but I thanked her and gave her a hug. She then pointed out no one was due back for at least three hours. She asked me what I'd like to borrow from her wardrobe. We sorted out a plain white halter neck top and denim mini skirt over a simple bra and briefs and blue sandals with a two inch chunky heel. Charlene helped me experiment with make-up, settling for Rose Quartz lipstick and smoky eyeshadow with black mascara and a foundation that matched my skin tone with a touch of Rose Passion blusher and nail varnish to match the lipstick."

"I bet that felt fabulous."

"It did. It felt wonderful to dress as the real me again. I spent the rest of my time squatting on Charlene's bed and reading the 15th birthday issue of Marie Claire magazine while we listened to Radio One."

The incident was so important to Mia every detail had been etched into her memory.

"And that carried on afterwards did it?"

"Yeah. You know, I just remembered. I read my five year horoscope out to Charlene. It said I was starting a winning cycle and would make a great lifestyle change. It said by 2005 I'd be riding a career crest. Shit. Well I did make a hell of a lifestyle change but the bit about this year being a career crest was wide of the mark wasn't it! What a fucking joke."

"So what happened?"

"We got away with it for five weeks. Then Len returned home earlier than expected one afternoon. Charlene intercepted him before he could come upstairs. That gave me time to change again but I missed some of the nail varnish. Len spotted it and realised what had been going on behind his back. 'I'll teach you to disobey me,' he shouted, 'and you, miss, will also pay for helping this, this pervert,' he added to Charlene."

I shook my head at the thought of this happening. Any hint of a smile on Mia's face disappeared as she related how Len had abused her.

"He then took my arm and forced me into my bedroom. He took off his belt and lashed out at me with it. The next day he took me to a friend of his who had a tattoo business and asked him to give me a British Bulldog tattoo that he thought would make it more difficult for me to go out in public as a girl. His friend was reluctant but accepted Len's assurance I was over eighteen — despite the fact he knew I wasn't. As I said in my statement to the police, the following weekend, he took me down to the Army Careers Office to complete an application form telling me the army would make a man of me. If I didn't sign up, Charlene would suffer even more for helping me. The sergeant told me the next stage would be for me to attend an assessment day in a couple of weeks."

The downcast look returned to her face.

"Surely he couldn't have made you join up?"

"He was threatening to punish Charlene more if I didn't. Charlene was angry with me for going along with Len's plan as far as I had. She asked if I wanted to go in the army and I had admitted that was the last thing I wanted to do. But what alternative had I had? I didn't want her to get into even more trouble. She pointed out any trouble she'd be in would be short lived while if I joined the army, it would be for years. The only long term solution alternative I saw was to leave home.

"I suppose you could have messed up the assessment day and got rejected by the army," I suggested, too late for it to have been any use.

"I didn't think about that! Anyway, I was over 16 by then so could do what I wanted. It meant sacrificing my plans for university but leaving home seemed the only option. The next day, while Len was at work, I packed my few possessions in a sports bag while Charlene went up to her own room. When she came downstairs again, she handed me another bag telling me I might find the contents useful. It contained my favourite items from her wardrobe. There were a couple of skirts and blouses, underwear, a handbag, make-up and pair of shoes. I caught the local bus to Ringwood where I picked up a coach to London."

"What did you do there?"

"I got off the coach at Victoria, bought a London A-Z and looked up the address of a hostel I'd found on the internet that would provide cheap accommodation for a couple of nights while I sorted out something more permanent. The following morning, I went to the Job Centre and other employment agencies to see what I could find. The most promising was temping as an Office Junior in a small advertising agency in Acton. They were impressed by my ten GCSEs. The pay wasn't great but I thought I could just about manage providing I didn't spend too much on accommodation or fares. They also wanted someone who could start as soon as possible and I was available immediately."

"That was lucky."

"It wasn't what I'd planned for my life but it was a new start. I found a bedsit about two miles from the office. It was a bit more expensive than I'd hoped but it had its own bathroom and cooking facilities. It was also on a direct bus route to work. The hostel, deposit and initial rent and food and other stuff I needed for the bedsit had taken a large chunk of the money I'd saved over the years, including from an insurance policy Mum had taken out."

I'd wondered how Mia could afford to put down the deposit on the bedsit – now I knew.

"After my first week at the agency, I found a shop in Islington I'd seen advertised in Exchange and Mart as supplying TV and theatrical items. They were very friendly and helpful. They told me about clubs and groups where I'd be welcome as Mia, including the Outsiders Club which took place every Saturday. I bought a copy of their catalogue and TVTS News a newsletter that listed lots of places to go and news about the TV and TS scene."

I knew the shop she referred to. I'd bought a few things there myself. I'd never dared go to any of the venues in TVTS News though.

She grinned as she continued: "I decided to go to the Outsiders Club that evening. I went to Oxford Street to find a suitable dress and pair of shoes. I didn't care that I was in male clothes. I found a fabulous blue knee length dress with a thigh high side split and long sleeves that would hide the tattoo Len had forced on me. I also bought new underwear to go with the dress. The shoes were navy three inch stilettos with a diamante trim. I found a handbag to match the shoes. I also bought jewellery and some sparkly make-up. The store staff didn't bat an eyelid when I asked to try on the dress and shoes and if some of the other shoppers stared, I didn't care."

I imagined her staring down any looks from other shoppers and daring them to say something.

"After shopping, I returned to my flat; prepared a meal then had a shower and did my hair. It was long enough to tie into a ponytail. Fortunately, Len had prioritised getting the tattoo and signing me on for the army over a trip to the barbers; though I'm sure that would have been next on his list. I got dressed, slipped on my new shoes, put on my coat and checked my mobile, purse and lipstick were in my handbag, picked up my keys and made my way down the corridor to the front door. Sooner or later, I was bound to meet one of my neighbours but I'd deal with that when it happened."

It reminded me of when I'd be leaving my bedsit before moving down to Bournemouth. Despite our differences, we'd shared many experiences. I could imagine us having become friends under different circumstances.

"The flat was only a few minutes' walk to Willesden Junction station and the tube to Aldgate. No one seemed to take any notice of me on the way which was a relief.

"The Outsiders club was near Aldgate station and I arrived about half past nine. I paid the reduced entry fee they charged for anyone dressed en femme, left my coat at the cloakroom and headed for the toilets to carry out a final check before going into the club itself. There were few people in the club at this stage."

My eyes were wide open at Mia's nerve.

"I bought a Bacardi and Coke then found a seat while I took in the atmosphere. It wasn't long before one of the other girls came over and sat down. She said she hadn't seen me in there before and asked if it was my first visit.

"I told her I'd just moved to London from Christchurch. She welcomed me to Outsiders and told me her name was Natasha. I gave her my name. Natasha looked late twenties, was wearing a huge blonde wig with exaggerated eye make-up, long scarlet evening dress and sparkling red shoes and carried a matching clutch bag. She asked me if I was transvestite or transsexual. I said I was TS, but hadn't started any treatment as I was waiting for my appointment at the clinic. She said she'd been on hormones for nine months but was more she-male than trans but the hormones were producing some nice tits and flashed them at me. When she asked if I was interested in men or women or other trans, I said men, paused then, added I wouldn't rule out other options."

Mia lit a cigarette before continuing. She sat back in her chair and looked me straight in the eyes, showing openness rather than challenging me.

"Natasha said that was a sensible response. Why limit yourself? She told me I'd get plenty of opportunities at the club with all the tranny fuckers. But she warned me not to give it away unless I got into a serious relationship with someone. I found out later the average was from £20 for a quickie, £50 for a short time back at his hotel and from £100 for overnight. Young ones like me could get up to double those amounts."

I understood the temptation of making what appeared to be easy money. I wondered, though, what effect it would have on your self-esteem; and about the dangers it would involve.

"I hadn't looked to make money from sex, but some extra cash would be welcome. Anyway, the dance floor filled up and I joined the other girls and let the music take me. A guy came over to dance with me. Our moves brought us close together and he rubbed himself against me. Then his hands held my waist, pulling me even closer before he took hold of my arse and fondled it. I slipped my arms round his neck and we kissed. As Natasha moved past me with her partner I heard her say "Go for it girl."

I remembered the first time I had danced with Roger and could imagine the buzz Mia would have felt.

"When the music changed, my partner asked if I'd like a drink. I asked for a Bacardi and Coke. We found spaces on one of the Chesterfield sofas. The guy introduced himself as Ed. He was wearing an open neck shirt and jeans. No rings or other jewellery — but that didn't mean a thing. He offered me a cigarette which I accepted."

Mia took a swig of Coke.

"He asked if it was my first time and I said it was and I'd just moved to London. Ed stretched his arm along the back of the sofa, behind my neck, then rested his hand on my shoulder. He asked where I was living and I told him border of North Acton and Willesden. When he asked if I had my own flat, I said it was hardly a flat, just a bedsit. About twelve foot by ten, single bed, wardrobe, little cooker and fridge and chest of drawers. But at least it has its own shower and loo."

"It sounds nicer than the bedsit I used to have near the Oval. I had to share a bathroom and toilet," I told her.

She smiled. "That sounds grim. Ed told me he lived near Hitchin which I'd never heard of. But he was stopping in a hotel round the corner from the club. Having stubbed out his cigarette his hand was now resting on my knee. He turned my head towards him and kissed me, probing my mouth with his tongue. His hand crept up my thigh under my dress. He asked if I'd like to go back to his hotel with him.

"I said maybe later, but I'd like to stay here for a while yet — I hadn't had a chance to dance like this before. I asked if he minded. He didn't, so long as I was dancing with him. He then asked what it would cost him to have me go back to his hotel with him. I hadn't thought about charging him but I remembered what Natasha had said. I asked whether he wanted short time or all night. He said 'All night' so I said £150."

Mia lit another cigarette.

"He hesitated for a second then agreed. We danced for the next couple of hours. Just after midnight, I told him I was going to the loos then we could leave if he still wanted to. I collected my coat from the cloakroom and we left the club. We walked arm in arm the couple of hundred yards to his hotel. Once in his room, he lifted the hem of my skirt and hooked his fingers into my knickers and tights and slid them down my legs while I undid his zip and took out his cock. He unzipped my dress and slipped it off my shoulders. I lowered my arms and let it fall to the floor. Ed discarded his trousers and pants and shirt and we climbed onto his bed.

"The next morning, I took the agreed cash, left the hotel and caught a cab back to my flat. I made a note to ensure I had spare knickers, tights, make-up and a toothbrush with me in future if I stopped out overnight again. I'd noticed quite a few of the other girls at the club had had bags with them containing changes of clothes — usually because they'd need to change back to male things before going home. Even after paying for the taxi and entrance fee and drinks at the club, I'd made a profit of over £100 for the evening. That made a big difference to my budget.

"Back at the flat, I redid my make-up and changed into a skirt and blouse and headed up the West End to buy another dress or two for future visits to Outsiders. Trying them on, I decided I needed to develop my bust if I wanted to wear the dresses I'd really like so I logged on line that evening and ordered a supply of HRT."

Mia buying black market hormones didn't surprise me. Whilst it wasn't something I'd recommend or condone, I understood only too well the desire to develop breasts. I wondered how she had concealed the growing bust when working at the ad agency.

Her face was expressionless as she told me about her time at Outsiders and she crossed her legs.

"Over the next few weeks I had encounters at least every other weekend, sometimes more frequently. The hormones soon took effect, probably because I was young. In fact, I had to wear tight t-shirts to flatten the developments for my day job. The Saturday before Christmas I saw a guy eyeing me up. He then turned to Harry behind the bar and had a quick conversation then ordered two drinks. He came over to where I was sitting and asked if he could join me; 'I gather this is your usual drink,' he said, putting a Bacardi and Coke down. I took a sip and said 'Yes, thank you, cheers.'

"He introduced himself as Vince. He said he'd been told I wasn't averse to men's company and wanted to discuss a proposition with me. I asked what sort of proposition, thinking it was likely to be kinky sex he was after. Not that it would be a problem. He'd said it wasn't what I was probably thinking. It was an opportunity to make best use of my talents and let me earn a lot more than I could picking up guys from the club. He told me he ran a very high end escort service. He used only the most attractive girls, 'Like you,' he'd said. It attracted the high flying international businessmen and women as clients. He had a small team and was looking for another girl and thought I might be right for the job. I was flattered and interested and asked him to tell me more."

I knew Mia had joined Vince's team; that had been in the documents I'd read and she'd mentioned it at the beginning. But I felt she needed to tell me the whole story in her own way and at her own pace; so I didn't interrupt.

"He told me to come to his office the next day at two pm and he'd fill me in on the details and passed me a business card. I put the card in my clutch bag and said I'd see him the next day. He then asked how old I was and I added two years and said I was eighteen. He then asked what my date of birth was and I told him 16th July 1984. He seemed content with my response.

"On the dot of two, I entered the office. Vince came over and offered to take my coat and said 'I think you've met Adam here.' I recognised Adam as a client from the previous weekend. Rather surprised, I said 'Yes, hi, nice to see you again.' He told me my talents, willingness to please and personality last Saturday had impressed Adam. He said they were all key things they look for in their girls. Adam was convinced I had the potential to meet their clients' requirements. He explained they had a team of five girls. If I joined, I'd be the sixth. I was flattered by Adam's report.

"He continued and explained their clients were high power business men and women from all over the world; Brits, Americans, Europeans, Arabs, Russian oligarchs, Indians, Japanese in fact from everywhere. They demanded the highest standards and that's what the agency offered. In exchange they paid handsomely for the girls' company. He said he was talking anything up to five thousand for a night — but he told me not to get too excited they had very high overheads to cover discretely promoting the service, the office and Adam and his own salaries and giving the girls the support they needed. It still meant I could earn between five hundred for an evening and a thousand for an overnight. He said if the clients tip extra, that was the girls' to keep. He asked how it sounded so far?

"It sounded great. But I asked what the catch was? He responded: 'No catch. We select the best, charge a lot, make sure the clients get what they want and ensure total discretion. You'll recognise some of the clients but don't even think about going to the press. You might make five grand for a story – but that's less than you could earn with us in a month or two so why spoil the deal?' He asked if I was interested. Of course I was interested. Who wouldn't be? So I said so.

"He told me the first step was for me to have medical checks to ensure I didn't have any infections. I'd repeat those checks regularly while I was with them. If those were OK, I'd move into the house the girls shared. They would deduct the rent from my earnings. He told me not to worry it wasn't a con. They marketed our services as high quality which meant we had to be used to elegant surroundings. Our clothes needed to be top drawer too. They'd organise a top to toe make-over including working clothes, cosmetics, perfume, jewellery and hair. He said that's what he meant about them having very high overheads supporting the girls. He asked if I was happy with that. I told him I was perfectly happy."

I certainly understood why Mia would be happy with such an arrangement. I still didn't interrupt her story. She had adopted an open posture and her eyes were maintaining contact with mine, without being challenging.

"He explained we needed to feel comfortable in top restaurants and clubs but also needed to be intelligent and able to hold our own in conversations on a range of topics including current affairs. Their clients weren't after dumb bimbos. The house had subscriptions to leading business magazines and newspapers and we were expected to read them; as well as design and beauty magazines.

"It also helps if you can speak different languages and are familiar with different cuisines. That way you know what to order for dinners and can advise the clients if they are unfamiliar with some of the dishes. We have conversational classes in Russian, Arabic, Chinese, Japanese, French, German and Spanish every day and organise trips to different restaurants for you to learn about the various dishes. He said he couldn't over emphasise their clients were demanding so they give us all the support they could to meet those needs. That's why they took a large part of the fee. They were up-front about it. He then said 'But, if you'd rather earn £150 a trick at Outlanders....' He knew the answer to that suggestion. Of course I wanted to join the team. Apart from anything else it would be my ticket to private surgery to shortcut NHS waiting lists."

"I can see why you'd want to avoid NHS waiting lists," I said; partly to let her know I was still actively listening to her.

"Vince warned me there had been occasions when clients had proved too boisterous. It was very rare but it was a risk. If that happened, they'd take care of us. They'd also have a word with the client and they could never book with us again. Clients were also aware if they hurt one us, any assurances about discretion stopped. That was the biggest deterrent for them. I pointed out getting hurt was a risk I was already taking at Outsiders and it sounded far less likely with them.

"He said it would probably take two weeks before they would send me on a date and asked if I could get to a clinic in Paddington the next morning at 8.30 for urine and blood tests; they'd gambled on me accepting their offer and made an appointment for me the previous week after my date with Adam. I was taken aback by their presumption but I guessed they could always have cancelled the appointment if I'd turned them down.

"He said the results should be through just after lunch so I could call them and, if they were clear, then I could hand in my notice at work. He asked how soon I could finish. As I was only temping, I could finish there and then and let the agency know. He said Adam would pick me up from work, take me to my bedsit to collect what I needed and take me to the house and asked me how that suited me. It sounded brilliant.

"The tests proved clear so, as soon as I got the results, I knocked on boss's door. I told him I'd be finishing that day. He offered to increase my rate if I'd reconsider. He told me he'd been considering making my role permanent. I asked if he'd give me a reference on that basis and he told me to type it up and he'd sign it. Well, a girl needs insurance. Adam collected me as arranged. It took less than twenty minutes to pack my two bags and clear out the flat. Then it was down to the office to hand in the keys. The letting agency said they'd check the flat the next morning and forward the balance of the deposit after any deductions for damages.

"At the house, I met the other girls: Angelina, Roxanne, Jessica, Erica and Melanie. They showed me my room and suggested I might like to get changed before joining them for dinner. Melanie was the eldest and the group leader. She and Angelina were post-op while the rest of us were pre-op or not planning to have any surgery at all. Over dinner, Melanie told me Angelina would take me shopping over the next few days for my working clothes, and a beauty make-over then arrange for me to have intensive 'finishing' training before they allowed me near any clients. I'd have to buy my own clothes and cosmetics after this first outlay — but I could expect to be given jewellery by satisfied clients especially any that rebooked me."

I could hardly believe the level of detail that had been involved in Vince's organisation.

"I worked out my clothes and make-up must have cost well into five figures. When I commented on it, Angelina reminded me we had to fit in with the clients' world and we couldn't afford to stint. She told me not to feel guilty about the cost; I'd soon have earned enough to pay back the investment."

She looked wistfully, perhaps remembering the surroundings she'd enjoyed at that time.

"Sounds like you had a fantastic wardrobe!" I said.

"It was. Once we'd done all the shopping and I'd had my make-over, Angelina took me to the photographer for my website portraits. The session took most of the day and we had a stylist on hand to touch up my make-up and hair. The results were amazing. In some shots I looked like the teenager I was — but nothing that made me look like a young schoolgirl, in others like a sophisticated lady about town. The agency would use them to appeal to the clients' different tastes.

"In the cab back to the house from the photo session, I asked Angelina about Vince's comment that some of the clients were women. She said one in five clients were female and enjoyed other women. Using our service offered them the same as it did for men: discretion and the combination of feminine bodies but with a bit extra if required. I told her I had no experience of sex with other girls. She looked at me in disbelief and said they'd have to give me some practical lessons, assuming I had no objection to making love with another woman. I'd never been attracted to another girl but it didn't bother me; in fact I was definitely curious.

"A couple of days later, Melanie and Angelina took me into Mel's bedroom after dinner. They said they would teach me some techniques for pleasuring female customers. They both stripped down to their undies and lay down on the bed and told me to join them – Mel in the middle and Angelina and me either side. Angelina then pointed out a woman's erotic zones including less obvious ones such as the nape of the neck, inner thighs and the bottom of the feet; ears, lips and, of course nipples and pubic areas. She demonstrated various techniques for stimulating the different zones — Mel's moans showed the effectiveness of the procedures. Angelina then invited me to try. As Mel writhed when I used my fingers, tongue and eyelashes on her, Angelina didn't need to correct my technique very often. Angelina then asked me to give her the same treatment — which I was happy to do. They then positioned themselves either side of me and rewarded me for being such a good pupil and told me I'd graduated but could probably use some additional practice to perfect my techniques.

"Mel then told me whilst most of the female clients wanted purely lesbian encounters some would want to be penetrated. In those cases Mel and Angelina resorted to a double ended dildo or strap on — but I'd be able to use my cock. They asked if I was comfortable having to use that hated appendage. I said I didn't think I'd enjoy it but would see it as part of the job."

I wondered if she was trying to shock me but, in fact, I was intrigued by her story and what she'd been through. I must have been staring wide eyed at her as she smiled.

"At the end of the second week, Adam took me out to a top West End club as part of my graduation process. At the end of the evening, he dropped me back at the house and came in to debrief me over coffee. He said he was very happy with my performance and he thought I was ready to accept client bookings. He then slid his arm along the back of the sofa we were sitting on and fondled my shoulder while he turned my head with his other hand and leant across to kiss me. I said much as I'd love to go to bed with him, I thought one of the absolute rules was we didn't use the house for sex with guys. He withdrew his hands, patted my knee and said. 'Good for you Mia. I'm glad to see you passed that last test.'

"My first date was dinner with Don, an American from the Deep South. He was president of a company producing components for the aerospace industries. We met at the Tara Hotel where he'd taken an Executive Suite. We had a drink in his room, ate in the Artist's Corner restaurant then moved on to the cocktail bar before returning to his suite. He seemed satisfied with my company as he tipped me an extra £50 and asked if I was free for an overnight stay on the Saturday evening. I told him I was sure I would be available and asked him to call the office in the morning to confirm. He then asked if I could provide some coke at the weekend. I told him I'd see what I could do.

"The other girls were still up when I got back to the house. They'd wanted to hear how my first date had gone. After satisfying their curiosity, I asked what the policy was on providing drugs for clients. Melanie said it was fine. It was quite a common request. She said we could get hold of whatever they wanted coke, E, crack, meth and it went on their bill. If you're caught with it, you could get done for possession but it's unlikely to be for intent to supply unless you have a lot. You don't have to get involved but most of the clients indulge sometimes and it would impact on your bookings if you don't. I asked if clients expected us to take it as well.

"Melanie said some would offer, some may expect us to accept, some won't worry if we don't. She usually took a small amount of coke with her and if they offer anything else tell them that's her preference; and only ever took any if she was with a very insistent client. She warned it can be extremely addictive so I needed to be careful. Melanie then said it sounded like I'd had a successful first date and let's hope it's the first of many more to come. We then went to bed.

"Next morning, I had a call from Vince to tell me Don had called and booked me again for an overnight on Saturday. He'd been particularly complimentary about me. Once we got off the phone, I called the beauty salon to book a hair do, waxing, eyebrows and nails. I had a late breakfast of cereal and fruit then dressed. It was our Spanish conversation session but that wasn't until two o'clock so I settled down at a PC and looked up what I could on Don's company and the aerospace industry.

"When I reached the hotel on Saturday night, I joined Don in his suite. I passed him the coke he'd requested. Having poured me a glass of Dom Perignon, he tipped a little of the coke onto a mirror and cut it using an Amex Black Card. He asked if I wanted a hit but I replied just being with him made me high enough. He laughed then snorted the coke and said I had real style and he planned for us to go out to a club.

"Don took my arm as we went down in the lift, the doorman hailed a cab for us and Don slipped him a note. As it was a dark colour, it had to have been at least ten pounds, just for hailing a cab. He rounded up the fare to a fifty and gave the doorman at the Shangri-la a ten for opening the cab door. The maître d' showed us to a private booth with a good view of the stage for the cabaret and a waitress I recognised from the Outsider Club came over and took our drink order – another bottle of Dom Perignon of course. While she fetched it from the bar, she left us with the menus. Don got some envious looks from other men in the club when we danced — which turned me on too. Don eventually suggested we return to his hotel. When we got back to his suite, he gave me a package. When I opened it, I found it contained a diamond bracelet. I thanked him for his generous gift to which he replied I was about to earn it. He proved to be an insatiable lover that night. I think we managed about three hours sleep interrupted by making love five times.

"The following week, I had my second appointment at the gender identity clinic. The specialist was annoyed when I told him I was taking hormones I'd bought off the internet. He advised strongly against it; it was almost an order to stop. I wasn't about to stop taking them though. I found a private gender specialist instead prepared to treat me, including providing prescriptions and organising blood tests — but, of course, you know Nicholas Wright, don't you."

"Yes — lovely guy."

"Anyway, I wouldn't be able to have surgery until I was eighteen. By then, I'd easily be able to save enough to have it done privately. I averaged two dinner dates and one overnight each week over the next several months so I was making about £8,000 a month. Until we got arrested and you know the rest."

It was a hell of a tale and the level of detail told me that Mia didn't only want to put her side of the story but make sense to herself of what had gone on. It certainly seemed cathartic.

I didn't condone the use of drugs, especially supplying them; which is what Mia had been found guilty of. But I felt there was a huge difference between selling drugs to schoolkids and junkies and providing a small amount to her escort clients. It was apparent, too, Mia would face more than the usual consequences of prison and that didn't seem just to me. Surely there should be a basic principle of equality of punishment with no increased or reduced impact due to irrelevant factors? In Mia's case, being in a male prison when she'd been living as a female for years was a huge extra factor.

"I can't imagine how you survived what you've been through," I said shaking my head from side to side. "I know I wouldn't have had the strength to do the same even with the support of my partner Roger."

She shrugged her shoulders. "I did what I had to do. Each new step didn't seem that bad. And, to be honest, I'm not ashamed of anything I did — which doesn't mean I want to go back to that life. I don't. I want to live as normal as life as I can. Mind you, I don't have to tell you no trans person can live a totally normal life."

"You're dead right there, you think your life is normal then something crops up to affect it because of a history you had no control over."

"Exactly Vicky. So, are you going to visit me?"

Without hesitating, I said "Yes, I'd be more than happy to."

She breathed a sigh of relief. "Thanks. It means a lot. You said you've got a partner, Roger was it?"

"Yes, that's right, we're sort of married and will make it legal when I get a Gender Recognition Certificate, with luck, later this year."

"Lucky you. Well look, I said I didn't want to keep things secret between us and I realise you won't want to hide things from Roger; so if you want to tell him things I've said then I don't mind so long as it goes no further."

"Don't worry, it won't."

Our time was up so we got to our feet and I gave her a hug. I didn't care if it was the 'done' thing.

As she disappeared through one door, I left the visitors' room, left the prison and returned to my car. I stood there for a minute relishing the fact I was free to go where I wanted and sad that circumstances had led to Mia being locked up.

# Chapter 25. Denise
## 27<sup>th</sup> January 2005

I had just unlocked the car when I heard a call "Vicky!"

It was Denise.

"I gather you've seen Mia. How did it go? I don't want you to breach any confidentiality, just get your first reactions."

"How long have you got?" I asked her.

"I'm off duty now – so it's more a case of how long have you got? Do you fancy a drink? There's a Costa's down the road."

Over coffees, I told Denise I agreed with her about Mia's position, I also felt sorry for her and I'd agreed to visit her. I also suggested the prison staff might benefit from some awareness training around trans issues."

"I agree. There are some dinosaurs in there. The Prison Service Director General seems to be keen on what he calls decency in terms of how staff deal with prisoners, but there's quite bit of resistance from some officers."

"Well, I don't suppose it's possible to change everyone's attitudes but if we can educate some of the others, it may make a difference."

"Would you be prepared to provide a workshop?"

"I suppose I could do it, maybe combining it with next time I visit Mia. But don't you know anyone else that's in a better position? Has anyone done anything like this before?"

"Not as far as I know within the prison service; but there is a new support group for lesbian and gay staff called GALIPS, I'm the local rep. I'll call Pete Allen, the chair and see if he has any ideas."

"If it goes ahead, who would organise it from your side?"

"I guess it would be down to me. I'll speak to the Governor and see what he says."

"OK, let me know. You've got my phone number haven't you?"

"Yeah, and thanks for your help."

We hugged then I got in my car and drove home wondering what I'd let myself in for.

I was sitting in the lounge deep in thought, holding a glass of Chardonnay, when Roger came in from work that evening. He kissed me, then took the glass from my hand and drained it.

"Refill?" he asked.

"Yes please. You know, I thought I'd struggled being trans but my life has been a bed of roses compared with Mia's."

"Let me get the drinks then you can tell me all about it. Or as much as you can share."

I took the refilled glass and took a sip, then recounted the story Mia had told me.

Roger only interrupted with the occasional "shit" or for me to clarify a detail.

As I recapped Mia's story, especially the losses and abuse she'd experienced, I struggled to get the words out as lumps formed in my throat and tears dribbled down my cheeks.

Roger's arms hugging me should have made me feel better but it only heightened the difference between Mia's and my fortunes; fortunes based on chance not because of anything either of us had done to deserve the breaks.

By the time I'd finished, the tears were flowing freely.

"So, I assume you are going to befriend and visit her." It wasn't a question.

"Yes. I don't feel obliged to do what I can — I want to. Denise has also asked if I can do a workshop on trans issues for prison officers."

"I can't think of anyone who would do it better than you. At the very least, just standing there and talking eliminates so many negative stereotypes the staff may have about what being trans is about. And, let's face it, Mia's history does rather reinforce some of the bigots' idea it's all about sex — and I'm not criticising her in the least for getting into the escort business. She only did what she needed to do to survive."

"So, you support me doing the workshop and befriending Mia?"

"Darling, I support whatever you do, you know that. And this is obviously very important to you isn't it?"

"It is. I believe Mia when she says she wants to sort out her life. She's at a low point, as I was when I tried to kill myself. You saved me then so perhaps it's time for me to pay that forward."

"Just remember, when I saved you, as you put it, I was being selfish I wanted you in my life. I always will."

He pulled my face to his and kissed me with a passion that left me weak. Then Roger's stomach rumbled which broke the mood and left us laughing.

"Damn," I cried as I recovered my composure, "look at the time. I haven't done anything for dinner. Looks like beans on toast or an omelette this evening."

Denise called me the following week to tell me the Governor had approved a workshop. She'd been in touch with Pete Allen at GALIPS. He'd passed her onto LAGIP, their equivalent in the Probation Service and Michaela Jeffries. Michaela worked for Manchester Probation and had done trans awareness workshops for probation staff.

It looked like a trip to Manchester might be useful. The city's reputation for a great LGBT scene was entirely secondary. Obviously ;-)

# Chapter 26. Manchester
## 5th February 2005

Denise and Ruth, her partner, joined us for the trip north. Or, more accurately, we went with them in Ruth's BMW X5. Goodness knows how much fuel it used but Ruth dismissed any suggestion of a contribution to the cost with a wave of the hand. My little Toyota Corolla was reasonably comfortable and much more relaxing for long drives than Roger's MGB, but it couldn't match the way the BMW ate up the miles or the luxury of the seats. The cavernous luggage compartment had swallowed our cases with ease and the high position gave a regal impression.

We'd booked rooms at a hotel close to the gay village. Michaela had reserved a table for us that evening at Taurus on Canal Street for dinner. We'd also booked a small conference room at the hotel to give us privacy for our meeting. Denise had persuaded her governor to cover the meeting room cost as part of the budget for the proposed workshop.

Michaela brought a USB pen drive with her, containing a presentation on trans issues she'd used for Trainee Probation Officers and at a National Probation Service Diversity Conference. We loaded the PowerPoint onto my laptop and Michaela ran through it with us.

"Bloody hell, they need to show that to every member of probation and prison staff," declared Denise when Michaela finished.

"I don't think I can match that presentation," I admitted, dejectedly. "Michaela's the one you need to do the workshop, not me, Denise."

"I'd love to, but I don't have the time. I get two days a month funded by the NPS for LAGIP work. That doesn't cover all of the hours I spend. My boss can't spare me any more time from my official job," Michaela said sadly. "I'll give you a copy of the presentation and you can adapt it, if it helps."

I couldn't believe her offer. "Are you sure? That's very generous."

"No problem. The aim is to educate people about the issues we face, isn't it?"

"Well, if there is ever anything we can do for you let us know. If you fancy a few days in Bournemouth or a bit of sailing, give us a call." I added.

"Sailing? Ah, now you're talking. I might well take you up on that. What do you sail?"

"Sunfast 37, are you familiar with them?"

"No, I've sailed mainly in a Contessa 32 around the Solent and a few cross-channel races and a Moody in the Ionian. I used to race dinghies in my younger days."

"Have you worked very long for Probation?" asked Denise.

"No, I started in November 1999 so a little over five years. It was my very first interview as Michaela. I'd been out of work for a few months; I lost my previous job when they found out I planned to transition."

"So how did you get involved with LAGIP and GALIPS?"

"LAGIP AND GALIPS?" asked Roger, looking confused, "and what was NPS?"

"Sorry, Roger, we love our acronyms. Lesbians and Gays in Probation and Gays and Lesbians in the Prison Service," Michaela explained, "NPS is the National Probation Service. Probation and the Prison Service now come under the National Offender Management Service or NOMS as part of the Home Office."

"Also known as Nightmare On Marsham Street — which is where the new Home Office building is!" added Denise, laughing. "Sorry Michaela, we interrupted."

"No problem, when I joined Manchester Probation, I found out I was the first openly trans employee nationally in probation. I published a message on the LGBT forum on Lotus Notes saying something like 'You've probably heard rumours there's a trans person joining the organisation. Well hi, it's ME! If you want any information on trans issues let me know."

"I then saw a notice about a LAGIP conference in 2000 at University of East Anglia in Norwich so booked a place. When I got there, a lesbian member demanded to know what I was doing there as it wasn't an organisation for trans people. I told her I was lesbian; so that was OK. When I said maybe it should include trans people, she said they'd already discussed that and it would not happen."

"Yeah, I've come across a few gays and lesbians like that," remarked Denise.

"Well, that was like a red rag to a bull," Michaela continued, "Next day was the AGM and they wanted volunteers to join a working group to look at the future of LAGIP, so, I put up my hand. They then wanted a volunteer to organise the next conference. I had experience of that too, so put up my hand again. The next conference was here in Manchester in 2003. In fact, the conference dinner was held in Taurus, where we're eating this evening. I did some lobbying in the meantime and at the conference. The upshot was at the AGM the next day, we voted on whether to extend the membership to include trans and bi individuals and the meeting carried the motion with only one abstention."

"I can imagine you being a force to reckon with," I said. "That's quite inspirational."

"I've thought, Vicky, the next LAGIP conference is in Brighton in April. Why don't you attend, I'm sure I can swing it with the committee. It's on a Saturday with the AGM the next day. You'd be welcome to come for the day and stop for the dinner in the evening — we can't offer accommodation though unless you come as a guest speaker. Now there's a thought. The Director General of NOMS is the guest of honour so you might have a chance to speak to him."

"Are you sure that would be OK?"

"I don't see why not, I'm vice-chair this year so certain the committee will agree. Why don't you attend as well Denise? I think Pete Allen will be there."

"It may depend on duty rosters, but I'll see what I can sort out."

"It would be good if you both came. Maybe we can put pressure on the DG about managing trans prisoners. He's also the Civil Service Diversity Champion after all. I've already questioned him over a lack of any reference to Equality & Diversity in the NOMS response to the Carter Report and got him to commit to it being important."

Denise looked shocked, "You challenged the DG? Christ, you've got more nerve than me, that's all I can say! I get nervous enough questioning one of my governors."

"Not sure my Chief Officer was too happy either — but I did it as a representative of LAGIP rather than a local employee. I'll also raise the issue at the next meeting of the NOMS Diversity Board. Now, is there anything else we need to discuss in private or shall we go for dinner?" Michaela asked.

Neither Denise nor I could think of anything so Roger popped back to our room with the laptop while the rest of us used the ladies.

It was only a couple of hundred yards from the hotel to Taurus bar and restaurant at the top of Canal Street. At the corner, I noticed the building we were passing had a sign announcing Greater Manchester Probation Area.

"Is this where you work, Michaela?"

"No, that's the Programmes Unit, I work at Headquarters near Old Trafford. We have about forty offices around Greater Manchester."

As we entered Taurus, a large gay guy greeted Michaela. "Good evening, darling, how are you?" he gushed, giving her a hug. "Your table is over in the alcove, I thought it would be more private."

"Thanks Polly — these are friends of mine from Bournemouth: Vicky, Roger her husband so don't get any ideas, Denise and her partner Ruth. I've told them this is by far the best place to eat in the Village."

"Of course it is, darling, I'll send Fiona over with the menus and wine list."

As Polly walked to the rear of the bar, Michaela turned to us.

"Polly and his partner own Taurus. We hold our monthly support group meetings downstairs so I'm often in here."

Right then, a tall individual in a short black skirt and white blouse wearing four inch stilettos offered us the menus. Her hair was blonde and big.

"There are also some specials listed on the blackboard. Can I get any drinks while you decide what you want to eat?"

We broke off the conversation to study the menus and placed our orders. Denise and Ruth ordered beer with their meals while Michaela, Roger and I shared a bottle of Pinot Grigio.

I wanted to investigate Michaela's sailing experience. I still couldn't believe she was old enough to have sailed for over fifty years — which she'd told us earlier.

"You said your dad took you sailing when you were young — do you remember much of that?"

"Bits and pieces. I was four or five at the time. There was this big lake near RAF Habbaniya and we would go up there most afternoons. The men started work early so finished just after lunch. I remember we'd go up in gharries as we called the lorries. There was a steep hill and sometimes the men had to get out and push. Dad would race his Snipe dinghy then take me out for a few minutes afterwards. I'd dive off the front of the boat with the painter and swim to shore.

"That was it for few years until I moved to London. A friend and I used to hire the twelve-foot dinghies on the Serpentine. We used to chase the ducks — which was excellent tacking practice.

"After that there was another long break 'til we moved to Cambridgeshire. I did courses at the County Council Sailing Centre at Grafham Water. Once you'd done one of their courses, you could join the centre's association for a pound a year and use their dinghies on Thursday evenings during the summer."

"What did they have?"

"Oh, usual range of Wayfarers, Toppers and a couple of cats."

"Good solid kit then."

"Yes, it was. Couple of years later, I got a decent pay rise at work which coincided with my friend from London getting a job at Grafham; it was at Littlehey Prison, Denise; so we decided to buy a dinghy between us and join the sailing club."

"What did you get?"

"Well, we tossed up between something sedate as my mate didn't have much experience and something that would be more interesting. We decided something like an Enterprise would be a sensible first step — but we thought we'd soon tire of that. We'd never been sensible so we chose a Fireball instead."

"You're kidding. That's what I used to sail!"

"My favourite dinghy! When my mate got moved to Feltham YOI, we tried a club halfway between us, but it didn't work out and the boat was getting old and kept needing work. These days I prefer cruisers, much more comfortable at my age."

After the meal, Denise and Ruth headed to a women's only disco at the Thompson's Arms while the rest of us visited Dotz piano bar, one of Michaela's favourite venues.

The doorman was dressed in a DJ but, to be honest, didn't look as though he'd be able to deal with rowdy customers as he seemed to be in his sixties, balding and cuddly rather than muscular.

"Good evening, Michaela," he greeted us as he opened the door.

"Good evening, Thomas," Michaela responded.

Michaela waved to the piano player as we made our way to the bar.

"Evening, Chris, these are two friends of mine from Bournemouth, Vicky and Roger."

"Hi folks, welcome to Dotz. What can I get you to drink?"

"I'll stick with white wine, what about you Vicky? Roger?"

"Same for me," I said

"And me," added Roger.

Chris opened a bottle of white and put it on the bar with three glasses.

As Michaela took out her purse to pay, Chris said "On the house."

"Thanks very much, Chris."

I must have looked surprised. When we sat down at a table, Michaela explained "I've brought lots of new visitors to Manchester in here over the years — Chris often refers to me as their membership secretary. He manages the club for his partner, Foo Foo Lamar."

We continued to chat about sailing and our transition experiences. Michaela had been in her 50s when she started. She had seen Nicholas Wright and had also used the team at Leicester. I wished I'd met her before my surgery. She'd have set my mind at ease over some of the concerns I'd had.

I managed to wheedle out of her that she had helped other trans staff to transition by advising their senior management teams and providing presentations to other staff; she'd just started attending national diversity meetings with the chair of LAGIP almost daring anyone to challenge her right to be there as the 'T' representative. She told us that when her boss had recently told her that she wanted to nominate Michaela for a national award in the inaugural NPS Diversity Awards in recognition of this work, she'd had to say there could be a problem as she was one of the judges. She did admit that her boss had rung the Head of Diversity and been assured that the nomination could go ahead as Michaela would just not be involved in judging that category.

"So did you win?" I asked.

"I can't tell you as the results are being kept secret until the awards ceremony next month," she replied with a straight face.

She'd also been the representative of the Probation Service at an event to mark International Women's Day and the opening of the new Home Office building. She wasn't boasting – just using the incident as an example of the progress the trans community had made in recent years. Even so, I was in awe of her achievements. Nothing seemed to faze her, and despite the difference in our ages, we seemed to have bonded so she seemed like a big sister or a favourite aunt.

We said goodnight to Dotz about 11.30 and made our way to Napoleon's. This was an absolute must for any trans person visiting Manchester.

The doorman waved Michaela through but then stopped Roger and me and asked us to pay £2 admission. Michaela then said "Vicky should be free Clive. Sorry Roger but trans people get in free, everyone else pays."

"It's the same at the Blue Peach, discrimination if you ask me," joked Roger.

Clive looked dubiously at me and insisted "£2 please." He then turned to Michaela, "you can't pretend she's trans. You know the rules."

"It's fine," I insisted, handing over a fiver to cover Roger's and my admission fees. I was delighted he was convinced I wasn't trans. Not that I was ashamed of my history but when someone sees trans people all the time and still doesn't 'read' you, it's fabulous.

We climbed the stairs to another bar and the dance floor.

"Hi Michaela, what can I get you?" asked the camp, slim blond guy behind the bar.

"Hi, Garry," she turned to Roger and me "What would you like?"

Roger decided on a beer but Michaela and I stuck with white wine.

"Two white wines and a beer, please, Garry."

Turning to us she said "Garry had the flat above mine when I lived in a tower block in Salford."

I don't know how many people we were introduced to that evening and I certainly can't remember many of their names — it was a blur. When we weren't chatting, we were on the little dance floor. Like the Blue Peach, the dance floor was surrounded by mirrors and transvestites were looking at their own reflections while they danced. Unless, that is, they were dancing very closely in the arms of one of the tranny chasers.

It had been a long day and about one, Roger and I decided it was time to head back to our hotel. Michaela said she would catch a cab home and we made our goodbyes but not before we got a promise from her she would come down to Bournemouth later in the year for some sailing.

Ruth wanted to see Old Trafford before we left Manchester. I had no interest at all in football. I suspect this was because, as a boy, I was expected to like it. But, in any case, as Ruth had been kind enough to drive us to Manchester, I was content to have a look at Manchester United's stadium.

Then it was out along Chester Road, around the M60 past the airport to the M6 and settle into a 70mph cruise south.

# Chapter 27. Workshops
## 18<sup>TH</sup> February 2005

I ran through Michaela's PowerPoint and amended it where it related to her own personal experiences or she had targeted it at Probation Staff. I was far from convinced I would be as effective as Michaela but Roger pointed out my personal experiences were as valid as hers. Even if I was only 80% as good as she might have been, that would still be far better than most people could provide. And far better than anything anyone else at the YOI could do.

I wasn't convinced but liked hearing him trying to boost my confidence.

Then it was the day of the workshop or, rather, workshops as the prison had now planned two — one in the morning, one in the afternoon.

Dressed in my most professional businesswoman outfit of skirt suit with feminine blouse, I'd had my hair and nails done the previous day and taken extra care over my make-up that morning. My presentation was on my laptop, I'd had to get special authority to take it in to the prison.

I took a last moment to review before I left the house, had I forgotten anything? I hoped not. The prison was providing a projector in the chapel where I was to hold the workshops, they'd promised a flip chart and markers and had duplicated some of the material I'd provided for breakout sessions.

I prayed everything would go well. Not so much for my sake. If I made a mess of it, I could live with the embarrassment but if I didn't get the message over clearly, Mia's treatment might be affected. If I got it right, though, maybe, just maybe, some of the officers might have a better understanding of what she was facing and be more sympathetic. It was quite a responsibility. Small wonder I was nervous.

Pulling up at the prison, I parked as usual; left my mobile in the car, as usual; walked to the entrance gate, as usual (well, almost as usual, I didn't normally wear high heels or a business suit). I approached the desk and told them who I was and I was there to do training. The officer's reaction wasn't at all like the reception I usually got.

Instead of looks down their noses, and dismissive responses, it was "Yes, ma'am, you are expected. Can I please see the authorisation for your laptop? That's fine ma'am. Do you have any prohibited items on you? No? Thank you, ma'am. Please go into the security lock. Once you're in, the door will close behind you and the one in front will open. Please take a seat there and your escort will collect you shortly."

I even got a smile.

As I passed through the second security lock, Denise appeared through another door.

"Wow, you look very smart today Vicky. Not that I expected anything less."

She unlocked the door from the waiting area and stood to one side while I passed through. The loud clang as she closed the door behind us made me jump. We were now in a courtyard surrounded by buildings, some with bars on the windows, on three sides, and a twenty feet high blank wall with rounded tops on the other. It was overwhelmingly oppressive.

The other side of the courtyard, another officer had come through the next gate.

"Coming through," called Denise and he left the gate unlocked for us.

Once again, the crash as she closed the gate behind us made me jump. It echoed around the courtyard like a peal of thunder.

"Not sure I could work in a place like this," I said.

"You get used to it," Denise assured me. I doubted I ever would.

"We go up here," she added, pointing up some stairs. By now we were encountering some of the prisoners. They seemed subdued which surprised me. "We don't tend to get violent prisoners here. Most of them are like Mia, they've gone off the rails but with a bit of help can get back on track. Not that any of them are angels."

After negotiating a few more gates, the clangs as they closed no longer making me jump quite as much, we reached the multi faith chapel. I connected the laptop to the projector and checked the presentation worked on the large screen. Satisfied all was OK, I had a last visit to the ladies before the attendees arrived.

They came in ones and twos, sometimes more. I'd expected a dozen or so, maybe twenty, for each of the two workshops but there were more, many more. I stopped counting after forty. I was conscious of them looking at me; probably wondering what I was going to say — maybe thinking that I looked too young to be able to tell them anything — or that anything I might say was rubbish. Were they there because they wanted to learn — or had they been instructed to attend? Would their attitude be hostile or would they just sit there in stony silence— challenging me to get through to them?

Most were in uniform but there were some in civvies. They looked older than many of those in uniform. I wondered who they might be.

This was getting scary.

Then it was time for me to speak. Shit. What had I let myself in for?

I took a deep breath.

"Good morning everyone. I'm Vicky Dalton and I'm here to provide today's workshop on Trans Issues especially as they relate to Transsexual Prisoners.

Several dozen heads turned in my direction as murmured conversations between colleagues faded to nothing; I could feel several dozen pairs of eyes scrutinising me; most of the faces emotionless — though Denise and a few of the others sitting near her gave me encouraging smiles.

"I'll cover an introduction to trans terms and labels, we'll look at brainsex; current views on causality; what transition involves; the legal position, including the Gender Recognition Act 2004; the ways trans people are treated and mistreated and the impact this may have on offending behaviour.

The mention of offending behaviour seemed to get their attention — now I was talking about issues that directly concerned them.

"We'll look at some statistics on self-harm and suicide amongst trans people and some suggestions for working with trans prisoners. So, let's start with labels. What labels do you know that relate to trans people?"

Two and a half hours later, we were into the question and answer session and I was fielding well-considered queries. When the questions dried up, I thanked the audience for their attention.

One of the 'suits' approached me. "That was an impressive talk and very informative. You've given us a lot to think about. I'm Stuart Campbell, the Number One governor here. Very glad Denise suggested these workshops. What would you think about doing more of them? Perhaps joining our diversity board? Can't pay you but can certainly cover expenses."

"I'd be very happy to help if I can. You probably know I visit Mia Evans."

"Yes, and I'm glad she has found such a good role model to befriend her. She could have gone either way but the reports I've had since you've visited her suggests we won't see her back inside again."

I was delighted to hear that from Mr Campbell. I was so glad I hadn't followed my initial prejudices over her involvement in drug dealing and had visited Mia. I felt a deep sense of satisfaction having, apparently, made a difference to her life and given fifty-odd prison officers a better understanding of what it means to be trans.

"Lunch Vicky?" asked Denise. "Your things should be safe in here if we lock the door."

The afternoon session was a repeat of the morning, though I felt my words flowed better with the extra practice. By the end, I was enjoying the experience of making the delegates think differently about trans people and what we go through.

I was on such a high by the end of the day I barely noticed the gates clanging as we passed through on our way out.

Going back through the security lock, I noticed the officer on duty had been one of those that had attended the morning session.

"Bye Vicky, that was a fabulous talk and you were brilliant."

Wow what a difference to the reception I'd received when I first came to visit Mia.

Denise gave me a hug and said she'd see me soon.

Back at the car, I took out my mobile and called Roger.

"Hi darling, how did it go? If I know you, it will have been brilliant."

"It was. Can't believe it. I'm on such a high but it's also bit of an anti-climax after all the preparation. How about going out to eat this evening?"

"Why not? Do you fancy the Bella Rosa?"

"Perfect."

I then called Michaela and relayed how the sessions had gone.

"That's brilliant Vicky, well done."

"I couldn't have done it without your presentation and advice so thanks for that."

"Glad it was of use. By the way, the committee has confirmed your invitation to the conference. They were more than happy to invite you. We would like you to do a ten to fifteen minute spot on your experience of working with Mia and providing the workshop. We can then arrange accommodation for you as a guest speaker."

I was astounded, but accepted the invitation.

When I returned to the prison the following week to visit Mia, my reception was in sharp contrast to the first few visits. The officer on the reception desk recognised me.

"Good morning Vicky. Are you here to visit Mia? She'll be glad to see you. Colleagues are still talking about the workshops you did. Those that missed them are asking if you'll be doing more."

"I hope to, but it's up to Mr Campbell."

Once Mia had joined me in the visitors' centre, I passed over a can of coke and some chocolate bars.

"What did you say in the workshops? Nearly all the officers have been much more friendly and sympathetic. They're even allowing me to order cosmetics and other female items from lists used in female prisons. I can use it in my cell but not at other times. Even the Number One Governor came to see me and said if I had any problems with other prisoners to tell the staff and they would deal with it."

I'd hoped to change attitudes but this was beyond my wildest dreams.

"I told them what trans people faced; it was inherent in us at birth and natural and not something we can fight. That the issues we encountered and the rejection, exclusion and discrimination we're exposed to made us feel rejected by society and it wasn't surprising if that made us reject society's values. I said if society treated us decently, it might have positive effects. I also pointed out the Gender Recognition Act showed we were now recognised as human beings in law."

"Well, whatever you said seems to have made a difference. What's the deal with the Gender Recognition Act? How would that affect me?"

"From October, you'll be able to apply for legal recognition as female providing you've been diagnosed as having Gender Dysphoria by a specialist and another medical professional."

"I've got letters from Tavistock and Dr Wright confirming that."

"You need to be over 18."

"I will be by October."

"And have lived in role for at least two years."

"Done that, providing they don't discount the time in male prisons."

"You need to sign a statement you intend to live as a female for the rest of your life."

"Well, I'm not going back to being male. This is me. Full stop."

"So, the only issue is whether time in here counts as living in role. Now you can wear female clothes in your own cell, I can't see why they'd discount it."

"So, if I get a certificate, I also get a new birth certificate. Is that right?"

"Yes."

"And the Prison Service has to treat me as female?"

"Yes, you become 'female for all purposes'. As the law puts it."

"So, they'd have to move me to a female prison?"

"I can't see how they can refuse to do so."

"Fuck me. Ooops, that wasn't very ladylike was it?"

I laughed at the incongruity.

"But there's a chance they may refuse my application if they don't accept being in a male prison as meeting the living in role criteria?"

"It's possible."

It would be a Catch 22 situation. If the Gender Recognition Panel refused to accept Mia's time in a male prison as living in role and grant her GRC, then the Prison Service wouldn't transfer her to a female prison and without being in a female establishment, she wouldn't satisfy the GRC requirements.

## Chapter 28. Birthday Party
### 5th March 2005

Friday 4th March was my 22nd birthday (and Pete's) so we planned a party on Saturday 5th at the Blue Peach. The usual crowd was there from the club and the support group plus Pete and his girlfriend Kerry. Once Kerry relaxed, she spent most of her time on the dance floor where she seemed to enjoy dancing with the mainly transvestite crowd. During breaks she chatted to some of them about their clothes and where they'd bought them and about their make-up.

Pete was content drinking and people watching. I caught up with him at the bar as Jacqui joined us to order a drink.

"Hi Jacqui, this is my brother Pete. Pete, Jacqui might be able to teach your outfit a thing or two. You should have seen how she dealt with a yob that tried to attack some of us a few months ago."

"Really?"

"It wasn't anything, what outfit are you with then Pete?"

"Artists' Rifles."

I saw Jacqui's eyebrows raised in recognition of the name.

"She says it wasn't anything but this guy took a swing at her having already assaulted one of our other members. Before you could blink, he was on the floor with Jacqui on top of him," I insisted. "When I asked how she'd done it, she just replied 'speed, aggression, surprise'."

This time I saw Pete's eyebrows raised as he tilted his head. Something was going on but I didn't know what.

"Regiment?" asked Pete softly.

"22," replied Jacqui, "but thirty odd years ago. I was part of the regular staff with 21 towards the end of my service"

"Yeah? Amazing. Where were they based back then?"

"Duke of York's Barracks, Chelsea."

"We're still there."

No wonder Jacqui had said we wouldn't have believed her when I asked how she'd learned to do what she had. Life never fails to surprise.

"Shall we find a seat?" asked Pete.

They headed for a couple of seats in a quieter corner and spent the rest of the evening talking to each other — interrupted only when they needed to replenish their drinks.

Jacqui's story shouldn't have surprised me. A lot of transwomen had taken up macho occupations to hide their feminine sides or to 'make men of themselves'. There were any number in the forces, oil rig workers, firefighters, police, construction workers, merchant navy and engineers.

I was sure Pete and Jacqui would be swapping stories and I would love to hear them too but didn't think she'd be prepared to share them with anyone who hadn't been through similar experiences. She'd see it as shooting a line.

Roger came over and put his arm around me and gave me a quick kiss. "Everything OK?"

"Fabulous, thanks darling."

"Pete seems intense with Jacqui, what's going on there?"

"Apparently Jacqui was in the same mob as Pete."

"What? SAS Reserves?"

"It appears she was a regular."

"She's a dark horse, she is."

"I think they're swapping stories of daring do!"

"Well, let's leave them to it, come and dance."

# Chapter 29.  Conference in Brighton
## 1st April 2005

I drove over to Brighton for the LAGIP conference. As I was one of the guest speakers, Michaela had organised accommodation. Roger had passed on the conference so I arrived on the Friday afternoon and joined the delegates for an informal welcome meet that evening.

Most of the group, including me, dispersed around Brighton's gay scene from about nine o'clock. I didn't stay out too late as I wanted to be reasonably fresh for my contribution the following day. It was one thing to give a talk to Prison Officers who had minimal understanding of trans issues — they'd probably believe anything I said, even if I was bluffing. This was an LGBT audience who would see through any bullshit.

Proceedings started with Michaela introducing the guest of honour.

The Director General then walked to the podium and, looking at Michaela said: "I first met Michaela at Greater Manchester Probation's Moss Side offices where I was talking to staff about NOMS and the plans to improve end-to-end offender management. She challenged me over the lack of any reference to diversity in our response to the Carter Report. When I answered her, she gave me *that* look."

Michaela looked rather embarrassed.

Over coffee, I joined Michaela and the DG.

"I'd hoped you'd forgotten about Moss Side." Michaela said.

"Not a chance, but don't apologise, you were right. We should have referred to diversity in our response and it was appropriate for you as vice-chair of one of the staff associations to raise it. I hope you'll always be a critical friend."

My presentation went down well and I had complimentary remarks from delegates. That meant a lot coming from those who already knew about the subject. Once I'd done my slot, I could relax and enjoy the rest of the day's proceedings.

After the conference dinner, and a warning to be certain to attend the AGM in the morning, delegates scattered around the gay scene again.

I left the hotel after breakfast, having said goodbye to Michaela and some of the other delegates and was back in Bournemouth by lunch time.

# Chapter 30. Round the Island Race
## 18th June 2005

The next few months passed with no significant dramas. Michaela came down and joined us on Summer Dreams for the Round the Island Race. We had a full crew with Dad and Pete also joining Roger and me.

Michaela hadn't forgotten how to handle the spinnaker from her Fireball days and we felt confident as a crew to drive the yacht hard and fight at close quarters with other competitors. We knew we had the skills to get out of any trouble. Our tacks were slick and, when we gybed the spinnaker, it hardly stopped drawing on one side before it was across and driving us along again on the other side as we sailed along from the Needles to St Catherine's Point.

I don't know about the others, but I felt so alive as we surfed down the front of waves, passing other boats who were sailing more conservatively.

One of the other yachts from our class kept luffing us as we tried to pass them. We threw in some smooth gybes which they struggled to match and when they made a real mess of one, we slipped past. This battle had cost us time but we were now heading for Bembridge Ledge. We saw another yacht ahead of us flying the white pennant that showed they were in the same class as us. We gradually made ground on them. Their crew was all dressed the same so it looked like they raced together regularly and probably had much more experience as a crew.

Nevertheless, by the time we hardened up for the beat up to Ryde, we were less than a boat length behind but far enough to windward of them they couldn't luff or backwind us.

Inch by inch, we crept past them, drawing ahead as we passed Ryde pier. Now it was the final leg back to the finish off Cowes. We noted our finish time and the sail numbers of the yachts ahead and behind us and texted these to the race committee. They would then have to make allowances for handicaps and work out the overall results.

In the meantime, we'd be heading up the Medina to the Folly Inn for showers and a meal before the water bus for the parties in Cowes and a visit to the club to find out our final position.

As we were sorting out our wash kit, I heard a call, "Ahoy Summer Dreams." Sticking my head out of the hatch, I saw it was Excalibur.

"Hi there. Are you mooring alongside?" I went out on deck, "Nice new mast I see. And you got round without broaching."

"Nice to see you too, Vicky. Well, we weren't handicapped by PeeWee this trip."

I took the line he handed me and passed it round a cleat at the bow then returned it to him to tie off on Excalibur.

Just then Pete came out of the companionway.

"Someone taking my name in vain? Catch," he said, throwing a can of beer to Craig at the helm, "Ben." Another can flew between the two boats. "Ray."

"Cheers Peewee," said Ray. The other two were too busy drinking to answer.

Craig then passed Pete the stern line and they made it secure.

Ben belched when he'd finished his beer. Well, what do you expect from guys? I shuddered at the thought I'd been considered one for nearly twenty years. Well, male, if not a guy.

"I needed that," said Ray.

We arranged to meet them all for a drink at the Folly Inn and see if we could find a table for the nine of us for dinner.

Michaela was no stranger to the Folly and was at ease chatting to the guys from Excalibur at the table. I told her how we'd all met — including Pete having fallen overboard and the SAS reserves connection.

Michaela lowered her voice and recited: *"We are the Pilgrims, master, we shall go always a little further: it may be beyond the last blue mountain barred with snow, Across that angry or that glimmering sea."*

"How the fuck do you know that?" asked Ben "Pardon my French."

I was confused, "what are you talking about?"

"It's the SAS poem inscribed on the clock tower at Stirling Lines," said Pete. "So, come on Michaela, tell us how you know it. Did you have a boyfriend in the regiment?"

"Not exactly. When I lived in London, I saw a poster saying if you joined the reserves they'd train you to parachute. I thought, that sounds fun. So, I applied."

"Not having that. No way would the TA have trained women as parachutists," protested Ray.

"Well, two points. The forces trained plenty of female SOE operatives in the war to parachute like Violette Szabo and Odette Sansom. But, in fact this was well before I transitioned."

"Transitioned, you mean like Vicky?" asked Ray.

"Yes, just like Vicky."

"Fuck me. How many of you are there?" demanded Ben.

"No one actually knows, certainly several thousand in the UK, perhaps tens of thousands."

"Never mind that, come on give with your story," insisted Ray, impatiently.

"Not much to tell to be honest. I signed up in February 68, did the usual bit of running to and from work with a full Bergan on my back, to improve fitness. But I got engaged not long after and started studying for Public Relations qualifications. Then one evening after training, we were in the mess for a drink and the previous group came in having done their parachute course. Every other one of them had a leg or arm in plaster and I wondered if I was doing the sensible thing. So I decided to leave, I only did about ten weeks in all, didn't get badged or anything. I saw one of the others from our intake about a year later. He told me out of the six that had joined the same evening, I'd left and two others had been killed while training. So I was glad I got out when I did. I have nothing but admiration for those of you that get through selection."

"Well, at least you tried and had a good reason to withdraw," conceded Craig raising a glass to her.

Our food arrived at that point so we all tucked into our dinners. We then dropped our wash kit off at the boats and took the water bus into Cowes. First stop was the results centre. We were delighted to find we'd made fourth place in our class in the race. Excalibur had been placed seventh in their class.

We collected our boat's souvenir tankard for having taken part. I offered it to Michaela but she said she already had one from a previous race in the 1980s.

After a few drinks in Cowes, we caught the waterbus back to our yacht. Excalibur's crew and Pete stayed in Cowes for a few more beers.

Personally, I was looking forward to something else when we got back on board. Ensconced in our cabin, Roger and I capped a fabulous day with some gentle lovemaking.

As I lay with Roger snuggled up to my back with his arms around me, his right hand cupping my breast and a finger and thumb playing with the nipple, I sighed.

"What's wrong?" Roger asked.

I turned to look at him. "Nothing, absolutely nothing. I couldn't be happier. I love you so much."

# Chapter 31.  Legally Recognised
## 31st October 2005

During the summer, I continued to visit Mia and I'd done a couple more workshops. The business was expanding, we were bidding again for the schools' contract from next spring and everything looked great.

Mia and I had prepared our applications for Gender Recognition Certificates. They were now ready to post to arrive on the day they would begin considering 'standard' applications; the first six months only dealing with applicants who had transitioned over six years ago.

On 31st October, when I got home, I found a C4 envelope postmarked Leicester on the doormat. When I opened it, I pulled out a blue tinted document. It didn't say much. Simply reference numbers then:

> *Gender Recognition Certificate*
>
> *Name Victoria Dalton*
>
> *Date of Birth 4 March 1983*
>
> *Gender Female*
>
> *Date    27 October 2005*
>
> *The above named person is, from the date of issue, the gender shown.*

I'd been legally female for four days and not even known.

Slumping into a chair in the lounge, I looked at the certificate in disbelief.

I was now legally female. *I was now legally female.* **Female!** I kissed the certificate then jumped up and did a jig. I didn't know whether to cry or laugh.

My celebrations were interrupted by my mobile.

"1462," I answered.

"Vicky, it's Mia. I've got my GRC, it came today."

"That's brilliant news, I got mine too. The Prison Service will have to move you to a female establishment now. If they play silly buggers over it, I'll get in touch with the Director General."

"Got to go, not much credit left on my phonecard."

"OK Mia, I'm thrilled for you. See you next Thursday."

"Thanks Vicky, I look forward to it, and thanks for all your help. Oh, and congratulations on your own GRC."

As soon as I rang off from Mia, I phoned Roger who was running a training session that evening.

"It's come!"

"What?"

"My Gender Recognition Certificate has come. They granted it last Thursday. I'm legally female."

"So, we can get married now?"

"Yes, yes, *Yes!*"

# Chapter 32. Wedding Planning
## 3<sup>rd</sup> November 2005

I'd already collated information about potential venues for our wedding. Mum and Dad wanted a church wedding; but neither Roger nor I were religious so we looked for venues with the character of a church and had found a few potentials.

We took Mum and Dad and Sandra to visit them.

"I can't see any decent venue being available for New Year's Eve, wouldn't it be better to wait until later?" asked Sandra.

"I don't want to wait a day longer than I need to and we'd then get busy again at work," I told her, "but, if we can't find anywhere suitable, maybe I'll need to rethink." I already knew we weren't wasting our time though.

"We might get lucky if there's been a cancellation, or something," added Dad.

"Perhaps," I agreed.

"Well, let's keep our fingers crossed," said Mum.

Roger kept quiet.

The first venue was a Victorian building. Its main room for the ceremony had been a chapel so it sounded ideal but, when we visited, we felt it lacked character.

Orchard Hall, the next venue would have been ideal for a summer wedding but as ours was to be on New Year's Eve, we thought there was a risk the marquee might be cold especially as it involved a short walk in the open from the main building.

Disford Castle was the third location. A grand hall, nearly three storeys high, with stain glass windows in a mock perpendicular gothic style gave the impression of a cathedral. It certainly ticked a number of the boxes. This would have been my reserve choice.

An old Manor House was the fourth venue on our list. The exterior was OK but the interior was bland.

I'd saved my personal favourite to last. It was a converted Victorian Barn next to a hotel. Externally, it wasn't special, but I loved the interior. It had high vaulted ceilings and a glass roof; chandeliers suspended from Oak beams and a Minstrel's Gallery ran around three sides of the main hall. The hall was connected to the hotel by a covered walkway; and the whole was set in about thirty acres of parkland.

It also impressed Mum.

"Now this *is* nice," she'd remarked as we'd walked in through the main doors.

"Oh yes," agreed Sandra.

Dad and Roger had the sense to say nothing but just nod in agreement. They simply had to sign the cheques!

Sandra turned to the Events Coordinator who was showing us around.

"Is it available on New Year's Eve?" she asked.

"Ah, sorry, we already have a provisional booking for that day. I can call the client to see if they've decided yet. They were to let us know by tomorrow. Let me see, it's for a Vicky Dalton. Oh, hang on, that's you isn't it?" she said turning to me.

Four other pairs of eyes looked at me.

I tried to look as innocent as I could, but burst out laughing.

"OK I confess! I came to have a look several months ago and thought it was perfect so put down a deposit. I prayed my GRC would come through in time and kept my fingers crossed that you'd all like it. I didn't say anything before as I thought it might tempt fate."

"Ever had the feeling you've been stitched up, Roger?" asked Dad with a chuckle.

"Most days with Vicky."

With the date and venue organised, we split up responsibilities for different aspects of the day between us. My spreadsheet from the commitment ceremony came back out and a lot more items added.

We decided on an afternoon ceremony followed by the wedding breakfast then a disco in the evening for a wider circle of friends. Dad wanted to pay for the whole wedding and I loved him for making this gesture of acceptance of me as his daughter. But James, Roger's dad, also offered to contribute and Roger and I insisted on covering the cost of the evening disco.

Sandra was to be my Matron of Honour with Katie and Claire as bridesmaids and Oliver as page boy. Roger asked Pete to be best man which surprised me as I thought he might want one of his longer term friends but they'd become close since Pete's apology after the rescue. Sandra's husband, Ian and three friends from the Blue Peach were ushers.

The venue would take care of the ceremony and reception other than the flowers for the hall. Sandra volunteered to look after those and organise the bouquets and button holes. My mum and Barbara, Roger's mum, would liaise over the invitation list. I'd given Mum names of personal friends we wanted to invite.

Mum, Sandra and I returned to the boutique where I'd bought the dress for the commitment ceremony. I chose a white strapless Empire Line with sweetheart neckline and a sweep train. The back had lacing and it had very pretty beading below the bust. To keep me warm between venues, I ordered a white faux fur stole to go with it. I didn't feel any guilt at all about wearing white. I may not be a virgin on the day but Roger had been the only man I'd ever made love with and it was he, after all, who had taken my virginity not just once but twice.

Sandra's dress was a full length with V neck in burgundy. Katie and Claire's were calf length in gold so their colours reflected the overall wedding theme. Oliver had a navy waistcoat and shorts suit with a white shirt and navy bow tie, socks and shoes.

I left Roger to organise the men's outfits. I didn't ask what he had in mind though I heard he was planning morning dress complete with top hats. Mum and Barbara were talking to ensure their outfits didn't clash. So far, so good. I was much more excited than I'd expected to be. I'd thought as we'd already had one ceremony this might be an anti-climax, but far from it. This felt like the culmination of everything I'd ever dreamed of — well, almost everything. I'd never be able to bear children which would have been the ultimate dream.

# Chapter 33. I Do!

## 31st December 2005

New Year's Eve dawned with heavy snow falling. A white blanket covered the grounds of the park in which the hotel and hall stood — how much more magical could it get?

Roger, of course, hadn't been permitted to stop at the hotel. He and Pete were at the house.

After a light breakfast, I didn't want any last minute bulges spoiling the look of my dress, Sandra and I headed for the beauty salon for the complete works. Mum and Barbara, the two bridesmaids and Oliver would come along later for their hairdos.

Back at the hotel, a relaxing cup of tea and a sandwich kept us going then it was time to get dressed.

"Wow," was all Dad could utter when he saw me. "You look beautiful, darling," he finally added before kissing me on the cheek. He made me feel so special.

With four inch heels, I was concerned about the walk from the hotel to the Barn even if it was covered. But instead of heading for the linkway, Dad took my arm and led me to the main entrance to the hotel. Outside was a horse drawn open sleigh.

"The venue has this for when it can be used. If there hadn't been any snow then it would have been an open carriage," Dad explained. "The bride absolutely has to arrive in style!"

I had a lump in my throat and was speechless as tears formed. I prayed I wasn't going to make my mascara run! I'd thought the day couldn't get any more magical but I'd been mistaken.

It was only fifty yards from the hotel entrance to the Hall but the sleigh took a turn around the gardens before stopping at the Barn. As I entered the foyer, Sandra, the bridesmaids and pageboy were waiting for me. Little Katie beamed at me and did a twirl to show off her dress. Oliver looked a bit confused and picked his nose.

Sandra took my stole then handed me my bouquet before lowering my veil and straightening my train then taking her position behind me. I put my arm through Dad's and, as the traditional Bridal Chorus sounded, we walked down the aisle. As I reached him, Roger turned and smiled. Although I didn't believe in any supreme being, I said a prayer of thanks to the universe for the man standing next to me. Nobody could ever have felt happier than I did at that moment.

Roger and I had discussed the exchange of rings part of the ceremony. We'd already done this at the commitment — so should we repeat it using the same rings or get new rings? As far as we were concerned our marriage had started at the earlier ceremony and neither of us wanted to replace the rings we'd used then. But nor had we wanted to remove the rings we'd already placed on each other's fingers. We decided we'd leave the rings on and for the 'with this ring I, thee, wed,' we would hold the ring on our partner's finger.

The officiator finally announced, "I now pronounce you man and wife." The legal aspects had, at last, caught up with what Roger and I had felt for more than a year. As we kissed, I felt as though I would explode with happiness.

The weak wintery sun was already setting as we went outside for photographs. We needed to hurry if we weren't all going to freeze. We did, however, include some with Roger and me in the sleigh and I was very glad of my stole.

Then it was back into the Hall to greet our guests. I was delighted to see Michaela had travelled down from Manchester to join us. I was also very glad the whole family, including Pete, who had missed the commitment, were here for our special day. He gave me a warm hug and whispered "I'm so sorry for having been such an arsehole when you came out. But you are a beautiful woman Vicky and I'm proud to be your brother." I kissed him on the cheek.

"That means so much, Pete. Thank you."

The celebrations continued culminating in bringing in the New Year as midnight rang out.

# Chapter 34.  Honeymoon
## 1st – 21st January 2006

Roger hadn't told me where we were going for our honeymoon; only that I needed to be prepared for the beach and for chilly mornings and evenings plus some hot days travelling. He'd had me sign visa application forms without letting me see the countries. He also organised vaccinations. I realised from the injections we could be heading for a tropical area. But I wouldn't have put it past Roger to throw in a few red herrings to confuse me. I noticed, though, he had sorted out his camera and lenses, including a long telephoto zoom — which had me wondering if it would include wildlife photography? A safari, perhaps?

After a leisurely breakfast with our parents, who'd also stopped after the wedding, we returned home and swopped my wedding suitcase for our holiday luggage. Roger carried me over the threshold, as tradition required for a new bride. We then drove to a hotel near Heathrow that offered parking and a shuttle service to the terminal.

When we got to the terminal the next morning and joined the check in queue for BA65 to Nairobi, Roger revealed our plans. We were to have eight days on safari at Treetops, Navaisha and a lodge in the Masai Mara then nine days at the beach at Mombassa and a final couple of days in Tanzania where we'd see the wildebeest migration and Kilimanjaro. It sounded incredible.

The flight arrived in Nairobi on time and we joined the passport control queue — the Immigration Officer greeted us with a huge grin — "Jambo! Kuwakaribisha Kenya, hello, welcome to Kenya."

"Asante sana," replied Roger. I looked at him in amazement. He winked at me, then whispered "It means thank you very much."

"Have you been to Kenya before?" asked the official as he looked at our passports.

"Once when I was a child," Roger told him.

"Never," I told him. "I'm really looking forward to it."

"I hope you enjoy your stay madam, bwana." He handed back our passports duly stamped.

"I'm sure we will. Thank you."

It was too late to get to Treetops that evening so we checked into a hotel in Nairobi for the night. After a light supper from room service, we went to bed. I was shattered. It had been a long day — waking up at six am and it was now a little after midnight local time or nine pm in the UK. The furthest I'd flown before had been our trip to Paris. Now here I was in the southern hemisphere albeit only by about eighty miles. According to a leaflet I found in the room, we were 4,237 miles from London. The flight itself had taken less than nine hours — but from leaving the hotel in UK to checking in here had taken us thirteen hours.

But once Roger and I got into bed, I somehow found some more energy. Well it was our honeymoon and we could sleep late tomorrow — or so I thought.

"Come and look at this view, darling," I told Roger when I drew the curtains the following morning. A magnificent splash of blue-covered trees was spread out over the gardens.

"They're Jacaranda trees, spectacular aren't they?"

"They look fabulous."

"It's about three hours to Aberdare. We have to leave our main suitcases at the Outspan Hotel and take the equivalent of an airline cabin bag each to Treetops. The rooms are small, what you might call 'compact and bijoux'. We've got a couple of places to visit en route."

"Oh?" I remarked.

"Mmm. You remember watching 'Out of Africa' the other week?"

"The Karen Blixen story?"

"That's the one, well our first stop is to see her house."

I'd been really taken with the film and Meryl Steep's and Robert Redford's performances. Seeing where it had been set would be a real treat.

"Where's the next stop?"

"Wait and see."

I could see Roger was determined to keep me on tenterhooks on this trip and only reveal details slowly. Not that I minded, it felt like Christmas, gradually unwrapping presents.

Karen Blixen's House was amazing. I was standing where they had made the film. Actually inside the sets (well, almost, they'd used the exterior in the film but they'd had to recreate the interiors in studios to allow space for the cameras — but it was still very exciting). I could visualise Karen and Denys talking in the lounge.

A few minutes after leaving Karen Blixen's House we pulled into an enclosure; a tall building with a veranda running along one side overlooked a paddock; and I got my first view of African animals, giraffes. We climbed up to the veranda which brought us to a comfortable head height for the giraffes. They came up to us and these gentle giants licked our hands, searching for food. They'd given us little pails of pellets which the giraffes took from us. Their gorgeous dark brown eyes looked at us as we stroked them and offered them the pellets. It was an incredible experience and I couldn't comprehend how anyone could kill such a lovely thing. Yet I remembered seeing a photograph of a hunter sitting by one she had shot, looking very pleased with herself.

I'd thought at the time how contemptible I thought she was. Touching one of these fascinating beasts reinforced that feeling. How could anyone think they'd achieved anything by killing a defenceless animal?

I could almost understand the macho need to 'prove' yourself by stalking a dangerous animal like a lion on foot; though it would be much more impressive if they took the shot with a camera rather than a rifle, especially when there were professional hunters ready to deal with the beast if the client failed or the prey threatened the client. As far as I was concerned, those people were utterly beyond the pale.

I must have shown how I was feeling because Roger turned to me.

"What's up?"

"I remembered that article we saw about someone having shot a giraffe. It upsets me to think of one of these lovely creatures being hunted just to satisfy her warped sense of achievement."

He pulled me to him and hugged me and the giraffe I'd been feeding stretched its head towards me and licked my forehead — it seemed to say 'thanks for caring.' In fact, it was probably attracting my attention to get more treats.

I stroked its nose and gave it some more pellets.

"Come on, time we were going."

I emptied my bucket of pellets where the giraffes could reach them, slipped my arm around Roger's waist and we returned to the minibus for our drive to Aberdare.

The traffic was horrendous with vehicles overtaking on blind bends showing a fatalistic attitude to survival. We passed several lorries and cars at the side of the road, the result of accidents, and a bus that had overturned. I didn't think there would have been much chance for the passengers and I held on to Roger, though what good that would do in a crash I had no idea! I was very relieved when we pulled off the main road and into the Outspan Hotel grounds.

We arrived in time for lunch. The staff removed our main cases from the minibus and stored them in the luggage room.

We had time to wander around the gardens where Roger and I found a small museum dedicated to Scouting in a cottage in the grounds. A board at the entrance informed us the cottage, called Paxtu, had been the retirement home of Lord Baden-Powell, founder of the Scout movement, and his wife, Lady Olave who had been the first Chief Guide. Although I hadn't been as keen a scout as Peter (I'd have preferred to have been a guide), I was still fascinated by the exhibits. Roger then revealed he had also been a scout.

"Baden-Powell is buried in a cemetery in the local town. Do you know what's on his gravestone?" he asked.

"Yes, it's the tracking symbol of a circle with a dot in the middle which means 'gone home'."

"Not just a pretty face are you?"

I put my arm around Roger and pulled him to me for a kiss.

It wasn't far from Outspan to Treetops hotel so we soon pulled up to what appeared to be a ramshackle construction. It was an L shape with a tower where the two legs met. The other end of the main leg (the vertical stroke of the L) was constructed around a tree.

A member of Treetops staff climbed onto the mini bus.

"Kuwakaribisha Treetops, Welcome to Treetops. My name is Joseph. If you will follow me, we have drinks for you in the bar where we will give you information about the hotel then give you your room keys."

We picked up our overnight bag and got off the minibus and followed Joseph. The bar had branches coming up through the floor and disappearing through the ceiling — well-padded with fleeces to protect heads and limbs.

A waitress offered us glasses of wine or orange juice, then Joseph attracted our attention once more.

"Again, welcome to Treetops. It's famous as the lodge Princess Elizabeth was visiting when she heard her father had died and she was now Queen. This isn't, in fact, the original hotel. Sadly, that one burned down in 1954. The hotel was rebuilt around the same waterhole you can see."

"There are several hides at ground level and the viewing platforms in the building. We have a number of animals that visit. A buzzer rings in your rooms when we get visitors during the night. There are from one to five rings depending on the animal at the waterhole — you can switch off the buzzer if you prefer."

"We also offer game drives including the popular Sundowner drive. This takes you to one of the high points in the park for drinks while the sun sets. Animals you might see include black rhino, leopard, elephant, and buffalo. There are also spotted hyena, the sykes, colobus and black-faced vervet monkeys. If you are lucky, you might even see rarer bongo antelope and the giant forest hog."

Porters had taken our overnight bags to our rooms for us so we went up to freshen ourselves then joined the Sundowner Game drive.

We climbed into 4X4s which then set off along the tracks. We hadn't gone far before the Toyota Landcruiser stopped. I saw buffaloes emerging from the bush to our left.

"Look darling, buffalos. Those horns are scary."

"They're one of the most dangerous animals in Africa and are reputed to ambush hunters following them," said the driver. "They're one of the 'Big Five' animals people try to see or hunt."

"What are the others?" I asked.

"Black rhino, lion, leopard and elephant."

"Which are we likely to see here?"

"Elephants and if you are lucky black rhino and leopard."

"Are they likely to attack us in the vehicle?"

"It's unlikely but you can never tell."

I hugged Roger closer.

The driver put the vehicle into gear and we drove a little further, emerging on the side of a valley. Over the other side, we could see a herd of elephants in the distance.

I squeezed Roger's arm.

"This is so fabulous. Thank you darling."

He was busy focussing a long lens on the distant herd but took his eyes away from the camera to give me a quick kiss, then concentrated on photographing the elephants — or ephalumps as we nicknamed them.

We eventually emerged onto the top of a grass covered hill. The lack of trees gave us a clear 360 degree view. Benches were scattered around and we were told we would be safe walking around but to stay in the cleared area.

I felt nervous knowing we were out in the open when our driver had told us how dangerous the buffalo were and there might also be leopards around. The views from the top of the hillock soon made me forget my concerns; though clouds in the distance concealed the peaks of Mount Kenya.

"When they settled the border between German East Africa and Kenya, they bent it around Kilimanjaro so each territory had one of the two highest peaks in Africa," explained our guide. "Please come and help yourself to drinks from the table for our sundowners."

We needed no second invitation. The peace of the place was disturbed only by the buzzing of insects as we watched the sun settle below the horizon.

Back at the hotel, we stood outside on the veranda overlooking the waterhole.

Roger gripped my arm and pointed.

"Elephants coming to drink," he said

They were soon joined by some warthogs and antelope, which were skittish; constantly watching for predators.

The dinner gong sounded and we took our places at the table.

Another couple were already seated as we joined them.

"Where are you folks from? My name is Dan, this is my wife Patty."

"Hi, nice to meet you. My name is Roger and this is my wife Vicky. We're from Bournemouth on the south coast of England. How about yourselves?"

"We now live in Texarkana — on the border of Texas and Arkansas, but Patty was born in the UK. We met when I was over there with the US Air Force based at Bentwaters flying A10 Thunderbolts."

"Warthogs? Not the prettiest of aircraft but I gather they were very effective," Roger responded.

"You know your aircraft, fella."

"My father was in the RAF so I grew up with an interest though I was still young when he left the service."

"What about you? What do you do?"

"I run a sailing business, chartering, training, and a chandlers."

"And you, pretty lady? Do you work or do you let your husband do what men should do and provide for the family?"

The hairs on the back of my neck prickled with the patronising attitude of the American but he wasn't going spoil such a perfect day.

"I work with Roger, we share responsibilities in the company," I turned to his wife. "Is this your first time in Kenya, Patty?"

"Yes, first time anywhere in Africa in fact."

"Same here."

After dinner, Dan and Patty attached themselves to us as we went out on to the veranda again. The smoke from Dan's cigar drifted over us so I moved upwind. Like so many ex-smokers I now hated the smell of tobacco smoke, particularly cigars.

Some antelope were drinking but seemed particularly skittish.

"Reminds me of going hunting as a boy with my daddy," commented Dan. "Would love to get a lion in my sights. You ever hunted, Roger?"

"Certainly not. I think killing animals for sport is disgusting," Roger replied. He was obviously as irritated by Dan as I was and not prepared to hold back on his views.

"It's one of man's natural traits right back to caveman days."

"Hunting for food may be one thing — but for sport is indefensible."

"Rubbish, it contributes to conservation. Hunters pay good money to hunt. That goes into the local economy and supports other work. Hunters are committed conservationists. As well as being able to demonstrate they are real men."

"That's utter nonsense. If someone wants to show how brave they are, then let them track the animal on foot then shoot it with a camera and contribute the same fee to conservation work," I said, Dan's attitude all evening had irritated me and I could no longer hide my views. It was a shame because I quite liked his wife.

"Come on Roger. Let's get some rest I'm sure there will be more to see later. It was nice to meet *you* Patty," I added.

During the night, the buzzer sounded several times and we jumped out of bed to go down to the viewing platform. When it sounded again about 4am, signalling another elephant at the waterhole, the fifth such visitor, we rolled over and went back to sleep.

The next morning, we avoided the table where Dan and Patty were sitting but we could still hear him expressing his macho republican views. I thanked the heavens they weren't on our tour.

After collecting our main bags from Outspan, our minibus hit the road again. Once more the traffic was chaotic. Our minibus weaved to avoid potholes even if it meant switching from the left side of the road to the right — while other vehicles just ran parallel up to fifty yards from the carriageway.

I was relieved when we pulled off for a break as I was beginning to wonder if we'd survive the trip.

"This is where the road crosses the Equator," announced Benjamin, our driver in that precise English taught to tour guides the world over.

"You'll see signs that mark the exact point. We'll stop here for forty minutes for a break and for you to take photographs if you wish. There is a café which has toilets but I advise you to take tissue with you."

"Stand with one foot either side of the line," I told Roger as he stood in front of a sign announcing we were now on the equator. We then watched locals showing how water in a bucket with a small hole in the base flowed out clockwise one side of the line and anti-clockwise if moved to the other side of the Equator.

Then it was back on the minibus for the next leg to Lake Navaisha. Paved roads soon gave way to dirt tracks and we left a dust cloud in our wake as we drove along. It wasn't the most comfortable of journeys as we were bounced around and I was very glad when we reached our destination and I could stretch my legs.

At the lake, we were given lifejackets then climbed onto long narrow boats for a trip on the water.

"Lake Navaisha is at the highest point in the Kenyan Rift Valley. Two rivers feed the lake and although it has no visible outlet, there must be an underground outlet, as the water remains fresh and, if it were evaporating, it would become salt," our guide informed us. "Joy Adamson, author of 'Born Free' lived over there in the mid-1960s." He pointed towards the shore. "Over four hundred species of birds have been identified here including one of the largest groups of flamingos. In the 1930s and 40s, flying boats used the lake as a landing place on the route between Britain and South Africa."

"Ooh, look at that cluster of islands over there with the birds sitting on them," I said to Roger. Then one sank – leaving me feeling foolish.

"They aren't islands, they're hippos," he laughed. "Over on the shore, there's a herd of wildebeest."

"And are those some of the flamingos?" I asked, as a flock of five long necked and legged pink birds flew over us.

"They are," he replied. "There are more over there — and there, and there."

"And, look at that pelican. It's scattering everything else out of its way as it tries to take off."

The  tips of its huge wings barely cleared the water on their downbeat as it seemed to run across the surface, eventually managing to scramble its way in to the air. I could imagine it yelling 'Gangway' at any other birds in its path.

"This is fabulous, I don't know which way to look, there's so much to see."

Back at the hotel, as we reviewed the photographs we'd taken, we couldn't believe the number of pictures we'd shot and the memories we'd already captured.

The next morning, we left Lake Navaisha for the drive to our hotel in the Masai Mara.

"Our trip today should take between five and six hours. Most of it will be on tarmac roads but the last hour, once we enter the Masai Mara reserve, will be on dirt tracks," Benjamin informed us.

After about four hours, we turned off the tarmac road and stopped at a Ranger control post which marked the entrance to the Masai Mara. I gripped Roger's arm anticipating the wildlife we could expect to see.

As Benjamin had warned, the road was now a dirt track. He had opened the roof of the minibus so we could stand up and take photographs. As we drove along, the orange dust we'd come to expect was stripping the varnish off my nails. The landscape was huge. Miles and miles of plains spotted with occasional thorny 'stay awhile' Acacia trees and strips of other trees marking the river courses; stretching to distant indigo mountains at the edge of the rift valley, all under brilliant blue skies.

We'd missed the main wildebeest migration; it was now back on the Serengeti in neighbouring Tanzania, where we'd catch up with it later in the trip, but we still saw a few stragglers.

"Oh look, a Zebra Crossing," joked Roger as one of them crossed the road ahead of us.

I rolled my eyes and nudged him in the ribs with my elbow.

Over the next few miles, we stopped to check out elephants, giraffes and antelopes ranging from large eland to the diminutive dik dik, barely the size of a small dog. Crossing river courses, we saw crocodiles sunning themselves on the banks while other animals nervously drank less than a dozen yards away.

At the hotel the staff welcomed us with hot towels to remove the dust of the road then showed us to our rooms. They led us down a footpath, through the gardens and past a series of individual lodges. Overhead the chirping of tree frogs and insects was set against the rustling of the wind. Butterflies and small birds flitted from flower to flower and tree to tree. Colourful lizards scuttled out of our way as we passed.

I thought back to our little garden in England where we could see squirrels playing; and perhaps a hedgehog would visit; where tits and finches might raid the bird feeders while gulls, pigeons and magpies swooped down onto the lawn for larger titbits. That, then, took me back to my little flat in south London where I'd be lucky to even catch sight of pigeons.

After refreshing ourselves, we dressed for the evening game drive in warm long-sleeved tops and trousers and broad brimmed hats or baseball caps to keep the sun out of our eyes and walked back through the gardens to the waiting 4 by 4. Roger and I were sharing the vehicle with another couple, Terry and Fiona from Northampton. Our guide and driver introduced himself as Gideon, which he said meant Great Warrior. As he was Masai, he said his name was very appropriate. I was a bit disappointed that he wasn't dressed in the traditional tribal costume but his safari jacket, trousers and bush hat were undoubtedly more suitable for driving in.

We'd hardly left the lodge when we stopped.

"Lion," whispered Gideon, pointing to a male lying next to some bushes. "We call it Simba in Swahili."

Four camera lenses swung towards the prone lion. Four cameras clicked rapidly as frame after frame was recorded.

"Look the other side," Gideon instructed.

"What are we looking at?" asked Fiona. Then I realised. Right at the side of the vehicle a female had come and laid down in the shade.

"Down there, Fiona," I said. She jumped back when she saw the lioness was only a couple of feet from her.

We sat there watching the two lions for several minutes before Gideon received a radio message that one of the other guides had seen a cheetah nearby.

He started the engine, causing the lioness to stand up and move away in disgust and those of us in the vehicle took our seats. He headed west, the sunlight striking the front windscreen of the 4x4.

On the way, Gideon pointed out other animals and told us their Swahili names: elephants were ndovu, giraffes: turiga, zebra: punda mitia, wildebeest: nyumbu and a dozen others that I've forgotten already. He was reluctant to stop though as these were common sights we could see at any time and he wanted to get us to the cheetah.

As we approached the reported sighting, Gideon slowed the vehicle and we had our first glimpse of the cheetah as it strode along next to the track ignoring us.

"Duma," Gideon announced pointing at it.

It looked magnificent, its whole body a sleek hunting machine with toned muscles tensed ready to spring into action. It leapt effortlessly onto a fallen tree and climbed to the highest branch to search the surrounding savannah for prey, its head slowly moving from side to side. At one point its dark brown eyes stared straight at us in the 4x4 before continuing to scan the plain — having discounted us as its dinner.

I have no idea how long we tracked that cheetah — nor how many photographs we took of it. We would drive a couple of hundred yards along the track; then stop and wait for it to walk past us; we'd overtake it again and repeat the exercise. Eventually, Gideon told us we had to return to the hotel as we were not allowed outside the compound after sunset. It was already getting chilly as the sun settled on the horizon and the effect of being at about 2,000 metres so we were thankful for our layers of clothing.

It had been a long day and I was shattered but I wouldn't have missed it for the world. The Masai Mara had already lived up to its reputation for incredible sights.

That night, as I lay in Roger's arms, I reflected, once more, on my life. Just thirty months ago I'd been hemmed in by four walls I could almost touch from my lonely bed. I'd had a job that was OK, but nothing special. Few friends, in fact no real friends, just colleagues. I'd spent as much time as possible finding the odd few hours here and there to dress — building an insurmountable wall to hide my true self behind the rest of the time. Scared stiff of being discovered and the dreadful consequences I expected to ensue. Scraping to make ends meet and leave enough to fund my secret lifestyle.

Thinking about my tiny bedsit on Clapham Road made me reflect on Mia. I imagined her in her cell in prison and the difficulties she'd been through. I shuddered when I remembered how I'd risked shoplifting to acquire some expensive make-up and, on one occasion, a bottle of perfume (admittedly only the sample spray) not to mention some lingerie. I could so easily have been caught and found myself behind bars like Mia.

How was it I had been so fortunate while she'd ended up in prison?

How had I gone from trying to take my own life to lying in the arms of someone who loved me?

How could I possibly now be on honeymoon in the Masai Mara?

If there was a purpose to life — what was mine that would deserve such riches?

I didn't accept I merited such good fortune and struggled to believe it would last.

Perhaps this was part of a perverse plan of an unforgiving God to show me immense happiness before tearing it away again as punishment for being an abomination, as the Bible said of crossdressers.

That awful thought sent a shudder down my spine.

"What's up?" asked Roger.

"I'm so happy I'm scared it can't last. I have this dreadful thought something will go wrong. I know I don't deserve you or what I have. I don't understand why you love me or even why you approached me in the dunes."

"Nothing will go wrong if I can help it. Does it matter why I love you? Isn't it enough that I do?"

"I know I'm being silly. But it's how I feel."

I knew it all came from being indoctrinated from an early age — boys are boys and girls are girls and that's how they should stay. All the biblical teachings about men lying with men and cross-dressing — not that I believe any of that stuff anyway. But even without religious crap, the way anyone who is different is considered abnormal or perverted.

"I know I've done things in the past I'm ashamed of and I deserve to be punished not rewarded."

"You've also been the victim in that though. Was it your fault your brain was female but your body was male? No. Even if you believed in religion, what do they regard as the most important, the body or the soul?"

I knew where he was going with this but played along.

"The soul, of course."

"And is your soul, your innermost being, male or female?"

"Well, I know not everyone thinks souls have a gender but if they do then it's female."

"Right, so, if the soul is more important than the body, are you male or female?"

"Female."

"So do those rules about cross-dressing or men lying with men apply? How can they? What religious rules have you broken that would invite retribution?"

"When you put it like that, I haven't. It still doesn't stop a lot of people thinking otherwise and I still worry about being outed especially in places where discrimination against LGBT people is common."

I knew there were places in the world where I wouldn't be accepted as female and our relationship would be seen as homosexual and punishable by death.

"Who cares what other people think? OK, so same sex relationships are illegal here in Kenya but you *are* female. Your passport says female. Your birth certificate says female. Your body is female — and I should know, darling. Everyone we've met treats you as female."

"I know. I said I was being silly."

I turned to face Roger, "Which brings me back to the question of why you love me. Why would someone like you love someone as silly as me?"

"Because you are not actually silly. Oh, I know you play the part at times but I think that's because you expect people to ridicule you, so you give them something to laugh at to deflect the hurt."

He was right, of course. If they were laughing at my antics, they weren't laughing at the real me.

"When I first saw you near the dunes, you intrigued me," he continued, "You were dressed as a guy but I saw your bikini under your t-shirt so I followed you. I wondered what you planned to do. When you got undressed, I thought you looked gorgeous and I fancied you. I thought you were incredibly brave to sunbathe in that orange bikini."

"Incredibly brave or incredibly silly?" I asked, realising, as I did so, I was doing exactly what Roger had said I did. I wished I could be like Michaela in Manchester with her obvious self-assurance but, then, she'd had 20 years of transition to develop her confidence. Maybe I'd get there one day.

"Whatever. When we talked, I wanted to protect and help you as you were obviously nervous. I had other friends who were trans, as you know, so it didn't bother me. The more we chatted the more I wanted to get to know you. There was something underneath I liked. You were intelligent and it took courage to do what you were doing. But I sensed a vulnerability I wanted to protect."

"Like my knight in shining armour?" I rather liked that image, me on the balcony of a turret with Roger climbing a creeper to reach me. I snuggled further into the security of his arms as he pulled fondled my hair.

"Maybe. Then, when you took my hand when I offered it to help you up, and held onto it as we ran into the sea, the way you responded to my kiss made me wonder how far you were prepared to go. But I also found myself not pushing things more than you wanted — which was unusual for me."

"So you picked up lots of strange girls did you?"

"A few. Some of the single girls on holiday wanted a fling while there and lots of the local lads happily obliged. But you were different."

"That's true."

He pulled his head away from mine and looked into my eyes. It was dark in the bedroom but I could still see that he was deadly serious.

"Well, yes, but that's not the way I meant. I'd experimented when I was bit younger with boys and girls and decided I preferred girls and, despite what you had between your legs, that's how I saw you. The aura you emitted was definitely female not male. I wanted to help you bring that out."

I thought back to my suicide attempt when, after two weeks of living as Vicky, I knew I couldn't go back to being David and couldn't see a future worth living.

"You certainly did that, nearly with disastrous consequences."

"Yes, and I was devastated when I realised you planned to kill yourself. When I recognised I couldn't face living without you, it made me face the fact I loved you."

"I still don't know why though."

"Because you are you. You are a beautiful woman. You have a fabulous smile. You make me feel good about myself. We laugh at the same jokes, we share a lot of the same interests.

I was about to object to his compliments but he put a finger to my lips so I shut up.

"As I said you're very intelligent and brave; you contribute a great deal to the business and the rest of the staff look up to you. We work well together and complement each other. Yet I still see some of that vulnerability which means I can still be your knight in shining armour and feel needed."

I was going to get a big head if he carried on much more but his words gave me a warm glow. He was obviously prejudiced, but if that's what he thought of me, then I wasn't going to object. I sighed as he continued:

"You are also a very caring person; you're loyal to your friends. You put others first even if you don't feel comfortable doing it — just look at how you befriended Mia. One of the other girls at the group said if you were a stick of rock, there would be 'helping others' running all through it and she's spot on."

Shit. Had someone really said that about me? I mean I do try to help people but sometimes wonder if some of the other girls see me as a do-gooder and are catty about me behind my back. I was a bit sceptical about Roger's comments and felt embarrassed at all the compliments but I loved hearing him reassuring me. He held my chin in his hand and kissed me lightly on the lips.

"You're also pretty good in bed. And I'm so glad you agreed to become my wife. I am so proud to be your husband. I'm the one with the good fortune."

I didn't know whether to cry or smile, so fastened my lips onto his and pulled him on top of me as I rolled onto my back.

All too soon, it was time to leave the Masai Mara. Having packed our bags, we had a last breakfast then climbed into the 4x4 for a final game drive on our way to the airport.

Well, I say 'airport' but it was little more than a dirt strip carved out of the scrub. It did, it is true, claim to offer the usual facilities.

The Duty Free Shop (it proudly announced its role on the top of the walls visible from where we stood) was a single storey construction about twenty feet long by ten deep made from corrugated roofing panels. The departure lounge had a thatched roof supported on eight round posts to give shade and benches providing a dozen or so places. Next to it, the security office was the most robustly constructed — it was about ten feet long by six deep, the lower third of the walls were made of mud bricks; the remainder was wooden, again with a thatched roof.

As for the toilet, it was a ramshackle shack, if that's not making it sound too well constructed, over a hole in the ground. The smell was appalling even from ten feet away and you needed to be absolutely desperate to use the facility. I wasn't that desperate. A few others got as close as the door before deciding they could probably wait until they got on board the aircraft.

I expected the airstrip to cater only to small aircraft so I was very surprised to see a four-engine plane approach overhead. Someone identified it as a Dash-7 and said it took fifty passengers.

"I hope those wildebeest clear the runway before the aircraft lands," Roger said pointing to some animals in the distance.

I watched the plane lining up with the runway as he spoke. I had visions of a serious accident and, as far as I could see, there were no emergency vehicles around to help. But, instead of landing, the pilot flew low along the runway, scattering the intruders and clearing the strip, before making another circuit and touching down. I realised I'd been holding my breath as it had made its final approach and landed and I exhaled in relief. I wouldn't like to imagine the consequence of 20 tonnes of aircraft colliding with 130 kilos of wildebeest at around 100 mph. I was certain it would be curtains for the animal but there would be serious damage to the aircraft too.

A group of schoolchildren, all in uniform but barefoot, had arrived at the airstrip. I thought at first they were going on a trip but they were there to greet the aircraft. As it taxied in. they waved and I could see the pilot wave back to them. That produced bright white smiles on their faces.

I nudged Roger. "Those children seem excited at the sight of the plane."

"I'm not surprised. I was the same at their age. When we were at Wittering, we'd cycle to the end of the runway and watch the Harriers flying back in to land."

As we took our seats on the Dash-7, I was glad we were on the side nearest to the children and I returned their waves when we prepared to leave. Once the engines started and the aircraft turned to taxi to the runway, the backwash hit the children who turned their backs to us for protection. As we took off, I could see the children returning to their coach, presumably to return to their lessons.

Our flights to Nairobi, then onward to Mombasa, were uneventful. The final leg by coach meant we arrived at the hotel about ten pm. As we entered the reception area, the staff greeted us with hot towels and glasses of refreshing orange juice.

"Good evening ladies and gentlemen, welcome to the Nyali Beach Resort. My name is Sarah. Please leave your luggage here and we will have it transferred to your rooms while you enjoy the buffet in the restaurant. Please collect your room key from reception and identify your bags for our porters."

Sarah then led us into the restaurant where we found a central island with dozens of cold dishes for us to choose from.

Above us natural branches and tree trunks supported the high roof like a wooden version of a vaulted cathedral.

"I hope nothing falls into the food," I whispered to Roger, pointing up at monkeys running around in the upper reaches of the roof. "But isn't this room fabulous?"

"It's incredible."

Once we'd all served ourselves, Sarah addressed us again.

"Ladies and gentlemen, this is one of four restaurants in the resort. It's where we serve breakfast and is one of the options for dinner each evening. It offers a carvery and buffet dinner, buffet lunch and afternoon tea and is part of your 'all inclusive' package. We also offer an Italian dining experience which is also in the 'all inclusive' package. Two other restaurants offer à la carte alternatives. There is entertainment in the courtyard outside this restaurant each evening which you are welcome to attend. If you have any questions, please contact reception or any member of staff. Thank you and I hope you enjoy your stay with us."

After dinner, we took our drinks outside and sat enjoying the balmy night, listening to the tree frogs croaking away and the sound of the surf on the beach barely fifty yards away. Overhead the full moon looked close enough to touch and millions of stars twinkled away.

"Make a wish," I told Roger.

"What?"

"Look, shooting stars, make a wish."

"Have you wished?" he asked.

"Oh yes."

"What did you wish?"

"I can't tell you, or it won't come true." In fact, I'd wished Roger never tired of me. I snuggled into his arms.

"Come on, let's find our room," I said.

As promised, the porters had delivered our cases to the room. We left the unpacking until the morning. All I took out was my washbag and nightie before brushing my teeth and cleansing my face.

I'm not sure why I bothered unpacking my nightie as Roger pounced as soon as I had undressed. Not that I was complaining in the least.

"*Wow!*" I heard Roger declare as he stood by the window the next morning.

"Come and look at this view," he told me.

Immediately outside our window a path separated us from an infinity pool. Beyond the pool was the beach which gave way to the deep blue of the Indian Ocean. A dive boat sat at anchor off shore, its canopy fluttering in the morning breeze and waves splitting either side of its bow. About a mile further out, there was a line of surf where the waves broke over a reef. A brilliant blue, cloudless, sky capped it all.

Hearing swimmers in the pool reminded me I was standing in front of the window stark naked so I dived back into the room.

"Close the curtains quickly," I shrieked.

Thankfully, I don't think anyone saw me.

After breakfast we walked down to the dive school next to the beach. Roger was already qualified as an Open Water Diver and he'd booked me on the course while he planned to do his Advanced certificate.

I discovered my training would entail almost full time study for five days. It involved theory, being tested on a section of the handbook each day, and practical sessions in one of the swimming pools. It really didn't sound like a relaxing holiday, but I had always wanted to learn to dive. Initial practice sessions under a tropical sky followed by diving on a colourful reef sounded so much more attractive than the local council swimming pool followed by a flooded quarry and scrapped vehicles back in the UK.

We were taught the importance of controlled ascents and decompression stops to prevent DCS, decompression sickness or 'the bends'.

"For every ten metres you descend, the pressure on the body increases by one atmosphere," Donna, our instructor, informed us. "So, at ten metres the pressure is doubled, at twenty metres it's three times the pressure at the surface. Under pressure, the tissues absorb nitrogen and we have to allow it to gradually come out again as we return to the surface."

185

We learned to calculate safe 'bottom times' at various depths and 'surface times' before it was safe to dive again depending on our previous dives and take account of residual nitrogen absorption for second or subsequent dives.

After dinner, we went out into the courtyard for the entertainment including, one night, an evening of games such as 'musical chairs'. By the time the original twenty or so participants had been whittled down to six, including me, it was getting competitive, with the various tables cheering on anyone from their group still in the game. Somehow I survived until it was only two of us left. My opponent was a Frenchman and the old rivalry between the two nations divided the audience into two camps. As the music stopped, the seat of the one remaining chair was pointing away from me but I grabbed the back of the chair and twisted it round and sat down.

"You cheated, madame," protested my opponent petulantly. It was musical chairs; cheating was allowed if not compulsory!

The next morning it was back to the dive school. I enjoyed learning the technical aspects and Alison, another of the students, and myself, found ourselves in a friendly competition during each of the day's tests. It was rare for either of us to get more than one answer wrong. One day I'd slip up, the next day she'd do so. On the final day of theory, we had to sit a written exam and score at least 75% to pass the course. Alison finished a minute or so before me and handed in her paper which Donna marked.

"Very well done, Alison," she remarked as she passed her scored paper back.

"How many wrong?" I mouthed at Alison.

She held up her hand with two fingers extended and a smug smile on her face.

"Brilliant!" I congratulated her. A few minutes later it was my turn to have my paper returned.

"Excellent work, Vicky," Donna commented. My eyes popped out as I saw my mark.

Alison raised her eyebrows in question.

I held up my hand and made a circle with the thumb and forefinger to create a 'zero'.

"Bitch," Alison mouthed. I poked my tongue out at her and laughed. None of the three guys on the course had come close to us, though all had achieved the pass mark.

We had now completed the theory and confined water elements of the course.

We'd learned how to assemble the buoyancy control device (BCD) regulator and tank; the pre-dive checks; how to clear our masks when water seeped in and remove and refit them in case they got dislodged; to buddy breath, sharing our spare regulator with a partner; how to remove the BCD under water and get back into it, in case we had to get through a confined space. In short, we learned how to deal with a lot of scary and potentially life threatening situations. But Donna had impressed upon us that if we remembered our drills we should be safe.

Finally, we learned the things on our feet were 'fins' *not* 'flippers'.

We now only had to complete two open water dives in the afternoon and we would be qualified.

On the boat we checked each other's kit following the mnemonic BWRAF: BCD; Weights; Releases; Air; Final check.

"All OK?" asked Donna.

We all gave her the 'OK' signal of finger touching thumb.

I took a deep breath — both metaphorically and literally. This was it. My first dive in the ocean. No turning back now; not that I wanted to. I was buzzing with excitement. I put one hand on my mask and regulator to ensure they weren't dislodged as I entered the water and rolled backwards off the boat. I hit the water in a cloud of bubbles and sank down a few feet before resurfacing. I looked round and saw my 'buddy' Alison and gave her the OK sign and was glad to see her respond. We then looked for Donna and signalled we were OK — this time with a hand touching our heads.

Having checked the other divers, Donna signalled we should descend.

I released air from my BCD and sank below the surface.

Looking down, I saw the sandy bottom twenty feet below us. Shoals of fish were darting this way and that, the colours were incredible, translucent blues and greens, bright yellows, brilliant reds, there were stripes and dots and mottled designs. Some were barely an inch long others a foot or more. The range of shapes included long sleek ones, some that were taller than they were wide – like the angel fish we'd had in a tank when I was a child, still others were like balloons. I laughed at the delight of the scene, blowing bubbles out of my mouth.

I recognised the orange and white striped clownfish, from 'Finding Nemo', darting in and out of the anemones tentacles. I felt an empathy with them as they all start as male and when the sole female in a group dies one of the males becomes female — so much for religious fanatics, and others, who claim 'changing sex' is unnatural.

We finned our way along the bottom following Donna. She regularly turned and checked with us that we were OK and signal to ask how much air we had left. It was just as well we had Donna to follow as I doubt if any of the rest of us had the slightest idea where we were heading or how to find the dive boat again — we were too focussed on the sights around us.

After about half an hour, I noticed a line going from the surface to an anchor and realised we were back under our boat. We ascended slowly then paused at five metres for three minutes to complete the decompression stop before surfacing. I removed my fins and handed them to one of the boat crew then climbed the ladder back on board.

"That was magic!" I said to Donna and anyone else in hearing.

"Did you see the lionfish?" Alison asked.

"The one with all the spines, sort of brown and white?"

"That's the one."

"Yes I did."

"OK everyone, calculate your residual nitrogen time and surface time so you know how long you need to wait before the next dive," Donna instructed.

As we prepared for the next dive, I noticed a helicopter hovering over another dive boat further out. I was about to mention it when the skipper announced.

"The helicopter you can see is taking part in exercises with the new Rescue Coordination Centre in Mombassa that will be starting to operate in May. It's from an American warship which you might just be able to make out in the distance."

I felt reassured that rescue would be at hand if we needed it — but hoped we wouldn't.

We stayed down a little longer on the second dive. As our group was swimming slowly along in one direction, I noticed almost all of the fish around us were swimming the other way. I wondered if they knew something we didn't. Were we heading into danger? Was there a shark or some other predator ahead?

I knew there were few species of shark that were a danger to humans and very few actual deaths by sharks; while man kills a hundred million sharks a year.

But that didn't stop me being nervous.

And excited.

In fact, we saw nothing threatening at all.

As we climbed back on board, the crew looked worried. Donna was talking to the skipper but I saw her glance over at me several times.

She came over.

"Sit down will you please, Vicky."

My heart sank. You only told someone to sit down when there was bad news. Very bad news.

"Why, what's happened? Is it Roger? Is he hurt?" I always knew something would happen. That our happiness was too good to last. I knew I didn't deserve him and fate was playing a game with me.

"He'll be OK. He was involved in an incident."

"What incident? Tell me." I was getting very scared.

"The other group encountered a shark and Roger's buddy panicked — he dropped his weight belt and ascended far quicker than he should. Roger tried to hold on to him to reduce his rate of ascent. When Roger realised he couldn't prevent his buddy surfacing, he let go of him and carried out his own decompression stop, then surfaced. The other guy had symptoms of DCS so needed treatment. The nearest chamber is in Zanzibar which is about fifty miles south of here. They don't think Roger is affected but, as a precaution, they've sent him to the chamber as well."

"Will Roger be OK?"

"I'm sure he will. He let go of the other diver around eight metres down, when it was obvious he couldn't stop him surfacing. Roger then sank down a few metres before he got enough buoyancy back in his own BCD. He then carried out a proper ascent including his decompression stop. As I said, he's being sent to the decompression chamber just as a precaution."

"You say it's fifty miles how are they getting there?"

"They called on the helicopter we saw earlier to take Roger and Edwin, the other diver, to Zanzibar."

"How can I get to Zanzibar?"

"We are sending a minibus to collect them tomorrow — but it's a hell of a journey. The road goes inland then back out to the coast then there's a ferry over to the island so it takes about fourteen hours. You can get there by air but only via Nairobi or private charter – but, remember, as you've been diving, you shouldn't fly for twenty four hours."

"How can I charter a plane? I want to be with Roger as soon as I can," I sobbed.

"Vicky, I understand, but you won't be able to be with him if he's in the decompression chamber."

"I don't care," I screamed. I had to be near him — surely Donna understood that.

"Hang on," Donna said, "let me check something." She fiddled with the dive computer on her wrist. "OK, we didn't go deep or stay down long. My dive computer shows a 'no fly time' of under an hour. So by the time you get to the airport, you'll be ok — but I suggest the pilot stays below two thousand feet even so. I guess a private charter would cost about thirty thousand Kenyan shillings, just over two hundred pounds sterling. If one is available."

"That's fine." I *had* to be with Roger. Whatever it cost.

"All right, let me see what we can do."

As we'd been talking, the boat had been making its way to shore. The other divers were in a huddle whispering amongst themselves and glancing in my direction.

Donna and I jumped off the boat as soon as it reached the beach and ran to the dive centre.

Abigail, the dive centre administrator was ready for us as soon as we entered.

"Right Vicky. I'll drive you to the airport where Jason, a friend of Blue's, is now filing a flight plan. You're lucky, he was at the airport this afternoon. He will fly you to Zanzibar airport. Then a taxi will take you to the chamber."

"Thanks very much." I didn't think to ask who Blue was.

"You'll need to take Roger's passport with you for the return trip. Do you have a visa for Tanzania by any chance?"

"Yes, we planned to fly up to Kilimanjaro next week so Roger organised them back in the UK."

"That makes life easier. Would you mind taking Edwin's passport with you? He'll need it to get back into Kenya."

"No problem."

"OK, well, Jason will stop overnight and can bring you, Roger and Edwin back tomorrow. He's doing it for 'mate's rates' which, in this case is just expenses: aircraft operating costs, landing fees and hotel for tonight. Is that OK?"

"What? Why? I don't understand." I was confused — why would someone do that for a stranger?

"As I said, Jason is an old mate of Blue's."

"Who is 'Blue'?" I was still totally confused.

"Sorry, 'Blue' is Andrew's nickname. Andrew Dawson? This is his company. He owns the dive centre. They're both Aussies."

At last I understood.

"Anyway, don't stand around here — get changed, collect your passports and anything else you need and I'll meet you at reception with Edwin's. OK?"

I suddenly realised I was still wearing a wetsuit so I stripped it off and ran back to our room my bikini, quickly showered and slipped on a sundress. At the last minute, I grabbed a change of undies for both Roger and myself and our toothbrushes and stuffed them in one of our cabin bags. I put our passports in my handbag and ran to reception.

Despite the assurances, I still worried about Roger as Abigail weaved her way through the chaotic Mombasa traffic, taking every opportunity to shave a few seconds off the journey time. She drove me through a side gate to the private aircraft terminal. An immigration officer checked my passport. I then saw a guy dressed in typical khaki safari shorts and military style shirt with epaulettes and button down patch pockets. He was a stark contrast to the pilots I'd seen on commercial airlines.

"Hi Vicky, I'm Jason. Sorry to meet you under these circumstances but I'm sure everything will be OK."

"It's very kind of you to help like this."

"Don't mention it. Gives me an excuse to get the old bird out and stretch her wings. I've done the pre-flight checks so we are about good to go. Have you flown in a light aircraft before?"

"No, never. The smallest was the Dash-7 from Masai Mara to Nairobi."

"Ah, well this will be very different. For a start we will need to stay low as you dived earlier and the aircraft isn't pressurised. Well, there we are," he said as we stepped through the door onto the apron.

A single engine aircraft sat waiting for us. Judging by the windows there were two rows of seats.

"It's a Piper PA-28. Cruising speed is around a hundred and eight knots, that's about . . "

"Hundred and twenty four miles per hour," I interrupted.

"Spot on. I thought you hadn't flown light aircraft."

"I haven't but I sail so I'm used to knots and nautical miles."

"Sailing. Oh yes that's using those flappy things on poles sticking up from boats. Isn't it?" he looked at me and I smiled despite my concerns for Roger.

"Climb in and fasten your seat belts. And put on the headset," Jason told me.

There weren't many controls or instruments — more than on a boat, but a lot fewer than I'd seen in pictures of commercial aircraft cockpits. I recognised a satellite navigation screen which was almost identical to one on Summer Dreams. I also identified the compass, altimeter and speed indicator and temperature and oil pressure indicators either from the units they were marked in or from their similarity to ones in Roger's MGB.

"OK?" Jason, sitting to my left, checked.

"Fine, thanks."

He then turned the ignition key and started the engine. The propeller in front of the windscreen turned into a blur and the whole aircraft vibrated.

"Nairobi Tower, Jasonair zero-one, Ready to taxi, south departure," he requested over the radio.

"Jasonair zero-one taxi to and hold short of runway zero-three using taxiway alpha. Contact tower on one-one-eight decimal eight when ready."

"Taxiing, holding short runway zero-three via taxiway alpha. Jasonair zero-one"

He leant forward and released the hand brake, then pushed the throttles forward and we gained speed, following the taxiway to the runway. We stopped short of the runway as a commercial airliner came into land. A Dash-7, perhaps the one we'd flown in from the Masai Mara, landed, its tyres screeching and leaving a cloud of burnt rubber in the air, as it touched down.

Jason ran the engine up to full power, holding the aircraft on the brakes then reduced the throttle and called air traffic control again.

"Mombasa Tower, Jasonair zero-one, ready for departure to south at runway zero-three.

"Jasonair zero-one Cleared for take-off runway zero-three."

"OK, here we go Vicky."

He advanced the throttles again, waited for the engine to stabilise then released the brakes. We accelerated along the runway and I watched the speed indicator build. Twenty knots, thirty, forty, fifty. At sixty, Jason eased back on the controls and we lifted into the air.

"See the lever marked 'flaps'?" he asked me.

"Yes."

"See the mark for ten degrees?"

"Yes."

"Move it to that mark please."

I did as he asked.

"OK, now move it to the zero position."

The altimeter wound up to two thousand feet. Jason pulled back slightly on the throttle.

"Put your hands on the control yoke. Just hold it lightly — like you would the tiller of a yacht."

"OK, pull back slightly on the controls. See how the nose is now above the horizon?"

"Yes."

"Now push it slightly forward and see how the nose goes below the horizon. That controls the up and down movement of the aircraft."

"I see."

"To turn we bank the aircraft rather than using the rudder — that would make us skid round. So slight pressure down on left and we turn left. Down on the right and we turn right."

"Got it."

"Damn. I've got a bit of cramp in my hand. Take the controls. OK we need to turn onto one-eight-zero which is "

"South."

"Ah, sorry, forgot you were a sailor. OK slight left hand pressure, watch how the compass is turning, level off just before it comes onto one-eight-zero. That was perfect."

"It's very much like on a boat, you have to come off the control before reaching the heading or you overshoot."

"Exactly. OK we need to maintain a cruising speed of one-zero-eight knots, a height of two thousand feet. Now we are clear of the coast, we can come onto a heading of one-nine-five. We'll run parallel to the coast until we get to Zanzibar. Are you OK with this?"

"Fine thanks."

"OK, then turn onto one-nine-five now. Lovely, you have a nice touch on the controls, a real natural." I smiled at the compliment.

I had to concentrate on maintaining the accurate heading, height and speed and, before I knew it, Zanzibar was ahead and a little to port.

"OK come slightly to port. See the smaller island ahead? And the headland on the main island beyond it?"

"Yes."

"Aim to cross the peak of the headland on a heading of one-eight-zero."

"OK."

Jason spoke on the radio. "Jasonair zero-one, Zanzibar control. Approaching from north under visual flight rules from Mombasa. Request landing instructions. Over."

"Jasonair zero-one. You are clear to land on runway one-eight. Turn left for identification."

I turned to the left.

"Jasonair zero-one. Thank you, we have you identified. Return to course one-eight-zero. And continue on finals. You are twenty four miles from touchdown. Report when visual with runway."

"Jasonair zero-one. Understood, continue on heading one-eight-zero. Report when visual with runway."

The runway appeared in the distance.

"Jasonair zero-one, runway visible."

"Jasonair zero-one we have you at ten miles. QNH one-zero-one-two, wind one-seven-zero at five knots."

"Jasonair zero-one, QNH one-zero-one-two, wind one-seven-zero at five knots."

Jason turned to me. "QNH is the local pressure which we set on the altimeter so the height readings are accurate. In fact it's the same as it was in Mombasa so we don't need to adjust it. The wind is pretty much a head wind when we land so we don't have to worry about it. We'll aim to land to the left of the runway centreline." He explained.

"OK reduce speed to ninety knots," Jason instructed me.

I eased back on the throttle. "Ninety knots."

"Flaps to twenty-five degrees. This is will slow us further so you may need a bit more throttle."

"OK flaps twenty-five degrees." The speed dropped to seventy so I eased the throttles forward a touch.

"OK we want to touch down just to the left of the centre line of the runway, as any crosswind is coming from that side and about a hundred yards along from the start of the runway. We don't have to worry about the length it's much longer than we need."

"OK — aren't you doing the landing?"

"You're doing fine. I'll be following through but you can do it. You've got one of the best touches on the controls I've ever seen. OK imagine a wine glass on the top of the dashboard and line up the point you want to touch down on with the top of the stem. Just easy touches on the controls. That's fabulous. Reduce speed to sixty knots."

We cleared the boundary fence with fifty feet indicated on the altimeter.

"Reduce speed to fifty knots, and cut the throttles completely now."

We floated down onto the runway, bounced a few feet then settled down.

"OK, you've done the hard bit, I'll taxi it. I have control."

I wasn't a fool, I realised Jason had been keeping me occupied during the flight rather than allowing me to concentrate on Roger's condition. Even so, I HAD flown the aircraft and landed it. And earlier in the day I'd qualified as a scuba diver so I now had qualifications under the water, on it and had, perhaps, taken a first step to a qualification above the water! It had been some day!

But now it was back to concerns about Roger and there was little in the taxi to distract me from worrying. So I worried. Even if he was OK this time I came back to that over-riding fear I would eventually lose him. It didn't matter how irrational those concerns were, they were real to me.

By the time we reached the medical centre, Roger and Edwin were completing the decompression process. As he emerged from the chamber I ran to him and hit him repeatedly on the chest.

*"Don't you ever do that to me again!"* I screamed, tears flooding down my face.

He just looked at me and pulled me into his arms and kissed me.

"I really thought I'd lost you. You can't imagine how I felt," I told him.

"Actually, darling, I can."

That brought me up short. Of course he realised. I'd put him in the same position. I felt terribly guilty.

"Sorry. I love you so much and couldn't bear to lose you. And I am so sorry for having put you through the same."

"Darling, you never have to apologise for caring. But how the heck did you get here so quickly?"

"I flew down in Jason's aircraft. Roger, this is Jason: Jason, Roger. Jason is a friend of Blue, the owner of the dive centre."

"And when she says she flew down she does mean she flew the aircraft most of the way. That's a heck of a girl you've got there cobber," said Jason.

"Don't I know it, Jason." Roger turned to me. "When did you learn to fly? How come I've never heard of this before?"

"Jason made me take the controls, it was my first time. He told me what to do, and, Jason, I do realise you were making me focus on flying to stop me worrying about Roger."

Jason just smiled.

Once Roger and Edwin had been cleared by the medics, and travel medical insurance details provided, we were free to leave for a nearby hotel. Edwin insisted on buying dinner for all of us as he had caused the incident.

The next day, after a leisurely breakfast, we returned to the airport. Roger and Edwin climbed into the rear seats while I sat next to Jason.

Jason requested permission to taxi to the runway. Having received clearance he turned on to the runway and asked permission to take off.

"Jasonair zero-one. Ready for take-off. Straight out departure."

"Jasonair zero-one. Cleared for take-off. Straight out departure."

"Jasonair zero-one. Thank you Zanzibar tower."

"Damn it. Seem to have got cramp in my hand again." Jason turned to me and winked.

I swallowed hard, reached forward, opened the throttle then released the brakes. As the aircraft reached fifty knots it lifted off.

"Hold it level until the speed builds a bit more. OK, ease back on the controls and maintain a ten degree climb. Flaps ten degrees. Hold this rate of climb, keep the speed at one-zero-eight knots."

"Fucking hell," exclaimed Edwin from behind me. I glanced back and saw Roger looking nonchalantly out of the window. He turned and winked at me.

"I never doubted you could do it. Wonderwoman."

"Level off at two thousand, Flaps zero, please Vicky. Heading zero-one-zero."

The flight passed smoothly and we landed at Mombasa's Moi airport with no problems and taxied to the light aircraft park. I closed the throttle, pulled on the handbrake then switched off the engine.

"Well done Vicky, you really do have a fabulous feel for the controls. You now need to get yourself a Private Pilot's log book. I'll sign off your first two flights," said Jason.

I suspect my smile reached from ear to ear. I grabbed Roger's arm as we walked to the small terminal where we had to show our passports.

As Roger hadn't actually shown any signs of DCS we booked a trip to snorkel with dolphins the next day.

As the dhow we were on left the jetty, the crew announced a prize of a t-shirt for the first person to spot a dolphin. I kept my eyes peeled and noticed other boats well ahead of us seemed to have turned towards the same place. Just then, a speck surfaced then re-entered the water with a slight splash. I pointed at the place I'd seen it. The skipper picked up a pair of binoculars and searched where I indicated.

"My God, you're right, there is one. How did you see it at that distance, I could barely make it out with the binoculars."

As we got closer, we saw several dolphins, some breaching then splashing back into the water, others swimming near us while yet more played with our bow wave.

Having readied ourselves for the water, we transferred from the dhow to smaller boats that took us ahead of the pod of dolphins so we could 'swim' with them as they passed under us. I say 'swim, but we were lucky to dive down a few feet and watch them dart past like torpedoes. We didn't have a hope of keeping up with them and they weren't in the mood to come and play.

Dinner back on shore was a fabulous selection of seafood, chicken and barbecued meats with fresh salads. Then it was back on the minibus for the drive back to the hotel.

At the Likoni ferry on the outskirts of Mombasa, it felt like we were being mobbed as hundreds of foot passengers and cyclists swarmed on board. I shuddered to think what would happen if the ferry was to capsize. The busy commercial port with ships from all over the world, and their inevitable food waste dumped overboard, meant the waters attracted plenty of predators including the few species of shark, such as the Bull Shark, that do attack men. I wanted to see sharks in open water but wasn't keen on coming face to face with a Bull.

The following day was our last in Mombasa. We couldn't dive within 24 hours of flying so we had booked a tour of the city. This included a cooperative where craftsmen and women carve all manner of souvenirs, particularly animals and native artefacts, which they sell either directly or via the shop on site or wholesale. The cooperative provides the basic infrastructure for the workers and visitors are free to wander around and watch them produce their creations. We bought a carving of a cheetah to remind us of the one we'd seen on safari.

After lunch, we visited jewellers we'd been recommended for Tanzanite. I bought a beautiful white gold necklace with a three carat pendant and matching drop earrings. A matching bracelet tempted me but that would have been too extravagant. I did, however, buy an eighteen carat gold signet ring with a small Tanzanite stone for Roger who was the other side of the shop.

As I handed over my credit card, I thought back to a conversation I'd had with a gardener at the hotel who'd told me he ran the five miles to and from work and their average wages were less than a hundred pounds per month. I also recalled the typical houses we'd seen on the outskirts of Mombasa and the shanty town on the edge of Nairobi. It felt obscene for me to be spending as much as I was in the face of such poverty. But I appreciated tourism was the second largest source of foreign exchange for Kenya and if we hadn't visited, then the country would be still poorer.

Even so, I couldn't help returning to my perpetual anxiety that I really didn't deserve all I had and it wouldn't last.

I entered my PIN number on autopilot, despite my black thoughts.

Our last stop in Mombasa was for tea at one of the grand hotels from the colonial era. I took Roger's hand in mine and slipped the signet ring onto the little finger of his left hand, kissed him and said "I love you. Thanks for everything."

"I love you too," he responded "even if you are sneaky buying me a present when I'm not watching."

He then took my hand and fastened the bracelet I'd decided to forgo around my wrist. "I can be sneaky too." It was fabulous and I gave him a lingering kiss. I felt tears forming — just how long would my good fortune hold? Perhaps I needed to see a counsellor about these feelings?

The next day, we left the hotel for the airport and a flight to our last stop in the south eastern part of the Serengeti where we would catch up with the wildebeest migration. En route, we passed close to Kilimanjaro and saw the snow lying on its peak.

Both Kilimanjaro and the migration were as spectacular as we'd been led to expect and were a perfect conclusion to a fabulous honeymoon.

# Chapter 35. Back to Earth
## 22nd January 06

Everyone at the office wanted to hear about the honeymoon and see the photographs. I was more than happy to oblige and share the amazing memories, including the scare over Roger. Looking through them, they reminded me of so many incidents that I'd already forgotten in the jumble of different events. I had to promise to tell them as much as I could remember.

I did, however, remind them if they wanted paying this month, I had work to do so they reluctantly got back to their own tasks and left me to get on with the payroll.

For some reason I felt quite deflated. The last year had been one major event followed by another culminating in our wedding and honeymoon. Now there were no significant events on the horizon, it was quite an anti-climax. It was, nevertheless, the life I'd dreamt of having but hardly dared hope I would ever achieve.

In Africa, Roger and I had just been a 'normal' couple on honeymoon. No-one, apart from me during my 'black-dog' sessions, considered me as anything other than born female and Roger, obviously, as male. We did the typically tourist things that everyone else did. There was no hint of my trans history — apart from having to be careful how I dealt with questions about my childhood; and that's exactly how I wanted life to be.

At the same time, I felt guilty about wanting to move on.

Was I deserting others that I could now help? Shouldn't I pay forward the help that I'd received when I needed it? Would Karma bite me on the bum if I failed to support others? Would my world come tumbling down if I didn't continue to help?

Did we want to lose touch with gay friends? In fact we wouldn't lose touch with gay and trans friends — they'd always be welcome; but there was a wider circle of acquaintances that could drift away.

It worked both ways, of course. Roger and I were no longer necessarily seen as queer by those that didn't know us personally. As far as they were concerned, we were a straight cis-gendered couple. This resulted in an unpleasant encounter one evening in the Blue Peach. We were approached by a camp gay guy. We'd never seen him in the club before and he had clearly had too much to drink.

"Can't you straights fucking well leave us somewhere of our own? Why do you have to invade our clubs for fuck's sake," he slurred. "If I fucking go into your straight clubs, I get abused or even fucking beaten up."

Georgina on the bar had noticed the trouble brewing and had called Graham the doorman over.

"What's the problem?" Graham asked.

"I'm sick to death of fucking straights coming into gay venues and behaving like they fucking own the place. Look at this pair – what the shit are they doing in here? Why can't they piss off to their own straight clubs, there's enough of them and few enough gay venues. Makes me puke."

"I think you've had enough for tonight, sir. Let me call you a cab," Graham told him.

"Fucking typical," the drunk ranted, "protect the straights and kick out the gays. Exactly my point."

I turned to him. "For the record, I am trans — so my husband and I are as entitled to be here as you would be when sober."

That shut him up and he started to mumble an apology holding his hands in the air. He was still saying sorry, or rather 'shorry', as he allowed himself to be taken out of the door and into a cab.

I had mixed emotions over the incident.

Most trans people want to be totally accepted and treated as the gender in which they identify so having been taken as a cis-gendered female even in a location where you'd expect to see transgender individuals was positive. His comment that Roger and I could now go wherever we wanted without problems was valid. Whilst LGBT venues were essential safe spaces for many gay and trans people, they were beginning to feel like a ghetto and I didn't want to be limited to areas where I was 'allowed' to be myself.

# Chapter 36. Preparing for the New Season

On the business front, one of the letters waiting for our return had been from the council. When I saw what it said, I turned to Roger.

"Do you want the good news first or the bad?" I teased him.

"What? Oh, give me the bad news first."

"We need to spend money on some more dinghies and find two more instructors."

There was a pause as he took in what I'd just said.

"We got the schools' contract?" he asked.

"We got the contract," I confirmed. Waving the letter at him. We jumped up and hugged each other.

We'd rebid for the contract to provide sailing training for local schools that we'd lost out on in 2003. This time, my trans history hadn't been a factor.

"Phew. Right then. What are we going to need? What did we base the bid on?"

"We planned on six boats for stage one and six for stage two. Plus another rescue boat. We can use our existing Lasers for single-handed race training — though we'll need to replace them next year. We allowed for two two-man dinghies with spinnakers and trapezes as well."

"And we need two more instructors?"

"Yes. Penny in the shop and Trevor in admin have expressed interest in training as instructors. Or we can advertise for people who are already qualified. If we train them up, we'll need to replace them in their current roles."

"I prefer to train people we already know." Roger ran his finger along the planning chart on the wall. "The schools' contract doesn't start until Easter so we have about twelve weeks which is plenty of time. They're both experienced sailors. They'll also need first aid courses."

"I'll speak to them later. We can release them from existing duties for a couple of days a week for the instructor training. I'll check when the Red Cross is running their training."

"OK, what about equipment?" Roger asked.

It would have been useful to visit a sailing exhibition to see what was available but we'd been on honeymoon for the London Boat Show and the Dinghy Show at Alexandra Palace in March would be too late. We did, however, already have a good idea of the market.

"The obvious choices are the Oppie or maybe the Hartley 10 for stage one and the Topper or Pico for stage 2. I'll arrange meet the manufacturers and see what discounts we can negotiate for a large order."

Roger nodded his head. "Yes, I think you're right — as usual. What about the two-man boat?"

"We're spoilt for choice there. Depends how challenging we want it to be and a bit of a balance between robustness and weight. If we want to make it easy to get on the plane and trapeze, obviously it needs to be light but we don't want it to be fragile as it's bound to come in for some hard wear and tear."

"If I know you, darling, you'd like us to get Fireballs."

I'd raced Fireballs before meeting Roger and they were still my favourite dinghy.

"Absolutely, they are easy to sail but challenging to sail really well. They get on a plane quickly and are good for training on a trapeze but the more sensible option may be the Laser Stratos; though I'm hearing rumours that it may be discontinued before long which would hit resale values. There are other options with trapezes and spinnakers though for race training. I'll get more information including costs."

"Fine. As far as the rescue boat is concerned, we can use one of last year's RIBs from shop stock."

"Fair enough. Well, I've got a bit to keep me busy then once I've sorted out the payroll run. I'll just let Penny and Trevor know their news.

We'll need to get their CRB checks underway so they are cleared to work with kids."

# Chapter 37.  T-Time
## 26<sup>th</sup> January 06

Although Roger and I were socialising more and more in the general community, I stayed involved with the T-Time trans support group. In spite of my concerns that if I didn't continue to support others, Karma would punish me, that wasn't the reason I remained a member. I wanted to be able to pass on my experience and show the others that it was possible to have a fulfilling and successful life after transition. I'd even been persuaded to stand for chair and had been elected unopposed. I wasn't sure if that reflected everyone's confidence in me or a reluctance to take on the work.

The group had exclusive use of the downstairs cocktail lounge at the Blue Peach until ten o'clock on Thursday evenings — so those members that wanted to could mingle with the rest of the customers afterwards or have a dance upstairs. The lounge had a range of comfortable sofas so made for quite a relaxed atmosphere. It also had its own bar staffed by Laura who worked for the Blue Peach as well as being a member of the group. The lighting was usually dimmed but we turned it up for our meetings.

At the first meeting in February, we had a couple of new members. As usual, we started with introductions.

Theresa, one of the new members, said she had a concern she needed help with. So, after some official group notices, I asked her to describe her issue.

"I transitioned eighteen months ago and have been living full time since then. I'm attending Charing Cross GIC and hope to have surgery in about a year's time. I recently transferred from the company's Gloucester office to Poole after some issues with other members of staff in Gloucester. The company felt it might be easier for me to make a clean start here where no one had previously known me as male. The problem is I get the constant feeling I'm not a real woman, that I'm fake. I keep expecting everyone to point at me and make fun."

She took a sip of her drink then continued.

"I think I'm reasonably convincing and I don't have very masculine features. I'm only five feet six and size twelve so well within typical female build. I don't think my voice is particularly masculine and, to be honest, I rarely get questioned when I'm on the phone. So I think I 'pass' quite well."

I looked around the room and could see some of the less convincing members grimacing in the knowledge that they were not so fortunate.

"I think it's that concept of 'passing' that bothers me. It suggests 'getting away with something' and pretending to be what I'm not. Well, none of us has a completely female body and never will. We can't give birth and our skeleton will always be seen as male. How do the rest of you see this? Does it bother you? How do you deal with it?"

I knew Laura had views on the issue so I looked at her and raised my eyebrows. She took the hint.

"I've never liked the term 'passing'," Laura replied, "As you say, it implies getting away with something and that's not how I see it. I prefer to describe it as 'not being mis-gendered'. While I accept my body isn't completely female my mind most certainly is and that's what matters. OK so I don't have a womb so can't give birth but is a woman who has had a hysterectomy or if she's had breasts removed any less of a woman?"

"No, and I take that point – but I still find myself doing male things and enjoying them which makes me question myself."

"Such as?"

"Motor racing, football, DIY."

"And no women do motor sports? No women play soccer? And all women should bat their eyelashes to get men to put up shelves or change fuses in plugs should they?" interrupted Rachel.

"No, but . ." Theresa started to reply as Rachel continued.

"It's not the 1950s any longer when women were expected to stay at home, do the cooking and sewing or only be interested in fashions or make-up. That sort of stereotyping belongs in the past."

"True, and I do like looking nice, but they are still more of a boy thing aren't they?"

"It's true more men take part in or watch motor racing or football but it doesn't mean women don't," Rachel continued. "I just see myself as a bit of a tom boy, personally I still like working on my classic sports car but it doesn't mean I can't be female and accepted as such — and I definitely love dressing up for special occasions."

"Maybe …"

I realised Theresa wasn't entirely convinced and I could tell from facial expressions that she'd expressed a concern that other members shared but hadn't expressed.

Jacqui had been sitting quietly during the conversation but she spoke up.

"I felt the same way as you Theresa when I started to transition. I wrote a poem at the time. It's pretty unsophisticated but I think it expressed what many of us feel at that stage. Let me see if I can remember it.

> *"Can you tell me what I am?*
> *Neither woman nor a man*
> *Not a sister, nor a brother*
> *Not a father, not a mother*
>
> *I can no longer live as a male*
> *Yet can I be a "real" female*
> *Am I to be trapped in the middle?*
> *Is there an answer to this riddle?*
>
> *Living as I simply have to be*
> *A woman is what I hope people see*
> *Yet when others, of me, do speak,*
> *Do they see me as a freak?*

As I said, it's pretty awful as a poem but it really was how I felt at the time."

I could see a number of the other members looking at Jacqui in astonishment. She was probably the last person we'd have expected to write poetry or to express any concerns about who she was. I thought I saw Laura wiping away a tear from the corner of her eye.

"Look, everyone is different and has a different combination of interests," Rachel remarked. "We are also all on a spectrum of masculine to feminine based on traditional values. As I see it, the laddish culture means a lot of young women are moving towards the traditional masculine behaviours, which I don't actually find attractive, but, if that's what they want to do, that's their choice. If 'one' is stereotypically macho male and 'a hundred' is ultra-feminine, I'd probably say I'm in the mid to high-eighties. Where would you put yourself?"

"I'm not sure, mid-seventies?"

"So still firmly within the female range?" Rachel interjected.

"Well, yes."

"So how is that pretending to be something you aren't?" Rachel challenged

"I know but it still doesn't stop me worrying."

"Oh, hell, we are entitled to worry after all the crap we're exposed to, growing up," I said. "I still have major self-esteem issues at times. I feel I don't deserve my good fortune and it'll all come tumbling down at some time. But I know most of that is due to the conditioning I was subjected to as a kid."

"You feel the same? But you always seem so confident and have your life together."

"Well, there you go. Blame the bastards that indoctrinated us — the religious bigots that taught we should accept what God gave us; that men lying with men is evil; and cross-dressing is an abomination — while quite a few of them were buggering the choir boys! Not that I'm saying all priests are paedophiles. Most of them are well intentioned and do a lot of good work, but religion is so often used as an excuse for intolerance. Remember the Evangelical Alliance's campaign against the Gender Recognition Act?"

"What about the feminist arguments — like we didn't have the same experiences as girls growing up?" asked Karen.

"That assumes all girls have a single experience that is different to boys — and boys all grow up with privileges over girls because they are male," answered Laura. "But that's so wrong in several ways. I'm certain my niece's experience of growing up in a four bedroomed detached house in a cul-de-sac in a pleasant village; going to a private school; belonging to a pony club and competing in gymkhanas is very different to that of one of several siblings with different fathers; where the mother is an alcoholic drug addict; on benefits; on a sink estate in an inner city. There is no single female experience of growing up. In fact I'd say there are far bigger differences between different social groups than between genders."

Like many of the other members, I was nodding my head at her comments.

"In any case, while I accept most males do have privileges, I doubt if that applies to someone who is trans," Laura continued. "I know most of us experienced being made to feel second class and were bullied and that seems to me to be much closer to the female experience than a male one."

There was a general murmuring of agreement from around the room.

"Good point," Jacqui added, "and I think the trans exclusionary feminists argue against accepting trans people because they can't accept there is a difference between male and female brains. Their argument was always that male and female brains were the same so there was no reason to discriminate. If transsexualism is caused by incongruity between brain sex and physical sex then it shows there must be a difference between male and female brains. If there is a difference, perhaps they are concerned it would be used as an excuse for discriminating against women."

"Hmm, you've given me a lot to think about," Theresa said pensively. "Thanks, that's very useful."

Looking around the group, it seemed the conversation had given most of the members something to think about. I suspected that many of them had occasional doubts about how others saw them. I knew I was vulnerable in this area and often wondered if folks really accepted me for myself or were laughing behind my back, just waiting for me to fall on my face.

# Chapter 38. Babysitting
## 10th March 2006

Sandra and Ian planned a long weekend in Rome and asked if Roger and I would mind babysitting Katie and Oliver. I was delighted to help, I loved being with my niece and nephew. It was easier for Roger and I to spend the weekend at their house rather than bring everything they'd need for the weekend to ours. So, Friday lunch time, I drove over to Eastleigh. Sandra and Ian's house was a semi-detached three-bedroom property in a quiet cul-de-sac. They'd bought the house as prices started to rise and, as Ian had recently been given a significant promotion, hence the trip to Rome, they had started to look at moving up-market.

"The coffee and tea are in this cupboard, mugs in this one," Sandra said.

"Sandra, this isn't the first time I've been to your house. I know where things are and if I can't find something, I'm sure Katie will know. If we can't find it, we'll do without."

"I know I'm fussing — but this is the first time we've ever left the children for a few days."

"They'll be fine. Won't we kids?"

"Yes we will," chorused Katie and Oliver.

"It'll be fun with Aunty Vicky," added Katie.

"OK, well there are some treats in the cupboard," Sandra said. "And some wine for you and Roger and help yourself to any other drinks."

"We … Will …Be …. Fine ! Now get into that cab or you'll miss your flight even if the airport is just down the road."

"OK. OK."

Sandra picked up Katie and Oliver in turn and kissed them and held them for Ian to do the same.

"Bye, darlings, see you in a few days. Be good for Aunty Vicky and Uncle Roger. Ian, have you got the tickets?"

"Yes love, and the passports and the Euros and the suitcase."

"Well, come on then," Sandra added as though he'd been the one delaying the departure. I shook my head then gave both of them a kiss.

We waved them off from the front door then returned inside after the taxi had disappeared round the corner.

"It's a lovely afternoon so would you like a walk through the woods?"

"Oooh yes," said Katie. "Will we see squirrels? Can I ride my bike?"

"Yes, you can ride your bike. If we're lucky we may see the squirrels and some other animals and birds. Shall we take some peanuts to feed them?"

"And some bread for the ducks?"

"Rice or bird food would be better for them but we'll take something. Now can you put your wellingtons on or do you need help?"

"I can do my own but Oliver sometimes needs help with his," responded Katie.

"Is that right Oliver?"

He seemed quite offended by Katie's suggestion.

"I can do them, I'm not a baby now, Katie."

"All right, now go to the toilet first both of you. And remember to wash your hands afterwards."

Coats and wellingtons on, I sorted out the stroller for Oliver in case he tired later. Then we set off along the footpath that led into the woods.

Oliver took delight in jumping into every puddle he found, like most small children. When he saw a blackbird land further up the path he ran towards it and was disappointed when it flew off again.

Katie, in the meantime was riding round, also splashing through puddles, holding her legs out wide as she did so.

Either side of the path were swathes of bluebells, glistening like tropical lagoons as the shafts of sunlight reflected off them.

"Can we pick some of the flowers, Aunty Vicky?"

"No darling, I know they would look nice at home but if everyone that came along the path took a handful, soon there would be none left. It's nicer to leave them growing so everyone can enjoy them."

"Mmm," Katie replied thoughtfully. "And, I suppose they'd only die in a vase after a few days wouldn't they?"

"That's right; but by leaving them here, we can come and see them for a lot longer. Listen. Can you hear that 'tap tap tap' sound? Do you know what it might be?"

"I don't know," said Oliver.

"Is it a woodpecker?" asked Katie.

"It might well be. Yes, look over on that tree there. Can you see it? It's green and red."

"Oh yes," cried Katie gleefully.

"I can't see it," moaned Oliver.

Katie took her brothers arm and pointed. "Over there, Ollie."

"Oh yes," he beamed.

We watched the woodpecker for a few minutes before it flew off again.

Then a little grey head popped up at the base of another tree. Two tiny ears twitched. Two tiny paws held a hazel nut.

"Can you see the squirrel, Ollie? Katie?"

We could see its teeth making short work of the nut before it was popped into its cheek to be finished later; perhaps to be buried and eaten during the winter.

Another hundred yards brought us out at the pond where a a number of ducks were swimming on the surface. I passed Katie and Oliver some of the food we'd brought with us and they cast it on the water for the birds to eat.

"Look over there, children, there's a kingfisher. Did you see it dive into the water? Aren't they beautiful?"

"There it is," cried Katie. "Look there, Ollie."

"I can see it. Oh look, it's got a fish," he said.

I sat down on a bench, an older woman was sitting at the other end.

"You have two lovely children," she remarked.

"Thanks, they are lovely, but they're not mine, I'm their aunt."

"Oh, I saw your wedding ring and assumed they were yours. Oh well, no matter. I'm sure you'll have your own if that's what you want."

I only wished she was right, but that was impossible. This was one of those situations I always hated. I could tell her the truth — that I couldn't have children — and risk getting into a conversation that might lead to outing myself. Or I could pretend I might well have a family at some stage.

This time, though, it wasn't just the dilemma whether to out myself that saddened me. It was not being able to have our own children.

"I can't have children myself due to hormonal problems when I was younger," I admitted. Well it wasn't untrue, just open to different interpretations.

"Oh, I'm so sorry to hear that. From watching you I think you'd make a wonderful mother."

I thanked her, but that compliment actually made me sadder. I wondered how Roger felt about not being able to have children. We'd never actually discussed it as it wasn't possible for us.

"Have you thought about adopting?" asked my neighbour on the bench. She then shook her head. "I'm so sorry that was very insensitive and rude of me. Please forgive my being so intrusive."

"Nothing to forgive. My husband and I haven't discussed it at all. We've kind of accepted that I can't have children and not looked at other options. Perhaps we should think about it."

"I know many men don't like the idea of bringing up other people's children but surrogacy is another option. That way he is the genetic father."

"Oh, I don't think Roger would have a problem with adoption as such. He's fine with children. We run sailing training courses for schools and he's great with the young ones and loves being with Katie and Oliver here. But you've given me something to think about..." I paused not knowing her name.

"I'm Mrs Collins, Gillian," she replied picking up on my hesitation.

"Nice to meet you Gillian, I'm Vicky Dalton."

"Hope to see you again, Vicky"

"I hope so. Come on children, Uncle Roger will be home soon."

On the Saturday, Roger and I took Katie and Ollie to a theme park. I watched Roger playing with the children and how natural he looked with them. He noticed me watching him and winked at me.

As we walked back to the car, he gave Oliver a piggy-back while Katie held onto my hand. It felt like we were a real family group and I loved the sensation. I hoped Sandra and Ian would find more excuses to go away and leave the children with us.

After we'd put them to bed, Roger and I settled down in front of a blazing log fire with some music on the hi-fi.

"Do you wish we could have children, darling?" I asked.

"I know you'd be a fabulous mother, Vicky, so yes, because I think you'd be more fulfilled — but it's never been the most important thing for me."

"You haven't answered my question."

"Darling, I'd have been very happy having children but as it's not possible I'm content as we are."

I turned his head towards me to I look straight into his eyes.

"What if we could have them?"

"If you're talking about adoption, I wouldn't rule it out — it takes a lot of thinking about though, for both of us."

"I met a woman at the pond yesterday who mentioned surrogacy — that way you would be the genetic father even if I can't be their genetic mother."

Roger looked at me with eyes wide open.

"How on earth did you get onto that subject with her?"

"She saw me with Katie and Ollie and assumed I was their mother. I explained I was their aunty and one thing led to another."

"How would you feel if our children were mine genetically but not yours? Would you resent it?"

"I don't think so — though I'd need to think about it and talk it through. Maybe I'll speak to Sandra — or maybe that counsellor I saw about my self-esteem issues; probably both. It would be nice to have our own family though wouldn't it? I'm sure your parents would love to have grandchildren to spoil; and I'm sure Katie and Ollie would like having cousins."

## Chapter 39. Sandra's Offer
### 22$^{nd}$ March 2006

Over coffee with Sandra the Wednesday after they got back from Rome I mentioned the chat I'd had with Gillian Collins.

"I've always thought you and Roger would be brilliant parents, which is why I wasn't worried about leaving Katie and Oliver with you. So are you seriously thinking of starting a family?" asked Sandra

"Yes. I'm not sure about adoption though. If we were to do something, I really like the idea of it being Roger's own child, genetically, even if it's not mine. So surrogacy might be a good option. Roger wonders, though, if I might subconsciously resent the fact it's his and not mine. I'm pretty certain I wouldn't, but who knows?"

"There is an option that at least means the child would be genetically related to you."

"How?"

"I'll donate the eggs for you. I should think that would make it as close as possible to one that would have been conceived from your own eggs, as both of us have the same genetic history."

"Would you do that for me? Wow sis. That's so generous of you." I hugged her so hard she had to beg me to let her breathe.

"I won't offer to carry the baby for you, so you'd have to find a surrogate mother but I can certainly provide the eggs. We know I'm fertile and we don't intend having any more children ourselves so I can't think of a better use for them. Ian has a secondment to the firm's Singapore office at the end of May and will be away for two months. I thought about going with him — but he's going to be visiting clients all around the region so I'm staying in the UK then joining him for a three week holiday at the end of his stint. I'll take the kids with me. I read an article on surrogacy a while ago and got in touch with a group for some information. I seem to remember I'd need to come off the pill during the process but there is plenty of time for that, then for me to go back on it ready for the holiday. Seems perfect timing."

"Sandra, how do you know so much about this?"

"I saw from the way you've been with Katie and Ollie since transition and particularly since your op, you'd make a marvellous mother. I thought, sooner or later, you'd get broody. So I did some research in case I could help. I met up with one of the members of a surrogacy support group and had quite a chat with her. One thing she did emphasise was that everyone involved should consider professional counselling. In fact I had a few sessions with the counsellor she recommended."

My chin hit the floor as I stared open mouthed at my sister, tears forming at the corner of my eyes. She took me in her arms.

"What are sisters for, if not to help each other?" she asked. "Besides, I fancy being an aunty myself."

That evening, after packing the dishwasher, I topped up our wine glasses. We then sat on the settee.

"Roger you know I saw Sandra today?"

"Yes."

"Well, you remember we were talking about surrogacy."

"Yes, darling."

"Well, she's offered to provide eggs if we were to go down that route. That means any children we might have would be genetically related to both of us. So what do you think?"

"When do we start? What do we need to do?"

"Well, there are the practical aspects — finding a suitable surrogate and that's likely to be the most difficult. Then there's harvesting the eggs and fertilising them — but Ian goes to Singapore at the end of May and he's away for two months. That gives Sandra time to come off the pill, for them to harvest the eggs then for her to go back on the pill before she joins him out there for their holiday — so that's perfect."

I reached into my handbag and pulled out a leaflet Sandra had given me and passed it to Roger.

"Sandra says it's also very important to consider the emotional issues and suggests we get in touch with this support group and go along to their meetings. They suggest that we should all also have individual counselling."

"It all sounds very sensible. I can't see any issues from my perspective — so long as it doesn't cause you any problems and affect things between us. But, of course I'll come to the group meetings and see the counsellor. What else do we need to do?"

"Apart from finding a surrogate to carry the baby, as I said, that's likely to be the most difficult and you'll need to provide the sperm at the clinic. Oh and you need to decorate the box room as a nursery."

## Chapter 40. Hannah from Heaven

Of course, it wasn't as easy as that.

When I rang the support group to get details of their meetings, I was warned that finding a surrogate might well take months. That didn't bother me too much; I was used to having to wait a long time for what I wanted. In the meantime we could sort out the other practical elements and get lots of advice by attending the support group.

Then, over lunch one day, I was chatting with Hannah, the mother of Jasmine, one of the youngest members of the T-Time support group. Hannah herself was only 34 years old and widowed — her husband had been killed in a car accident four years earlier. We'd become good friends over the past few months and regularly met up for meals, I told her of our plans.

"What's actually involved in surrogacy?" she asked.

I explained the process as I understood it.

She took a sip of wine from her glass, sat back, her head tilted to one side and her eyelids partially closed, looking pensive for what seemed like an age. I took a sip from my own glass. Hannah then looked straight at me, hesitated a second then said: "I'll be your surrogate if you want. You saved Jasmine's life when you befriended her and showed her that it was possible to transition and be successful."

I couldn't believe my ears and needed to check that I'd heard her correctly.

"What did you just say?" I asked, staring at her.

"I said I would be your surrogate if you want. It's the least I can do for you, after what you've done for Jasmine and me," she confirmed.

I was dumbfounded.

"You don't have to do anything; you don't owe me a thing. That's what we are here for — to provide mutual support," I protested.

"I know that but I *want* to do it. Not just because of what you did for Jasmine and all the other members. I felt so helpless when Jasmine told me she wanted to transition. I didn't know where to turn. All I could see was my child saying if they couldn't be who they really were then they didn't want to live."

I'd known that feeling myself and I couldn't help shivering when I remembered my own attempted suicide.

"You showed us how she could be Jasmine and where to look for help and she's never been happier. This is something I can do; something I feel comfortable doing. It means I'm taking back control of at least part of my life not just riding along as a passenger. Please let me do it for you," she continued, taking hold of my hands in hers.

"That would be incredible," I said, "but you need to be absolutely sure. It's not something to decide on the spur of the moment. You also need to discuss it with Jasmine."

"I know Jasmine would be more than happy for me to help you. But, yes, I'll speak to her about it."

When she phoned the next day to say that Jasmine was enthusiastically in favour of the plan, Roger and I invited them both round to the house for a chat.

We insisted that we cover all of her expenses in spite of her protestations that she was comfortably well off from insurance her husband had had. Hannah, Roger and I then met up with Sandra and Ian so everyone involved could get to know each other and feel included in the process. Ian wasn't in the least concerned. He said our arrangements really didn't affect him at all and, as long as Sandra was happy, it was fine with him.

We arranged for a solicitor to draw up an agreement based on the advice we got from the group, although we all knew it couldn't be enforced in law. That didn't seem important as we knew Hannah was motivated by gratitude and Sandra by sisterly love.

The four of us, Roger, myself, Sandra and Hannah joined the support group and arranged to have individual counselling as well for a few weeks. It also seemed sensible to arrange another meeting for everyone before Sandra visited the clinic for the harvesting and a final one before the embryo was implanted to ensure that we were all still entirely happy with the arrangements. Our agreement meant all of us had to be happy to continue.

Thankfully, we did all want to proceed.

By the end of September we had confirmation all was well and we could expect an April baby. We had also had extra embryos stored in case the first pregnancy failed or to provide us with the option of a larger family later as Hannah had already told us she'd be happy to carry another baby for us.

I couldn't believe it. It felt like the missing piece (or pieces) of the jigsaw were about to fall into place.

As well as attending the support group most months, Hannah and I got together at least once a week as her pregnancy progressed and I took every opportunity to take note of her experiences so I could contribute in the future to mums' and toddlers' groups.

## Chapter 41.  Mia Released
### 23$^{rd}$ August 2006

Mia was released on parole in August. Her A level results had come out the previous week; she'd achieved A star in English and French and A in German. Her place on a Business Management Course at Salford University was secure.

She spent the weekend in Manchester so she could enjoy the Pride weekend and finalise her accommodation arrangements in Salford in the Halls in Peel Park.

Mia then came to stop with us for a couple of weeks. She was a very different person to the Mia I'd met on that first visit to the YOI. She had really knuckled down to her studies over the last eighteen months and was back on the track she'd planned before Barry had been arrested and Social Services had shipped her off to live with her birth father.

She had an appointment with Dr Wright and I decided to have a day off and go with her to say "Hi" to Nicholas and Cassie and update them on my own developments.

When the door to Dr Wright's office opened for him to invite Mia in, he saw me.

"Hello Vicky, everything OK? I'll have a quick chat after I've seen this young lady."

"So give," Cassie demanded when the door closed behind Mia.

I wiggled my left hand for her to see the rings.

"Roger?" she asked.

"Of course," I smiled. "I think you know we had a commitment ceremony in 2003? Well, as soon as I received my GRC, we organised a proper wedding. That was last New Year's Eve; then we had a three week honeymoon in Kenya and Tanzania."

"Huh. Bet you didn't wait for the honeymoon to test your equipment though."

I pretended demureness, lowering my head then looked at her from under my eyelashes — but I couldn't maintain the look so giggled.

"Dead right. We had a romantic weekend in Paris as soon as I was allowed to use it."

"Lucky girl. So what else is happening?"

"You remember my brother, Peter, had rejected me?"

"Yes, that was sad."

She looked concerned at this.

"Well, he's fine with me now. In fact he was Roger's best man."

Her face brightened immediately.

"Oh, that's brilliant. I love a happy ending."

"Ah, but that's not the best news."

"No?"

I paused as she looked at me questioningly.

"No. Roger and I are having a baby. My sister donated eggs which Roger fertilised and one is now developing into a baby courtesy of a surrogate. We'll see how we go but there are other embryos stored in case we want more children."

"Bloody hell, Vicky, you really have turned your life around haven't you? Well good for you girl. I see so many in here that just give up or wallow in misery or blame everyone else for their problems. But you've taken your opportunities and whilst I know you'd agree you've been lucky finding Roger, you've made the best of it."

Mia came out of the inner sanctum beaming from ear to ear.

"Nicholas has given you your referral," I said, pre-empting her announcement. "It's written across your face."

I hugged her.

"Thanks for all your support, Vicky. I don't know what I'd have done without your help. Even those talks you gave made a difference to how the staff treated me. I owe you big time."

"You don't owe me a thing, Mia. But all I ask is if you're ever in a position to help other trans people you pay the help forward. We need to support each other."

"Absolutely."

I brought Nicholas up to date with my news.

"Glad to see things are working out so well for you, Vicky. You seem to have been a positive influence for Mia as well. Please keep me in touch with your news in the future."

There was another visit I wanted to make so we returned to the car. We headed south then along Chelsea Embankment, over Chelsea Bridge and through some back doubles, taking side roads to cut across between main routes, eventually emerging on Clapham Road. We turned into a side road and I pointed to a window.

"That was my flat Mia, not the most salubrious as you can see."

I turned round and drove through more back doubles to the leisure centre where I used to work.

It had been nearly three years since I'd left so there would have been a fair turnover of staff — but I knew my old boss, Andrea, was still there as we spoke occasionally on the phone.

I gave her a call on my mobile.

"Hi Andrea. Are you in the office?"

"Vicky, yes, why?"

"Look out of your office window."

A face appeared and I waved. I heard a screech of delight as she disappeared.

Mia and I walked into the centre.

I immediately recognised Sally on reception.

"Can I help you?" she asked.

"No thanks, Sally, we're here to see Andrea."

"Do I know you? You look familiar but I can't place you."

I couldn't resist being wicked.

"I trained you to work on reception about three years ago."

"No, you must be mistaken, that was the assistant manager, David."

"That's right. I used to be David, now I'm Vicky."

Her eyes opened so wide I thought they'd pop out and her mouth did the same.

Just then Andrea came into the reception area.

"Vicky!" she exclaimed and gave me a huge hug. "Why didn't you warn me you might visit us?"

"We weren't sure how long we'd be at Nicholas Wright's and I wanted to surprise you. I think I've confused Sally," I told her.

"Well you asked me not to say anything to the rest of the staff so I didn't."

Sally looked from me to Andrea and back to me then to Mia.

"Come on through to the office I'll get coffees," said Andrea.

"Bye Sally. See you later," I said as we left the reception area.

Mia planned her surgery for the Easter break to minimise the impact on her studies so I was able to drive up to see her before the baby was due. She looked as happy as I'd felt and I was glad to see her. I stayed for a couple of days after she'd had her op.

# Chapter 42. Thomas
## 27th April 2007

Roger and I were watching television when Hannah phoned to say she was on her way to the hospital. The nursery had been ready for some weeks – though both Roger and I kept buying extra toys and mobiles and the like. There was a chest of drawers stuffed full of baby clothes and all the sterilising bits and pieces were ready in the kitchen and the latest pushchair was in the hall.

I had to remind Roger several times to watch his speed as we rushed to the hospital — the last thing we needed was to arrive there in an ambulance. Hannah could have had the baby on an NHS hospital but we chose to use a private clinic. They had been quite happy for Roger and me to attend ante-natal classes with Hannah and to attend the actual birth.

When we reached the hospital, Hannah was in her private room and looking quite relaxed — though I did wonder if she was like a swan, serene on the surface but churning up inside. I walked over to the side of the bed and gave her a hug then took her hand in mine. Jasmine was sitting in a visitor's chair next to her mum.

"Are you OK?" I asked.

"I'm fine, Vicky. It's not the first time I've done this you know," Hannah squeezed my hand as she smiled at me. It seemed wrong for her to be reassuring me, I was there to support her.

"These are for you," Roger said as held out a bouquet of flowers for Hannah together with a thank you card.

"Oh they're gorgeous and smell lovely, thank you."

"It's us that need to thank you, Hannah," I remarked.

Jasmine stood up.

"Shall I see if I can find a vase for those, mum?"

"Yes please, darling," said Hannah.

In the end we needn't have hurried to the hospital as baby Thomas waited until twenty past three the next morning to make an appearance, tipping the scales at seven pounds six ounces.

We had to keep out of the midwife's way during the actual birth but I held one of Hannah's hands while Jasmine held the other and Hannah squeezed hard.

The midwife confirmed that all was well with both Thomas and Hannah, that everything had gone quite normally and there were no causes for concern. She then gave Thomas to me to establish skin to skin contact and Roger and I could see our son clearly for the first time. Knowing that we were going to be responsible for this little bundle was awesome and very scary. Jasmine took photos of us with Thomas.

Hannah was, unsurprisingly, tired after the birth so we reluctantly said goodnight after giving her another hug and a kiss and thanks. I went along to a room that I had booked for the night for Thomas and me while Roger took Jasmine home. He would return the next morning to collect us and take Hannah home.

Both sets of grandparents came to visit as did Sandra, who brought Katie and Ollie to meet their new cousin. Even Pete dropped in with a gift for his nephew. My parents would have accepted our children regardless but I was really pleased Thomas was genetically their grandchild — even if the lineage wasn't as straightforward as usual. Oh well, I rarely did things the 'normal' way so nothing new there.

Thomas was a perfect baby, rarely waking us at night. I think I settled into motherhood quite well and changing nappies and making his feeds became second nature. Whether I'd have been as happy if he'd been waking up several times a night is another matter. But, as he slept through most nights, that wasn't an issue.

Hannah also visited regularly — and became an honorary aunty. One really pleasant afternoon in August, we were having a drink in the garden and Thomas was on a blanket on the lawn. He was lying on his tummy and reaching for a toy and babbling with delight as a butterfly flew past.

"Thomas is doing really well, isn't he?" remarked Hannah.

"He certainly is — and he's such a delight," I replied. "Aren't you darling?" I added as I tickled his sides.

"Are you still planning to have another?" Hannah asked.

"Yes. If we can."

"When were you thinking of?"

I looked at her. She had the hint of a smile as she looked back — then lifted an eyebrow.

"I do hope you are not thinking of finding someone else as surrogate. I'd be quite offended you know."

"I hardly dared ask you. Are you sure?"

"Of course. Unless you weren't happy with the arrangements last time."

"God, No. They were perfect as far as we were concerned. I just didn't want to impose on you."

"You wouldn't be imposing. You do so much for others — especially for Jasmine so it's my privilege to be able to do something for you. And don't tell me again that I don't owe you anything. This is friends doing things for each other because we want to, not out of any feeling of obligation. Agreed?"

Well, what could I say?

"Agreed. Thank you so much."

I still found it difficult to accept that people wanted to do things for me. I still struggled to believe that I deserved their friendship. I wiped away a tear from my eye, joined Thomas on the rug and buried my face in his tummy.

"Who's going to have a sister or brother then Thomas?"

He just gurgled and smiled at us.

When I told Roger that Hannah had offered to help again, he was as delighted as I was.

"You do realise if the children have their own rooms, we won't have anywhere for visitors to stay don't you?" I pointed out to him.

"Are you suggesting we need a bigger place?"

"How would you feel about moving? I know this used to be your gran's house and she left it to you."

"I'm certain she intended it to be a help not a millstone to carry. I'm sure she'd be happy for me to move on, especially under the circumstances. Why don't you contact estate agents tomorrow and see what you can find? The business is doing well so we can afford something larger."

I took Thomas with me to view potential properties. One of them was in a small village a few miles inland from the coast.

The estate agent was waiting outside as I arrived.

"As you can see, the development is off the main road through the village, this road loops around the back of the original houses so there's no through traffic," he said.

Instead of identical boxes, each property seemed to be individual. Some had three bedrooms, some four and number 63, the one I was viewing, had five. All were set back from the road with perfectly manicured lawns in front and, in the case of No 63, a block paved drive leading to two integral garages. The house looked at least twice as big as our current home.

First impressions as I went through the front door were of an airy hallway with an atrium up to the first floor at the side of the staircase.

"The downstairs cloakroom is through there," the agent told me. "Next to it there is a study or a family room which looks out over the garden."

It was as big as the entire bed-sitter I'd had in London and could immediately see the advantage of keeping it as a playroom for the children.

"Then we have the lounge. As you can see, patio doors lead out into the south facing garden," he intoned.

The main feature of the room was a Cotswold stone fireplace. I could just imagine roasting chestnuts over a roaring log fire in winter. We would, however, need to buy some new furniture as our current three piece suite would be lost in this room.

I stepped out onto the patio which led down to the lawn.

"Look Thomas," I said, "lots of grass for you to crawl about on." He gurgled and reached for my nose. At the bottom of the lawn, an archway led through a rose hedge with what appeared to be a kitchen garden beyond. As I reached it, I could see strawberries ripening, raspberry canes and various other bushes together with different fruit trees. At the bottom of the garden was a Hawthorn hedge with fields beyond ensuring that the garden wasn't overlooked.

"It's a lovely garden," I said to the agent who was looking at his watch as I turned to face him.

"Yes, the current owners have obviously put a lot of thought into it. Shall we go back inside?"

We went back in gain through the patio doors and the agent continued his spiel. "The lounge leads into the dining room through folding double doors so you can open up the combined space for entertaining and, as you can see, also has patio doors — ideal for summer entertaining."

The current owners had an oval table with eight place settings with space to spare around it so unless we had the entire family to dinner, it would be more than adequate.

The agent showed me into the kitchen. Again it was light and airy with a large window over the sink looking out to the front of the house. There were lots of storage and work areas and I could imagine creating spectacular dishes for family and friends. Much as I loved our current home, the kitchen was small and if the dishwasher door was open, I had to squeeze past it and there were limited work surfaces. I'd be well and truly spoilt by this kitchen.

"The utility room has plumbing for washing machine and an outlet for a tumble dryer and a Belfast sink plus additional storage cupboards," recited the agent. There were a couple of dog baskets in the utility room and I could see it would be perfect for changing out of muddy boots after a walk.

"It then leads out to the side of the property where there is storage for recycling bins."

I was pleased to note that there were gates at the front and rear corners of the house so Thomas and his future sibling and possibly pets, wouldn't be able to run out into the road from the garden — or play with the bins.

We then looked at the first floor. The master bedroom had an en-suite bathroom and a walk-in wardrobe. A second bedroom also had an en-suite but with shower rather than bath and the three other bedrooms shared a family bathroom.

As we went back downstairs, the agent pointed out the door to the garages. He showed me through.

"Some similar houses have converted one of the garages into another room," he said. "And, at the rear of the second garage, is a storeroom for gardening equipment."

It was a fabulous property and I had fallen in love with it. I knew Roger would be happy with it too as it ticked all of the boxes we'd discussed.

The village, too, was perfect for a family and I couldn't have dreamt of anywhere better.

There were three pubs, a garage, a combined shop and post office and a fourteenth century church with a tower. A village hall stood next to one of the pubs, with a sports field behind it where they'd play cricket matches and hold the village fête in the summer and a bonfire and firework display for Guy Fawkes night — the bonfire obviously well away from the cricket wickets. There was also a small primary school the children could attend in a few years and a doctors' surgery.

I called Roger there and then and asked if he could come and see the property and checked that the agent was happy to wait another half an hour or so.

Roger was as enthusiastic as I had been so we made an immediate bid of just under the asking price. We'd have paid the full amount if the vendors had insisted but they accepted our offer.

We moved in a few weeks after Charlotte was born on 3rd September 2008.

It was a new start for all of us. None of the neighbours knew of my history. As far as they were aware, I had borne both Thomas and Charlotte, so it would never occur to them I might be trans. I wasn't worried about being outed for my own sake — or ashamed of being trans; but I didn't want the children to be subjected to any problems.

I was more than happy to spend most of my time looking after the children and getting to know the neighbours; although I still went into the office to handle the payroll and marketing. The staff delighted in seeing the children and spoilt them rotten each time.

Charlotte took after her brother and was little trouble. Not having carried the children for nine months, I was better placed to deal with them without the strain of my body recovering from pregnancy and Roger was a great dad too. He was always there when needed, getting up in the middle of the night on the few occasions when required. In the end, I missed the interaction of work and decided to return part time. We employed an au pair, Irina from the Ukraine, allowing me to spend afternoons in the office. It seemed the optimum solution.

As far as I was concerned our family was now complete and perfect. Perhaps my fears that my good fortune couldn't last were being proved groundless.

# Chapter 43. End Game
## 21st July 2008

I'd kept in touch with Mia while she'd been at university and she'd stayed with us during some of the holidays.

She'd become a regular at family barbecues while visiting us and everyone accepted her, despite her colourful past and we'd become best friends. She helped in the business when she came to visit so, when she needed a placement for her Business Management course, Roger and I were happy to offer her a position. We were confident that a fresh look at the operation would be beneficial to all concerned.

She would have been welcome to stay with us but after her time in prison, she valued her freedom to come and go as she wished and found a bedsit in town. When she began to turn down invitations to get together, I was convinced she had found a partner. I found it strange, though, that she was reluctant to share any details with me.

Then, during the late summer, I started to notice Roger was becoming secretive too.

He'd been on the phone when I walked into his office. Usually, he'd just wave to me then continue his call. This time he cut the conversation short with "Have to go, I'll call you back later…. Yes…. You've got it…. No, I don't think so……"

I couldn't hear what the other person was saying but it sounded like Mia.

"Who was that?" I asked.

"Kay at the council about next year's schools training schedule."

It was plausible — but he didn't sound convincing. As far as I knew, Roger had never lied to me before so I was surprised to find myself suspecting him now.

Then, when I called in at the office the following week, Mia and Roger were in a meeting that, again, ended as soon as I appeared on the scene.

Mia hadn't even stayed in the office for a coffee together; which we'd normally do, the three of us chatting generally and throwing ideas around. This time she'd looked sheepish as she closed the door behind her.

What was going on? I wondered. At first I just told myself I was being stupid; that I was imagining things.

But it continued for several weeks and I really started to get paranoid. My old obsession returned. My life had become too perfect and I was sure it was about to fall apart. But Roger and Mia? Would Mia really betray me after all the help I'd given her? I wouldn't have thought so, but could I ignore the evidence of all the secret conversations.

Then Roger and Mia were away together on a business trip for five days. It was, ostensibly, to look at centres for flotilla holidays in the Ionian. It was one of the suggestions that Mia had come up with as part of her proposed strategy for the business so, obviously, it made sense for her to go on the trip.

Roger had tried to persuade me to join them, but he realised full well I could hardly leave the two children and we couldn't take them with us. So were his attempts to get me to go a smokescreen? OK they had come back with specific proposals and a potential deal so they had done some work out there. But had it been all work and no play? Had there been dinners for two under the Greek skies? How could I tell? Was I being stupid?

When I asked Pete if he thought there was anything between Roger and Mia he said there wasn't and that I had nothing to worry about, but the way he said it, I knew he was hiding something.

Hating myself for doing it, I even went through Roger's pockets and his wallet. I checked his credit card and bank statements but found nothing unusual. I wanted to believe that there was nothing to worry about but there was still that niggle in the back of my mind.

It wasn't as though Roger was any less attentive towards me. We still made love, he still took me out for romantic dinners and bought me bunches of flowers. But, was this to cover his tracks, because there were still unexplained absences, those terminated phone calls and meetings. Had something happened on that business trip? There was no way to tell. The hotel bill had been for two separate single rooms. But did that prove anything? Not at all.

I was scared.

I loved Roger with all my heart.

I didn't want to lose him.

But was I now just a boring housewife for him? Did he need more?

Was he feeling tied down by the children?

What should I do?

Should I challenge him?

What made it worse was that it would soon be the fifth anniversary of our original commitment ceremony and I'd wanted to have a big celebration that evening. When I raised it with him, he made a feeble excuse about preferring to leave it until the fifth anniversary of our actual wedding and we should just go out for a private meal this year. Yet we'd both considered the commitment ceremony as our real wedding day.

Then there was Mia.

She was now avoiding me and finding excuses to be elsewhere. Excuses I knew were rubbish. For goodness sakes, she said she'd been for coffee with Karen from the group when Karen had been having lunch with me. How careless can you get? And Roger was out of the office at the same time. I could tell when a bitch was getting laid and Mia definitely was.

Then to cap it all, I saw the two of them hugging outside the hotel where Roger and I had had our wedding.

I'd been visiting to book the hall for a party to celebrate our fifth wedding anniversary even though it was still a long time off. As I was about to park, there they were, coming out of reception obviously very happy in each other's' company. I turned my car around and drove away, wiping away the tears that ran down my cheeks as my worst fears had been confirmed.

I pulled off the main road and parked in the entrance to a farm field and just sat there staring into space.

I considered my options. I could confront Roger over dinner that evening, but was there any point?

The evidence I'd seen was conclusive. If I confronted him, the inevitable outcome, if my suspicions were confirmed, would to be a break up. Where would the children go? Conventional wisdom was for them to be with the mother. But, in this case, genetically, Roger had a more direct link than I did. As it seemed he and Mia were now an item, they'd actually be better placed to look after Thomas and Charlotte than I could.

As devastated as I was by developments, I'd always known my happiness was bound to end sometime. I'd known all along that I didn't deserve it. I had so much to be grateful to Roger for. I didn't want to lose him. Of course I didn't want to lose him. But I knew there was no way I could keep him if he now loved Mia.

If I was to lose Roger and someone else was to receive his love, then no one deserved it more than Mia to make up for the awful start she'd had in life. I didn't blame either of them. You can't help who you fall in love with and people change. I'd changed since having the children. I'd given them my attention so Roger had lost out; though he'd also given them his attention too, so it worked both ways.

But where did that leave me?

Did I want to live without Thomas and Charlotte?

Absolutely not.

Did I want to live without Roger?

No.

Despite his apparent infidelity, I couldn't see myself loving anyone else. If, indeed, I could find another man prepared to love a transwoman. Especially a transwoman with two young children.

I was back to 2003, when I couldn't face the future. This time, I'd have to make sure I finished the job. At least I knew the children would be well looked after and they were young enough to get over me quickly.

Sitting in the dunes where I'd first met Roger and where I'd made the earlier attempt to end my life. I removed the painkillers from their blister packs and dropped them into the bottle of vodka. After staring at the bottle for a few minutes, I shook it to make sure the tablets had dissolved.

A yacht sailed past about three hundred yards off shore. It reminded me of the times Roger and I had enjoyed sailing Summer Dreams. A lump formed in my throat as I remembered the trip to Ouistreham, the Round the Island Races and the trip back from Salcombe when we'd helped rescue Pete. We'd faced challenges on each of those occasions but had overcome them.

I thought about how my parents — and Sandra and Pete — would react. I felt sorry for what I was about to do, no doubt they'd feel they should have done more even though they'd been so supportive. Mia and Roger would probably also feel guilty — with good reason. Could their new relationship survive such culpability? How would that impact on Thomas and Charlotte?

No doubt the press would also report my death in a sensational way. I could imagine the headline would be something like 'Sex Change Suicide'. They'd almost certainly dead-name me, referring to me as David and digging up my past. Was that how I wanted to be remembered? Was that the legacy I wanted to leave Thomas and Charlotte?

Shit *No!*

Mia had also faced huge problems in her life but hadn't given up, so how could I consider doing so? OK so maybe she deserved happiness — but so did I and I wouldn't give Roger up that easily. She would have to fight for him, if that's what she wanted, I wasn't going to make it easy for her.

And, if, in the end, Roger did choose Mia, I would survive. Maybe it wouldn't be easy — but, transitioning hadn't been easy. I'd taken a huge step into the unknown; but I'd come through that and it hadn't been as bad as I'd feared. Yes, Roger had supported me and that had been crucial; but I'd also found inner strength. I thought back to my counselling sessions and how the therapist had helped me deal with my low self-esteem. Was I really worthless without Roger?

Hell *No!*

I stood up and poured the vodka onto the sand, dropped the empty bottle in a bin at the car park then drove to the hairdressers for the appointment I'd made the previous week. If I was going to fight, I'd better look my best!

"Taxi's here, Vicky," I heard Roger call as I finished my make-up and made the final touches to my hair.

"You look lovely as always, darling," Roger told me as I picked up my bag and wrap at the front door.

Could he really be so two-faced if he was having an affair with my (former) best friend?

"Where are we going?" I asked.

"It's a surprise."

It turned out to be where we'd had our wedding. The taxi parked immediately behind a horse and carriage standing outside the main entrance. I wondered what was going on; maybe someone else was having a wedding reception. If so, I hoped things worked out better than they had for me. Well, that wasn't fair. I'd had a wonderful six years with Roger and I'd always known it wouldn't last.

It was, however, an ironic location for us to face up to what was going on — but I had determined to do so over dinner. My biggest regret was the impact any breakup might have on Thomas and Charlotte.

"Does this remind you of anything?" Roger asked as the taxi stopped.

"Yes. We had a sleigh for the wedding."

"Well, I couldn't manage the snow, so it'll have to be the carriage."

I was confused. Not that being confused was anything new for me. This made no sense if he was planning to leave me. Could I have got things so wrong? In a daze, I climbed into the carriage which then drove around the park and pulled up outside the barn where we'd been married.

As we entered the great hall there was a huge cheer from all our friends and family. I turned to look at Roger as my chin hit the floor, his eyes twinkling with delight at having surprised me.

Mia and Pete were standing together just inside the door, holding hands.

Roger then took my hand and slid a ring on my finger to nestle against my engagement and wedding rings. It was a white gold eternity ring with a single blue Tanzanite and small diamonds either side.

"Happy anniversary, darling."

Sandra handed me a glass of fizz. "You look like you need this."

The end?

# About the Author

Helen identifies as female with a transsexual history. She started treatment in 1998, transitioned and started working full time (for Greater Manchester Probation) as female in 1999 and underwent surgery in 2000.

She was the first openly transgender employee nationally in the Probation Service and provided workshops on trans issues for probation and prison staff (amongst others). Any similarity with Michaela Jeffries is far from coincidental!

She chaired a number of trans and LGBT support groups and helped form a:gender, the pan-civil service trans network and is one of only three 'Honorary Life Members'. She served on national and local Diversity Boards within Probation and National Offender Management Service and has received a number of awards for work with trans individuals. She is a counsellor specialising in trans clients. Overall, she estimates that she has met well over 1,000 transsexual individuals and many more who do not plan to transition permanently. Many of the incidents in Summer Dreams are from her personal experience or those of other individuals she has met.

Her story prior to retirement is covered in her autobiography: "A Tale of Two Lives: a funny thing happened on the way to the Palace" available on Amazon https://www.amazon.co.uk/dp/B079Z1QVYF

Helen has a number of other novels in progress some of which also feature transgender protagonists.

If you enjoyed Summer Dreams, follow Helen on Facebook at:

https://www.facebook.com/helendaleauthor/

or her website

http://www.helendaleauthor.info

Printed in Poland
by Amazon Fulfillment
Poland Sp. z o.o., Wrocław